# MYTHOTENEBRAE

## A COLLECTION OF STORIES

### Storm Constantine

**IMMANION PRESS**
Stafford England

**Mythotenebrae: A Collection of Stories**
**By Storm Constantine**
© 2020

http://www.stormconstantine.co.uk

Cover by Danielle Lainton
Interior layout by Storm Constantine
Interior illustrations by Danielle Lainton, except for those on pages 166 & 195, which are altered screenshots from Storm Constantine's transmedia project in the video game Rift and page 212, which was drawn by Storm Constantine when she wrote the story "The Testament of the Kehllcomm" in the late 1970s.

Set in Garamond

ISBN: 978-1-912815-12-8
Catalogue Number: IP0163

An Immanion Press Edition
http://www.immanion-press.com
info@immanion-press.com

# Contents

# INTRODUCTION

Welcome to Mythotenebrae – the sixth volume of my collected short stories. There are fifteen of them, many of which are previously unpublished. It's long been my aim to sort out and polish up all the juvenilia I have stored on my back up drive. In this volume, I've completely reshaped three of these stories, one of which I wrote during my O Level exam when I was 16. An old piece indeed! I've also included several recent pieces that were accepted for publication by other editors, but then their proposed books were cancelled, or their publishing houses closed down. So I trust there will be a lot of material that is new to the majority of readers.

The full history of each tale is at the back of the book, in terms of when and where (if applicable) they were published, but I've added a brief description of the history of each story along with it, explaining its inspirations and/or how it developed. As we're releasing this book around Samhain 2020, it seems only fitting that the first story in it has a Halloween theme.

May you enjoy this collection as much as I have working on it. Samhain Blessings upon you all. May your ancestors make their presence felt in the happiest way and give us positive energy for 2021. I suspect most people need it.

Storm Constantine
October 2020

# THE BONE FIRE

*Story History:*

This piece was written for a Halloween-themed anthology, edited by Steve Jones. Compiled in 2018, it was published by Skyhorse Publishing in *"The Mammoth Book of Halloween Stories"*.

I enjoy tinkering around with existing folklore and in this one reinvented the goddess Hekkate a little, and her mythical children. When I was writing it, I felt I was actually in that world, as a young girl exploring the expanding margins of life.

Jenna's chant to Hekkate is adapted from a quote by George Carlin: *"There are nights when the wolves are silent and only the moon howls."*

When the sun threatens to die at the end of the year, it's up to us to keep it alive during the long dark. When it's weak, the rule of light weakens too, and the dark may slip through a veil we cannot see. Here, far away from the world of the blind, we do what we must. We make our own light.

Our village, Door's Dale, lies in a hollow, surrounded on two sides by ancient forest. A road pours down from Heron's Cop, to the east, and wanders through the village to the setting sun, and the slow rise of Acre's Hill, in the west. At Hallow's Eve, in the fields, where once the wheat and barley blew, we raise the bone fire. Its flames mimic the sun in summer, and through our intent, keeps the solar eye alive throughout the long darkness. You wonder what we burn upon the fire? Must be bones, mustn't it? Do you want to hear?

Summer had been good that year; the Kindly Ones had turned smiles to us rather than blades: they who live in the trees, in the clear cold brooks, and beneath the fields. We knew, however, that winter would be harsh, for in August the fields had been hidden often by thick fog, and the geese and ducks had left early, heading south. Woodpeckers had been spied, in their green and red coats, sharing a tree – always a sign. Among the hedgerows, I'd noticed spiders had spun their webs larger than usual, and the house-walker kind was heading indoors in crowds, to scuttle about in the evenings and be eaten by cats. So, as a precaution, the bone fire would be bigger than usual too this year.

Jenna Harne was my friend. We were fourteen years old, tugging at the leash of childhood, knowing it must eventually snap; if we tugged hard enough perhaps that would be soon. We loved Hallow's Eve, but who didn't? It was a time for games and celebration, feasting and dancing and dressing up. I would guise as a Kindly Woman that year, with a face of green and a robe of leaves, with bees in my hair, albeit made of wire and sheep's wool rather than real ones. Jenna's costume was that of a demoness, of red and black rags with a crown of late roses she'd dyed almost to soot by standing them in ink. Her face was painted red, with gouts of black around the eyes and mouth. She looked wickedly lovely.

In the early evening, we'd walk the lanes between the farms, each carrying a basket and a lantern. At the crossroads we passed over, we would place an apple and a gobbet of raw meat for She of the Four Faces, but when we came to a house or farm where a turnip lamp was lit upon the step, we'd knock at the door and ask for gifts for Those Unseen. At the end of our journey, we'd eat what we'd been given – small sweetmeats – and say, "This for you, dear ghost, enjoy its taste through me." If we carry out this task every year, then the ghosts and demons themselves do not have to, and it's safer for everyone. We dress up to fool the real spirits, for they are partial to children, especially at Hallow's Eve, for then the Kindly Ones and their friends from beyond the veil are full of tricks and mischief, as we are. If we wear a guise, they take us for one of their own and pass us by.

Jenna and I set out as usual, with apples and wrapped meat in our baskets and our lanterns on sticks. I wore a cloak of green, and Jenna one of crimson. We sang songs to warn people of our approach. As younger children, we'd loved this part of the event the most, but now, with that leash tethering us to innocence wearing thin, we were eager to return to the village for the main celebration. On this night, we'd be allowed to drink cider. Jenna wanted to flirt with boys and show how well she could dance. At the end of the evening, she'd allow someone to kiss her. I hadn't quite caught up in that respect and was looking forward to the feast more than anything, and being able to pretend I was an adult, but in a different way. I'd walk around as if I had property and animals, my head held high, my gown trailing in the grass.

At the first crossroads, we placed our offerings at the stone cross – me the apple, Jenna the meat – and Jenna chanted:

> "*Hekkate, Hekkate, bring me tonight*
> *sweet love in the light of the bone-fire,*
> *when your dogs hold their tongues*
> *and only the moon may howl.*"

I rolled my eyes and sighed. Even I knew Hekkate was not a goddess interested in love, since she was the four faces of the moon, from light to dark, and was friendly with Death. "Maybe she'll give you a corpse to love," I said.

"Don't be stupid, Emlie," Jenna snapped. "I want one of her sons, for she lends them sometimes and puts them in the body of a boy. Tonight, I want something better than a sweaty, snotty barn-boy."

"Idiot," I said, and we linked arms and walked away.

We called at six farms and, after the seventh, intended to return to Door's Dale. Earlier, we'd passed many other guiser groups on their rounds of the farms, but now, on our way to Kettle Farm, the lanes felt empty and desolate. A snowy owl swept across our path and Jenna said, "There's winter's sentinel." Anything could be keeping pace with us behind the high hedges on either side of the lane. We shivered and hugged each other, laughing in delicious fear.

A lamp burned upon the porch step of Kettle Farm, but when we knocked the door there was no answer. Jenna put her hands in a funnel against the kitchen window and peered through. "No one here," she said.

"Maybe they've gone to the feast already," I said.

"Perhaps, although there are two pies on the table. They wouldn't forget those."

"Maybe they're for later. Shall we go?" I was beginning to feel more than mildly frightened. The night felt so still, watchful, and we were alone out here. Would our guises hold? I adjusted my crown of bees.

Jenna picked up her basket and lamp, but before we could go back down the track, someone came around the side of the house. We both shrieked and jumped, then began to laugh. It was a boy, probably a son of the house, dressed in a costume of black, with the white bones of a skeleton painted over it. He was tall and had long black hair that was greyed with ash. His face was painted white like a skull. He might be beautiful or hideous, it was impossible to tell, but struck me as graceful. He bowed to us extravagantly and said, "Ladies!"

"This house has no gift for us?" Jenna said archly. "Would you scorn a Kindly Lady and her friend from Hell?"

"My bones can't hold a gift," said the boy.

"What about those pies in there?" Jenna insisted.

"You must know I can't go in and steal those without being invited."

"Oh well . . ." Jenna's banter faltered. "Let's go, Emlie."

I felt that boy standing there behind us all the while we walked down the farm driveway. I didn't think he was a son of Kettle Farm, but more likely a guiser, like us. They had a lot of boys there, true, but he'd felt different somehow.

"What a fool," Jenna grumbled, once we'd reached the lane.

"Could have been Hekkate's son," I said.

"Her sons aren't idiots."

For a moment, I wondered why she was so grumpy, but then she began to sing, and I joined in, and the spirits kept their distance.

We reached the field just as the bone fire was being lit. It was built of branches and unwanted lumber, but there were bones in its heart – those of the first lambs eaten in the spring and kept for this time, as well as the flayed bones of beloved old dogs who had died, because the dog was Hekkate's sacred animal. Fiddlers were playing and capering about, and the air smelled of burned sugar, apples and turned soil. Torches on tall poles blazed wildly, providing the traditional hellish light. A large crowd had gathered, people from the village and all the outlying farms. Jack of the Lantern had been brought from the church, where he was kept all year in a box under the floor stones, and was being paraded around by Farmer Docken, he who owns the most land in our parish. The lantern was an ancient human skull, in which a candle burned; the sun caught in bone. Jack grinned at the fire, his eyes alight with the writhe of captured flame. He was, for that night, lord of the land, our lord, who protected us. The priest had come to join us, as he always did, although he'd left his saints at home.

Jenna and I joined a group of our friends and began to dance and sing. Jenna indulged herself in some mild but apparently unsatisfactory flirting. "They're all so dull," she confided to me. Hekkate's son was yet to materialise.

Then I nudged her arm. "Look, the skeleton."

On the other side of the fire, close to the trees of Tedder's Wood, stood the tall boy we'd met at Kettle Farm. He was drinking from a cup and appeared to be eyeing up the revellers. "I think he's a stranger," Jenna said. "What's he doing here?"

"Perhaps the answer to your prayer," I said.

"Let up on that!" Jenna snapped. "He must be a relative of the Kettles. Hekkate's son would be different."

"Can't we just pretend he is?"

Jenna sighed. "Don't be silly. Come on." She took my arm, and we went over to him.

"Hello," Jenna said boldly. "Are you with the Kettles? We met you at their farm earlier."

"Yes, I'm from that farm," said the boy, somewhat unconvincingly, I thought.

Close up, you could see his wide dark eyes and the fine shape of his lips, even though they were caked in white paint. He smelled like burning, like a hearth fire in winter. Once again, he bowed to us, "Lady of Hell, will you walk with me around the fire?"

Jenna took his arm. "All right."

I was about to protest, "What about me?" then realised the folly of it. The time had come to let Jenna make her own entertainment. Somewhat downhearted, I began to walk back to our friends, but then another boy stepped into my path. It was the night for it, of course. He didn't smell of burning, nor was he very tall, but his eyes were pale without being blue, and his teeth when he smiled looked sharp. "Why aren't you in costume?" I said.

"I am," he replied. "I'm a spirit of the hedgerows."

"I see." I noticed then, as if it had just appeared, he wore a wreath of berries and twigs on his head. But he felt comfortable to me, as if I'd known him as a kind friend for a while.

"What's your name?" he asked me.

I told him.

He offered me a berry sprig, and his arm, which I took hold of, and suddenly Jenna was forgotten. Skipping along beside this unexpected prince of the night, I rejoined the party, and danced till my shoes were blood, as the saying goes.

Eventually, the flames burned lower and people were yawning. Only the stalwart few were left to dance and sing till dawn. And dawn is a long way away at Hallow's Eve. I'd drunk enough cider to be tipsy and was wondering if I wanted to kiss my prince or not. He was certainly handsome, a little older than me, and my friends were all clearly fascinated by him. His name, he'd told us, was Tom, and he was the son of a traveling woman, who was visiting several parties that night and would eventually come to fetch him. He had his arm about my shoulder now. I'd lost my crown somewhere and my hair hung loose. I felt beautiful and grown up and didn't want this magical night to end.

Jenna's mother came up to me. She was wearing her cloak, as if she was about to go home, and I saw that Jenna's red cloak hung over her arm. "Where is the little strumpet?" Jenna's mother asked, but not angrily. "I found this dropped on the ground near the woods, and it's all muddy. You know where she's gone off to and who with?"

I said I really didn't know, but imagined she was somewhere with her bony boy, perhaps being initiated into mysteries of life I didn't yet care for.

"Well, I can't just leave her out here and let her come home alone, at the Kindlies know what hour," said the mother. "Help me find her, children."

So we split up into pairs to search the fields and the nearby woods. I hoped I wouldn't be the one to find her and her boy. I didn't want to see what they were doing.

Tom came with me and asked me what was going on. I told him what had happened at the farm and by the fire. "He said he's with the Kettles," I said.

"Then you should have told her mother."

I spluttered a laugh. "No! I couldn't!"

Tom stopped me, put his hands upon my arms. "Remember what night it is."

"What do take me for? I know it's a night of spirits. But I also know that boy wasn't Hekkate's son."

Tom blinked. "What?"

I told him the rest, Jenna's prayer.

"She asked for that?" he said.

"Yes. Why?"

"You should be careful what you ask for on Hallow's Eve. You know why you wear the costumes. People you meet in the smoke might not be who they say they are, and they can hear the words inside you."

The atmosphere between us had dampened, and I felt I'd offended Tom in some way, and now he saw me as silly and frivolous.

"She's only larking about," I said, peevishly. "He wasn't a spirit, or a goddess's son. Simply a boy visiting the Kettles. It's just a party."

Tom's voice was sour and cold. "Which is, of course, why your priest leaves his collar on the altar this night, and Jack surveys the land."

"Tom, don't be like this. We were having fun."

He paused, looked at me for some moments, then smiled. "Of course. Shall I kiss you now?"

"I suppose so."

It was the kind of kiss you remember for the rest of your life, so you can tell of it in detail to your great grandchildren. Perhaps the memory has grown better than the reality, but to a young girl that night, in the dying smokes of a Hallow's Eve bone fire, and the scents of the land strong in witcheries, it was the kiss of a king of Faery.

When he had done with enchanting me, Tom held my face in his hands and said, "What do you want for the future, Emlie? Make a wish."

"I will, but surely I mustn't speak it."

"You can tell me."

So I told him my heart's desire, for my own land, and a long, low house, and a high-stepping mare, and three black-haired daughters who looked like witches.

"It's yours," he said, and kissed me again. "Now, I must go, because my mother is calling."

"I can't hear anything."

"Sometimes calls are from the heart, not the mouth," he said.

Then he ran away and left me alone among the trees. I wasn't very pleased about that but found my way back all right. No one had found Jenna, though.

By this time, her family were panicking and there was talk of kidnapping and murder. I had to tell them what had happened at Kettle Farm and that we'd seen the boy by the fire. My mother slapped my head for not mentioning it earlier. The Kettles were approached and – to no one's surprise – didn't know who the bone boy was. All their relatives were accounted for.

We searched all night and found nothing, but in the wan, mist-haunted morning, the Docken twins found Jenna by Bride's Mere. She was wandering as if blind, her hair like a thatch and her costume torn to tatters. She was muttering a weird song and didn't seem aware of other people around her. Rob and Lily Docken brought her to her family. The priest was called from wading in the nearest pond, where he and other men had been dredging. He put his hands on Jenna's head and said she'd been assailed, although, when she was later examined by the women, there were no marks to be seen upon her. She didn't seem frightened or hurt, only dreaming. Her song, when we could understand it, was a song of love.

As for the bone boy, he'd vanished, having no doubt had his fun, though why Jenna's mind had gone away with him, I've no idea.

In the copse beside the mere, Amy Proudtoe found a pile of human bones – old, brown ones, as if unearthed from a grave – with a skull on top, laughing as skulls always must. We knew then that this had been his costume. The priest confirmed it. Jenna had dressed too well. Her disguise hadn't failed, it had succeeded, or so people said. The bony boy had taken her for one of his own. If he hadn't, they'd have found *her* bones, her cold flesh, not his discarded costume.

The women carried the old brown bones to the embers of our Hallow's Eve fire and found its dying yet still-beating, blistering heart. Here, they placed the demon's guise, and the priest said a few words he'd never speak on a Sunday in his pulpit.

*"Hide your children well, in costumes of ghosts and witches. Or a denizen of Hell might come to them, dressed in human skin and bones to make a human guise."*

He kept Jenna's mind, that boy. It never came back and neither did he.

As for me, Tom had known who and what I was, and that I'd

never made a prayer at the crossroads, at least out loud. His mother had heard my heart, not Jenna's demand, perhaps, and had preferred my desires to hers.

Even to this day, I leave offerings to She of the Four Faces at the crossroads, and I work always in her name, doing her business. But she never sent him back to me, even when I earned my land and house, and bought my high-stepping mare, and gave birth to the first of my black-haired daughters who look like witches.

Jenna had a child too, nine months from that Hallow's Eve. It looked healthy and normal enough, but it only lived a day.

# HAVEN

*Story History:*

I've always loved the music of fairy tales, the particular rhythm and syntax they have, and I've written quite a few stories in this vein. "Haven" was inspired by the experiences of a friend, who fell in love with the wrong person. There was a gulf of difference between her and the object of her adoration – socially, culturally and spiritually. Being of a magical persuasion, her presence in this man's life was almost an irritant, because he professed he had no interest in the subject and did not believe in anything he couldn't behold with his own senses. I wonder whether he was secretly scared by the unseen, the weird. For my friend, venturing into this man's world was a culture shock – she'd always had a very Bohemian and unconventional life, and the way ordinary people lived was baffling to her. Suffice to say, things did not end well. As a kind of consolation, I wrote my friend this fairy tale. It was published in *"Splinters of Truth"*, by NewCon Press in 2016.

There was once a city that lay close to the ocean, at the edge of a vast delta land. Diamond-bright water and verdant isles glistened beneath the light of a mellow sun, and silver clarions sounded from the high towers of the city, proclaiming across the lands of this world and beyond that all was right in the kingdom. Banners the colour of saffron unfurled upon the lofty poles that rose above the towers. They moved slowly in the balmy breeze, which was scented with the aromas of the mellow flowers that grew upon the islands of the delta and in the tiered gardens of the city itself. Did this city have a name? Yes it did. Its name was Haven.

There were no thieves in the city, no dark alleyways, no terrible areas of mystery, no dragons, no ghosts. Only light and the dreamy smiles of those who were truly content in that gilded world.

The prince of this city, Garland, was loved by all whose gaze fell upon him. He was the beloved only son of the king and queen, and wherever he walked in the courts and echoing chambers, so petals of the rose were strewn at his feet. His words were recorded by a retinue of scribes, his witticisms and words of wisdom distributed throughout the kingdom so that all might share in his bright spirit. He towered over all, both in presence and in height and there were none in the kingdom more loved or more celebrated than he.

The king had ordered his artists, at the moment of the prince's birth, to paint the scenes of his son's life as it would be, and these pictures adorned the walls of a long gallery within the palace. Prince Garland would move among these pictures, secure in the knowledge that all was as it should be, and all would proceed as it was ordained, the path from birth to death. He could see his own passing, far in the future; he lying as an old man, pale upon his last bed, surrounded by his wife, children and grand-children, adored and safe in those final moments. And in the meantime life was good, pictures of bliss; those around him caught in poses of attention upon his words. He would not ride into battles, because the kingdom was peaceful. He would not take for himself an exotic and mysterious foreign wife, because it was already decided whom he would wed – a genteel lady of the court, of suitable pedigree. He would not have adventures, because it was dangerous to wander beyond the kingdom. He would make no changes to, nor leave true mark upon the world, because no one within the kingdom desired it to change. Haven would continue as it always had, beneath the light of that mellow sun.

But where would be the story in this bland, contented life devoid of storms and uprisings? You are right – there is nothing exciting to tell. But only if Haven's dull existence remained unchanged. And it is the nature of the world to alter.

Occasionally, the prince and his friends would ride out from the city and gallop through the marshy pools to the forest at the other side of the delta. Birds would fly up in a clatter as they passed, and silver water spray out from beneath the horses' hooves. Some of the young men would carry the banners of Haven, which streamed behind them, and some would blow upon silver trumpets so that no one could be in any doubt about who rode across the land. They were a beautiful company, full of laughter. They rode to hunt the white harts that roamed the forest, slinking like ghosts through the trees. There were no ghosts in Haven.

And, as is the way with tales of this nature, upon one of these excursions the prince became separated from his friends. How this happened no one afterwards could truly say. Perhaps a wind came up that blew the branches of the trees against his horse's eyes so that it frighted and veered off along a different path. Perhaps a strange magic twisted the paths between the mossy trunks. But however it happened, for a short time he was alone, and you can be sure a man such as he was vulnerable in that situation.

As he rode, the tall oaks crowded in around him. They were so ancient, time appeared to have twisted them out of shape. They loomed and watched, rustling even when the wind was still. The path became very narrow and led at length to a glade, in the centre of which was a grassy mound. The prince thought that the light in that place was unnatural, and a shiver passed through his skin. He smelled magic, even though he had no idea what that was. He noticed that the only birds in the glade were crows, blacker than the night of the moon's dark. Their raw voices seemed to mock him. He noticed that an intoxicating scent rose from the ground, earthy and potent. And it seemed to him, very faintly, that a strange music filled the air, music not of this Earth. He could barely hear it – a distant choir and the tinkle of metal chimes moved by the slightest of breezes. Part of him spoke loudly in his mind: *turn back, turn back*. But another part did not heed these words. He rode into the glade and halted his horse upon the forest lawn. And he waited.

As many of you know, there is another world that exists alongside our own. In all respects, these two worlds are different, yet some would say they are the same. The people of Haven did not speak of the other world: they shunned it. Children in Haven were not told tales to frighten them should they misbehave, so they never feared the darkness. The people of Haven denied this other world existed, in fact, and the strength of their belief was so powerful they were kept safe from its influences.

Others, who lived in different kingdoms, referred to this world as the realm below. To some, it was an underworld, grim and terrible, while to others it was the land of endless summer, where the citizens lived eternal lives, bathed in the light of a sun that was not a sun, but something else.

On this day, when the prince of Haven strayed from the path, the queen of the underworld awoke from a bizarre dream she was having. She stretched upon her canopied bed and rose up from it. She was assailed by a strange feeling that seemed to make tight the very fibres of her being. She too could hear a distant music and was discomforted by its tone. She felt in her bones that the planets shifted in their positions, and that if she were to venture into the upper world she would see their new pattern in the sky, and this would mean something. So she clad herself in a robe of crimson, and bound her black hair with a rope of inky pearls. She crept like a thief through the halls of her palace, past the king of the underworld as he slept, and came at length to the narrow stair that led to the world above. She came out of the hill in the centre of the glade where Prince Garland sat upon his nervous horse, and she thought to herself, "what have we here?"

The prince, when he first caught sight of this creature rising from the earth, experienced a shock in his flesh, for she was so *other* to all that he knew. He was unsure whether to be frightened or appalled or disgusted. He recognised her as a witch, even though he didn't really know what that was, for he had never been told tales to frighten him as a boy. He could see that she possessed weird beauty, but this was a beauty he had never seen before, so alien and discomforting. She was nothing like him, he knew, and if he had any sense at all he would put spur to flank and gallop his horse out of the forest in any direction. But when he looked into the woman's black eyes, he saw within them a kindred soul, a heart that beat as his did.

And so they stared at one another for some minutes, she circling the stamping, head-tossing horse, her body stooped over in a predatory crouch, tendrils of her loosely-bound hair brushing the ground. And he gazed down his nose at her, his eyes aflame, still and straight in the saddle and he waited that she might speak. But she didn't, so at length he said, "Lady, are you lost within the forest?"

The woman looked into his eyes, and he wondered if she did not understand his language, but then she spoke. "Am I lost?

Truly, I don't know. I have just come to this place. It is strange to me."

"Who are you?" he asked, and she replied,

"I am the queen of another land, far from this world, yet so close. The sky called to me, for it had something to say, so here I am."

"The sky cannot speak," said the prince.

"Can it not?" asked the woman.

Prince Garland knew that however he answered that question it would not be with words she'd want to hear.

She laughed at his silence and said, "Perhaps you are the sign the sky spoke of."

This announcement troubled the prince greatly, but in a hidden place within him, because he could not imagine what kind of sign this creature might be looking for. There had been no Granny or Nurse in his childhood to whisper to him of the denizens of the other world, so he had no way of knowing what faced him. He was a prince of Haven, untouchable and celebrated. There was nothing to fear. When he spoke, flowers fell from his lips and people sank to their knees before him. When he smiled, clouds moved from the sun. And so he smiled and so he spoke in flowers. "My lady, if you are really a queen, then you should not be alone in the forest. Come with me to my city and my people will care for you until you know whether or not you are lost."

The woman raised her eyebrows at him. "Your city? I cannot go there, sir. The stones of your domain would crumble before me."

"Those stones have stood for a long time," said the prince, smiling still. "I do not think you are a risk to them."

The woman narrowed her eyes at him. "I will not go to your city. If you would speak with me, you must do so here."

"Speak with you?" The prince laughed. "It is only courteous of me to assist you, that is all."

"As you wish," said the woman, "but now you must go, because the sun sinks beneath the trees and soon the night will come, and that is not your province."

The prince looked about him and realised that she was right. He thought the time was earlier but already the shadows lay long around him. He felt as if he had conversed with this woman for hours, but of course that was not possible. "I wish you safety," he said, "and that you find your way."

The woman said nothing to this, so he turned his horse and urged it back along the path, until presently he heard the voices of his friends, who had been looking for him. The sound washed over him like cool clear water, and he felt that something was removed from him, something dark, something tainted. He looked back over his shoulder at the forest, where now the shadows clustered like hags, and he thought for a moment he heard that strange music, and a scent came to him, like the essence of the earth.

The ways of enchantment are weird and unfathomable. They come in many forms. The most potent and devastating of witcheries is the natural calamity of love. And sometimes love comes disguised as something else, and sometimes it is wrapped in fear, and other times it comes as a warrior, invincible and merciless, to smash the towers of our very existence. Unbidden, unnoticed, and certainly unwanted, such a warrior crept like a thief into Haven, that city where no thieves roamed.

Prince Garland returned to his parents' palace and put out of his mind the strange encounter in the forest. Perhaps it was unfortunate, during this crucial time, that his betrothed was away from the kingdom, engaged in the polite social activities to which ladies of her station are accustomed. But this meant the prince was in one way alone, as alone as he'd been on the forest path.

That night, as he retired to his chamber, a dire wind came up from the east, bearing with it the scent of earth and the sound of a wolf howling. When the prince went to the window casement, the sky looked purple rather than black, and the stars were fierce. The moon was a thin sickle, sharp enough to cut a man's throat, and the air was cold.

The prince pulled long velvet drapes across the casement. He did this roughly, as if to shut out something terrible. He went to his bed, but he could not rest. He felt as if there was something he'd forgotten to do, but he couldn't remember what it was. And all the time the wolves of the wind circled the tower where he tried to sleep. He had never thought of wolves before, but he could imagine them now, white as ghosts, their long paws pacing the swirling air.

When he did sleep, his dreams were frightening, of being

awake and trying to sleep. Eventually, the sun called him from these dark visions, and he woke truly. A man from a different kingdom might have known by then that something had changed in his life, but Garland lived in Haven, and nothing changed there. So the uncomfortable feeling in his flesh and bones spoke only of illness to him. He wondered whether he should visit the court physician. But then...was something calling to him? He felt in his fibres he was being drawn. Without conscious decision, because he never thought of such things, he found himself at the stables, asking for his horse, and presently he was riding out across the delta. Alone.

He fled like a voiceless prayer into the dark forest of listening trees. His horse gasped and froth flew from its mouth; its eyes showed white all the way around. Presently, as if guided by unheard voices or unseen hands, horse and rider came to the grassy mound and there, sitting atop it, was the witch queen of the underworld.

"Lady," gasped the prince. His horse, shuddering, sank to its foreknees and he slipped from its saddle.

"I have thought of you," said the queen. "Strangely, I have thought of you."

The prince strode to her and enfolded her in his arms, which at once felt so right, yet at the same time wrong. He wanted to embrace her yet squeeze the life from her for making him feel this way. She lay quiescent against him, breathing as a frightened wild animal might, when held dazed against a human breast. The voices of the court, of his betrothed and her ladies, rang distantly in Prince Garland's ears. For a while he heard their laughter, and it was tinny and tawdry. What lay against him now in comparison seemed pure and honest. "You are lost," he said, "and I am urged to succour you. Come with me to my father's city."

"Come into your world?" murmured the queen. Her voice sounded slurred, slightly drunk. "But I do not know it."

"We shall be great friends," said the prince. "And I shall help you learn."

"Take me with you," said the queen.

Behind them, the prince's horse was much recovered, standing once more proud and strong. The prince lifted the witch queen onto his saddle and climbed up behind her. In this, way, with the night of her hair streaming upon the early day, he bore her back to Haven.

Once the royal court laid eyes on her, they believed that the peculiar woman spoke the truth and was of royal bearing. Clearly, her mind was befuddled, and she had somehow lost her way, not just in the physical world but in her mind. She was not mad in a disagreeable way that might have to be hidden and controlled, but distant and confused.

They installed her with the ladies-in-waiting who tended to the queen, the prince's mother. The queen summoned the visitor to her.

"What is your name?" she asked.

"Pavonia Nocta," replied the witch, a name she made up on the spot, because no being of earthly flesh should know her true name.

"We shall call you Vonny," declared the queen.

Even the ladies, staring at the dark vision of midnight hair, creamy skin and crimson robes, balked at this homely name. The witch would never be Vonny to those who came to fear her. She was Pava.

In most tales of this nature, you'd expect the prince to fall desperately in love with the witch and want to marry her. Trials might be set for her to prove she was royal. Or she might be bewitched and exiled by rivals to wander the earth, until some kind soul found her and restored her memory or her sight to her – whatever might have been lost. None of these things happened.

Pava spread her poppy skirts about her and sat beside the queen, watching the ladies. Sometimes, she would glance out of the arched windows, where the shadows of flying crows darkened the glass. She appeared bemused, but content. She waited to see what would happen.

Prince Garland, meanwhile, laughed and played with his friends, indulging in all the pursuits considered suitable for young men of his age and station. Naturally, his thoughts wandered occasionally to the strange woman he had brought into the city, but he told himself he was merely concerned for her well-being. One afternoon, he sought her out, to ask how she was faring. She was in the rose garden where there were so many heavily-perfumed blooms that people who walked there could barely breathe. You could make perfume merely by holding a bottle with a bit of oil in it open to the air. The sweetness of Haven, hanging like ropes of silk in the sunlight.

"My lady," said the prince, bowing. "Are you well? Are you happy?"

Pava had been walking around the labyrinthine paths, perceiving a pattern there that the inhabitants of Haven did not. "I am interested," she replied, crushing a white rose with one hand and bringing its murdered petals to her nose. "What a strange world this is."

The prince felt a needle of sorrow make a stitch within him. As he'd suspected, her mind was addled. "Have you remembered your home?"

Pava frowned. "I'm unsure it's yet appropriate." She smiled at him.

He took her hands. "But are you happy?"

She looked at his hands over hers. "Oh yes, I'm not sad. There is a lot of light here, isn't there? Doesn't it make you tired?"

The prince felt something give way within his breast as he gazed at her smile, which seemed unbearably innocent, and listened to her mad words. He must protect her.

"What is your name, prince of Haven?" she asked.

"Garland," he replied, even though he was sure she must already know this fact.

She laughed and raised a hand to reach above him, let the torn petals drift down over his head.

Later, in a salon daubed by sunset, surrounded by women who twittered like little birds, Pava considered the prince, Garland. He was similar to a tree, she decided, not the kinds found in the underworld, those willows with branches like white hair, or the strange growths that were half fungus, half wood. No, he was a summer tree of the upper world, resplendent with bright foliage, the sun caught within his leaves. He would smell of sunlight and his touch would burn. Despite this, she would like to touch him and sensed he felt the same about her, except a mass of twittering birds roosted in his upper branches and he couldn't hear anything sensible or true because of their din.

Pava thought about going home, but then decided to stay a while longer because the upper world and its people intrigued her. Sometimes, when she walked the gardens and terraces of the palace, all the people she passed appeared to be wearing masks, grotesquely smiling masks. Beneath them, these people might have no features at all. Garland too wore a mask, but she suspected that what lay beneath his was something far more beautiful than the stylised, frozen smile he wore. Before she went home, she must look beneath his mask, otherwise she would be forever curious and restless.

One night, she turned into a black cat and slipped like a dark fluid through the palace, up stairs, along corridors, past rooms where people slept and did not dream. She followed her nose, which being a cat's nose at that time was very sensitive. She was drawn to the chamber of the sleeping prince, and realised then that he slept the whole time, even when he thought he was awake. She jumped onto his chest and purred into his face. Experimentally, she sucked in some of his breath to see what it tasted like. Nothing. Still, he looked beautiful, and his mask wasn't there. What lay beneath though was the face of a child, an idiot child who could not dream and was never truly awake. Sadly, she kissed him – sad, because that kiss would wake him, and she knew he wouldn't thank her for it.

Garland shifted in his sleep, mumbled a little, uttered a short gasp. Then, making a chewing noise, he rubbed his nose and turned on his side. He began to dream.

Before morning, a crack appeared in the north tower of the palace, but because such things never happened, no one in Haven noticed.

Prince Garland woke late and felt strange at once. He realised eventually this was because he was grumpy, out of sorts, and he never felt that way. Dimly, he was aware of being very uncomfortable about something, but he didn't know what. Gloomily, he went to eat the breakfast his servants had laid out for him.

After breakfast, he remembered he had dreamed, and the dream had been shocking. The Lady Vonny had come to him in his room and taken off her crimson robe. Beneath it, she wore no petticoats, no underwear. Her skin had been white as the moon but for the black triangle above her thighs, and her dark red mouth, her star-deep eyes. She had done something unspeakable – leapt onto his chest and crouched there, her breasts in his face. And in the dream he had thrown her off, only to lie on top of her, spear her with the ferocity of a hunter bringing down his prey. She'd cried and hissed like a cat.

Now, even the memory of that dream aroused him and made him feel uncertain. His breakfast plate was chipped and the milk in his tea slightly sour.

That day also the Lady Talina came home, she and her maids erupting from white carriages drawn by snowy horses, filling the air with their tweeting laughter. Talina had brought gifts with her for everyone except for the blood, night and snow woman who had come to the palace. Talina had been bred to mate with Prince Garland. There was no other life she could imagine, and it was also unimaginable that he'd want anyone else but her. And yet...

In the cathedral-like throne room, as Talina went to pay her respects to the king and queen, with her betrothed at her side, she noticed the shadow moving slowly behind the columns on the left side of the thrones. A tall woman dressed in a dark red robe, with skin like new cream and eyes and hair like the night. The woman looked at her directly with an expression of curiosity and triumph. At her side, Talina felt Prince Garland flinch, as if someone had stuck something sharp into his side. He put a hand over his breast. The woman amid the columns had paused, standing like a wondrous ghost in the few shadows that were allowed in the palace. Although it seemed that shadows were growing about her.

Who was this creature? Talina, in her relatively short life, had never experienced jealousy, envy, insecurity or fear. Now she felt all of them at once, and her body felt obliged to collapse, since it could only recognise these feelings as the symptoms of illness.

Gazing down upon his fallen betrothed, Prince Garland thought how pale she looked, how small her features were, her brow smooth and slightly glazed, like porcelain. Talina was a little doll, empty inside. She was not exciting like a black flame, like the wind given voice, a creature of blood, night and snow. Then Garland chastised himself for these uncharitable thoughts. This was the woman who would be his loyal companion until he died. He bent to lift her, but by then others were already attending to her.

A part of Garland, a new, untutored but instinctive part, advised him he should take the Lady Pavonia Nocta out of the city and return her to where he'd found her. She represented danger to him, even though he lacked the knowledge to form that idea into words. But despite this resolve, he wanted instead merely to follow the Lady around the palace, watching her from a distance as she wove her dreamy journeys. Where she walked, moss grew deeper into the ancient stones, ivy tumbled down from high balconies like a woman's unbound hair, and the mortar between stones grew damp and friable. Walls became infirm and listed. More cracks appeared. Poppies pushed up between the flagstones. The balmy summer became so hot that crops shrivelled in the fields.

People became irritable and, when they looked at their neighbours, saw reason to find fault and criticise. A man murdered his wife. A wife murdered her husband. One midnight, when the heat was so strong several babies suffocated, two girls threw themselves consecutively from high towers, smashing on the hard flagstones, which splintered beneath the impact. The bodies looked like smashed poppies. That same night a group of young noblemen got into a brawl. One was killed by a sword. Later, another drowned in the Great Canal as he stumbled drunkenly home.

Because events of this nature never happened in Haven, and despite the fact its inhabitants were ill-equipped to perceive darkness, even when it threatened to turn out their lights for ever, inevitably people sought the help of the king and his council. These worthy gentlemen were as perplexed as anybody else and had no idea what was happening or why. Prince Garland, listening to the debates, could think of only one thing and was surprised no one else appeared to have thought the same: these horrible things had only begun to happen since Pavonia Nocta had lived in the city. But he could not speak his suspicions aloud, because to do so might result in Pavonia Nocta being sent away, and he could not bear the thought of that.

Awake or asleep, he was consumed by thoughts and visions of the dark lady. He could not bear to remain in Talina's presence now, for even the smell of her across a room nauseated him. Cloying, too sweet, somehow rotten. Pavonia by contrast was like a cool stream of dark water to ease his senses that the cauldron of the day tormented. Nightly, she visited him in dreams, although he was too reticent to approach her by day. His nights were riotous orgies of physical pleasure and he woke from them exhausted.

Even the dullest and most unimaginative of people have instincts they cannot control. The citizens of Haven became afraid. Darkness had seeped out of the palace and now wandered the streets at night, streets that were no longer peaceful, where thieves and whores roamed, where spiteful laughter could be heard, and the splash of heavy objects falling into the canals.

"The Lady Pava walks," people would whisper to one another, and sometimes – sometimes – she would actually be seen, gliding slowly through the night, her dark red gown shedding crimson petals, her long feet unshod, her hair around her like a shawl. Where she walked, cracks appeared in pavements and walls, flags fell limp, flowers died. And other flowers grew up in their place with strange colours: the purple of veins, the red of blood, the blue of dead flesh.

The courtiers, the king's council and the royal family took longer to believe the tales than those who lived in the city about them. When the queen heard the rumours, she pronounced, "Nonsense, there is a plague! No woman alone can cause that."

The king called a meeting of the sombre priests from the cathedral and eventually one of them, the youngest of their company, dared to suggest that Pavonia Nocta might be responsible for the calamities befalling the city.

"How can one woman do such a thing?" the king demanded.

"I have read," said the young priest, nervously, "that beyond the world we know there are other worlds. We never see them but sometimes they might... *leak*."

The king fixed the priest with a frightening stare. "You are saying Lady Vonny is a *leak*?"

"She is Lady Pava," said the young priest quietly, "and yes I am."

His colleagues tutted and pulled on their beards, but then the oldest of them said, "In my youth, I heard of such things." His voice was merely a creak, a sigh, his body curled over like an unborn child's, but for all its thinness his voice carried weight among his peers.

"What shall we do, Brother?" they asked the old priest.

"Say many prayers," said the old priest, who then fell asleep in his chair.

"I want praying in the cathedral though day and night," ordered the king. He gestured to his personal guards. "Bring to me this woman, if that is what she is."

"Father," said Prince Garland in a shocked, low voice. "Please, it cannot be her. She..."

"Quiet!" said the king. "You brought her here, my son. Perhaps you should be the one to rid the city of her."

Pava found the city was changing more to her liking. She enjoyed strolling through the summer nights, away from the twitterers at court. She knew that wherever she trod Haven came alive beneath her toes. Some of the inhabitants were more interesting to her now and she would smile at them as she passed, bestow her blessing. Prince Garland, though, she could only reach in dreams. He wore a suit of armour over his real self, crafted generations before, and she could not breach it. Perhaps it was because of that pale, milky scrap he was due to marry. Pava had sent blights to confine Talina to her bed, but her limp influence remained. More often, Pava found herself thinking of home, the dark lord who was her counterpart, the infinite rivers, the endless mountains and the forests shuddering with magic. Was it perhaps time to leave after all? And yet, whenever she thought this, she saw Garland's face, the child inside it, the potential bandaged tight within his heart. Perhaps she should lure him to her home, but she knew this would not work. In her realm, he would melt into a ghost, until he was only a whisper and a sigh. Garland was not robust enough to take the steps down into the dark. This saddened her.

*I am bandaged too*, she thought, *by an unlikely dream. A future that cannot happen.*

Yet still she could not pull away from Haven and because of this, and the strength of her, the city became ever more like her. She did not consider that the people who ruled might not like this change.

And so, that day when the meeting took place in the cathedral, she was called from her bed in the afternoon. The guards who came to her flinched as they crossed her threshold. The elegant, womanly chambers were now bereft of light. Creepers had fingered in through the windows, the glass shattered. Furnishings had become deepest crimson and indigo and black. White lace upon the cushions was now like dead bracken. Candle wax had dripped into shapes resembling deformed homunculi that clung to the stems of tall candle-pillars, or lolled melting in their bowls. The bed was like a grave, but plush with rotted satin. Pava's maids were now vixen sharp with knowing eyes and pointed fingernails. They laughed at the guards and skittered to the shadows in the corners of the rooms.

"What is it?" Pava asked, rising up from her bed, a perfect vision of blood and night and snow. She raised a hand to silence her maids, who were cheeping and chittering with threat.

"The king demands your presence," said the bravest of the guards.

Without further words, Pava glided past the guards and through the door so they were forced to run to keep up with her.

Pava knew that a significant moment had come and had no fear of it. She strode to the throne room with plaster falling from the ceilings in her wake. She absorbed the light of torches in the long passages so that darkness prowled behind her.

The entire court was gathered in the throne room where a thousand candles had been lit. Pava could hear croaking coming from the cathedral across the city: the priests' prayers. There was the king and his queen seated on thrones that were now almost too hard and uncomfortable to bear. Beside the king stood Prince Garland, interestingly pale and haunted.

Pava said nothing but stood before this company, intrigued as to what they might say. She noticed then, the young priest in his white habit, standing a short way behind the king's throne, his hands folded into his sleeves. She knew from looking at him that he was braver and more awake than most in Haven, and that he had taken a lamp and gone deep into the lower chambers beneath the cathedral. He had climbed down the damp, twisting stairways so far he'd reached the mildewy libraries that had been hidden away there, long before Haven had grown up above them. In crumbling documents and mouse-chewed books he had found words like 'witch', 'underworld' and 'curse'. He thought he knew her now. She smiled.

"You are accused of treason," announced the king, pointing at Pava. "For hundreds of years our city has stood unstained, pure and joyful. Until you came. Until..." And now he got to his feet and his voice thundered out across that vast chamber in a way it never had. "...until you bewitched my son and had him bring you here."

"He came to fetch me," Pava said. "I *did* warn him. I told him bringing me here would break the city." But there was no note of apology, fear or contrition in her voice. She spoke the simple facts.

"So you confess your crimes?" asked the young priest, stepping forward. He appeared disappointed, but then he had found words such as 'torture' and 'rack' in his researches too.

"Crimes? No," said Pava. "I warned him, but he insisted."

"You could have refused," said the queen harshly, "if you knew there was something to warn about."

Pava shrugged. "He intrigued me." She paused for a heartbeat, then said, "I suppose now I should leave."

The king and queen appeared confused in the face of Pava's sanguinity. They glanced at one another. And perhaps, in another story, they might simply have banished her from the city, and the buildings would have mended themselves, the people too, and Garland would have married his lacklustre maid, and everything would have gone back to how it was. Only, two things happened.

First, Garland uttered a terrible cry of "No!"

And this word was a key in the lock of a door behind which was fervour and cruelty.

"Burn the witch!" yelled the young priest. And then everyone was shouting it, but for the king and queen, and Garland, and those of their courtiers who had the most dignity.

Chips of coloured glass fell from the stained-glass windows. Three ladies fainted, one after the other, as if struck dead.

"Your grace!" bellowed the priest. "Execute her! Burn her! Burn the evil from our midst."

The king opened his mouth, but what he was about to say will never be known, for opening his mouth was enough for the guards and lesser courtiers to surge forward, led by the priest. They lifted Pava among them and ran with her out of the throne room. The quieter courtiers followed them, less hastily.

After this maddened crowd and its bewildered observers had left the chamber, the king and queen sat in shocked silence for some moments. Garland, on his knees, wept beside his father.

"My dear?" said the queen to her husband, in an exhausted voice.

The king merely raised his hands, sighed. No king of Haven had had to deal with such a calamity for thousands of years.

Then Garland leapt to his feet, crying, "I must save her!" and ran also from the chamber.

Pava could have changed into a raven and flown away, for she knew they meant to burn her, but as she had no fear of fire, decided instead to remain and see what would happen. They carried her to the cathedral square, where all the priests came out like a herd of sheep in their white, woollen habits. Guards restrained her as the crowd searched for wood to burn, a stake to which to bind her. People came running from all over Haven, taking up the cry of "burn the witch!" They brought with them kindling and lumber, which they threw onto the mounting unlit bonfire.

And then at last Pava was dragged up the pile of wood and tied to the stake. She neither struggled nor protested, merely watched the crows circling the high towers. Already the air smelled of burning. The young priest put torch to wood and quickly flames leapt up greedily. Bells were tolling, people shouting, some weeping.

Pava intended to enjoy the flames, then turn into smoke and go home. She knew she'd no chance of waking Garland now, so must accept defeat. She'd let these bleating sleepwalkers have their spectacle, something to remember her by, for in murdering her they slaughtered any chance of regaining their blithe innocence. A small revenge for their insolence. But then, as the edge of her crimson gown took light, she saw Garland riding fast towards her, his horse pushing through the crowd.

*Oh dear*, she thought, sighing, as Garland leapt from his horse and began scrabbling up through the burning wood. *He will quite lose his beauty*. His hair and clothes were alight, his hands reaching for her. He'd not make it. Kindly, she leaned away from the wood, extended her body into a long snakelike thing and held out her arms so he could take hold of her wrists.

"Poor boy," she said to him, for she could see now he was truly awake. "I can't let them burn you too." So she blew upon him, blew him backwards onto his horse, to the moment before he'd started climbing. Then, flexing her shoulders she sprouted the wings of a great raven, burst her bonds, rose up with a mighty "caw!" and flew away.

At once, a rainstorm filled the sky from nowhere, pelting down like spears. Flames hissed and died. People cowered, fell beneath the weight of the water, crawled to safety. Some were crushed in the struggle.

Garland alone remained still, upon his horse, staring at the sky. The rain was his tears, a deluge of them, given to him by her. He felt released.

While thunder crashed and the storm tore into what remained of his city, Garland turned his horse and made for the main gates. Later, some people said they saw him, riding away, and that his horse sprouted wings, so he took to the sky, followed her, his witch.

But this didn't happen. Garland merely rode away and found another life, somewhere else, full of texture.

As for the queen of the underworld, she returned to her realm, and in the way of all the best stories lived happily ever after. But sometimes, she'd wake up in the morning, with deep bruises around her wrists, and know he was in pain.

# Dimmed by a Scattering Cloud

*Story History:*

This piece was written for a friend's anthology, which unfortunately never got to be published, so here is the story's first appearance. It's based upon an experience I had when holiday in Southwold, Suffolk with some friends in June 2018. I wrote it after a visit to a restaurant in the seaside town. The characters are inspired by people I saw there, but I have no idea what those people were like in reality. I'm simply a person who makes up stories from situations and individuals that stimulate my curiosity and move me to write. On the day following the meal, the town really was engulfed in an eerie sea fret, but I never saw my visiting goddess wafting through it. However, even though this is fiction, I had to ensure she finally got her dessert. The title is adapted from a fragment of a poem in an old folktale of East Anglia.

The anthology it was due to appear in was based on local goddesses in folklore. As far as I know, there is no goddess resembling the character in this story within East Anglian folklore, but she fits the feeling of that wonderfully haunted landscape well. I never saw again the mysterious couple again, but I could imagine how it might have gone, if I'd seen that girl once more, if the dream had continued...

When she came into the restaurant, I noticed first the paleness of her; skin white as frosted glass and with the same dull bloom. Her hair was also white – I thought naturally so – yet not like the hoariness of age. Weirdly dusty in appearance, it hung round her face onto her shoulders, straight, parted in the middle. She had a narrow, sensitive face and her eyes were unusually dark. Her body was loosely encased in a long summer dress the colour of buttermilk, with a handkerchief point skirt.

Behind her came the boy.

They sat at a table almost opposite where I was sitting. For a moment they remained still, then a waitress came to them, handing out menus, and it was as if they woke up – *began*.

At that moment, the girl became a character to me; I had only to learn her story. I am always alert for stories.

I was dining alone on the first floor of *The Tall Ship* hotel, where I was staying. The place was busy, as Saturday nights at a seaside town in the holiday season always are. Torrential rain had brutalised the day, but the ripening evening was more cordially drenched in low sunlight. The streets still shone wet; the puddles were golden. Now I sat with my back to the window.

Having just made my order, I watched the girl. There was nothing else to do other than wait for the meal. She stood out from the crowd of hot, boisterous families and rowdy groups of friends. I couldn't see as much of the boy, as I was seated too far to the left of him, but it was plain he was trying to amuse his companion. He fidgeted, laughed so hard and loud I could hear him clearly. She smiled at him in an odd, courteous way, but from where I sat I could see she would not meet his eyes. First date? Had they met on the Internet, only to be disappointed by reality and made awkward in its company?

The boy's dark hair was cut in an achingly modern style, brushed forward along his scalp. His shoulders were broad, and his dark shirt, drawn tight across his back, appeared expensive. He looked athletic. I had no doubt his face would be attractive.

My first course arrived; an exquisite rendering of potted shrimp. Along with it came warm, freshly-cooked bread and sumptuous yellow butter. I indulged my senses slowly, savouring the flavours and textures.

Shortly afterwards, a first course was brought to the girl and her companion. She had chosen oysters and now raised the great half shells to her pale mouth and devoured them neatly. I have never been partial to oysters, unable to grasp what others find appealing about them. Still, her choice intrigued me. Perhaps she was trying to impress the boy with her sophistication. I could not see what he was eating.

Pale, glacial, a being of frost and sea foam, the girl sat erect, made little movement, but I noticed she drank steadily the almost colourless wine the boy had ordered. I decided she must be the daughter of rich parents, perhaps had recently left boarding-school. There was something strangely old-fashioned about her, so unlike the young people I saw around me every day. He was perhaps a couple of years older than her, but it was difficult to tell precisely from this angle.

She became aware of me watching her and, even though I'd been discreet in my observation, glanced at me now and again. I could tell she didn't mind, didn't even care why this mature woman dining alone was interested in her. Perhaps she liked to be watched.

My main course arrived, a neatly eviscerated lobster, appearing rather like some kind of crypto-zoological dissection, but divinely cooked.

The boy was still trying desperately to interest the girl, but I could see he wasn't having much success. She wasn't rude but simply didn't respond in the way someone should, dining out with a friend, lover, or even *potential* lover. Did he bore her? Was she wishing she'd never agreed to this invitation? It was obvious he had invited her rather than the other way round for the simple reason he was the one trying to make the occasion work.

Their main meal arrived. Before it went down on the table, I saw he'd ordered steak, while hers was something pale in sauce, possibly sole. As she consumed it, with obvious relish, she continued to drink. He ordered another bottle. I noticed that her skin had become rosy, either from the wine or the humidity in the air. This wasn't a natural colour but rather like a rising of blood beneath the skin, as you'd imagine a vampire might look filling up with the juice of a victim. Yet she consumed only white fish, bread, and a salad of green and maroon leaves. Her hair, too, appeared to have taken on a yellowish hue and was becoming faintly unruly. Despite this slight unravelling of her image, the bizarre *colouration*, she remained contained, her movements economical.

She was like an animated doll, a complex automaton, but I felt this was only a front or an affectation. Behind the exterior, a swift mind was at work. This, I intuited from the glances she cast in my direction. It was as if she was aware I could truly *see* her and was in some way pleased or gratified. What was her purpose? Had she ensnared the boy?

The boy took longer to eat his meal because he was still attempting to be interesting. I felt sorry for him and also embarrassed on his behalf. He really should stop.

Then, halfway through their main course, the story began to lose its drama, because it became clear the boy gave up. Perhaps, without knowing it, he'd heard – or felt – my thoughts. Silence fell between them. He even took out his phone, glanced at messages. Now, she seemed to become aware she'd lost him and made some effort to reignite his interest. Her movements became more animated. She laughed. Her colour was still up. She appeared more like an ordinary girl, But, alas, all this was too late. The catch had slipped the hook.

I was waiting for my dessert when he signalled for the bill and paid it. She appeared subdued again now, but her colour had not faded. He stood up from the table, glanced at me. He was indeed handsome. When the girl stood up, some moments after him, her skirt revealed her legs and I saw they didn't match her slender body. The thighs were unusually big, even if the calves were of normal size. She followed him out of the restaurant.

That was the end of my story, I thought.

After I'd finished my leisurely dinner, and had drunk coffee and brandy, it was almost 11 o'clock. The little town had fallen quiet – no night clubs here, or any other bright and noisy venue to keep people out late in the evening. Now the sun had gone, the air was damp and cold. Not unusual for the ancient fenlands of England at the start of summer. I went for a walk before retiring to my room for an early night – I'd hiked far that day over the marsh dykes and looked forward to curling up in bed with the novel I was currently reading. But I wanted to walk off my meal first.

As I strolled through the narrow streets, I pondered the weight of history around me – all that might have lapsed into the marshes and the sea. This area was renowned for sunken towns, since the cliffs were forever collapsing, taking churches and dwellings with them. But not recently. There were stories of bells that still rang beneath the waves, warning of storms and death. Phantoms were alleged to walk the marshes and ghostly carriages to career along the lanes. Demonic black dogs could appear to slaughter or to guide the lost. These phenomena were easy to imagine, especially in the dark.

In the winter time, this flat, misty land might be eerier still, but now, as June unfolded its green, the fields and marshes were incredibly lush, almost wantonly so. The canopies of the trees reared heavily against the sky – perhaps the same trees that had observed and survived the storms of centuries past that had washed away entire villages. The land had a long memory, I felt, and while it might lack the dramatic vistas of mountains and sheer forests found in other parts of the country, it was almost unnaturally fecund, soaked in an uncanny atmosphere you could breathe in, absorb.

And thus my thoughts were led to the strange girl I had seen in the restaurant. *Was* she strange, or did I merely want her to be? She had mermaidly aspects, but also something else – the hint of the blood drinker, the suggestion of frost and foam. An uncanny creature. She hadn't wanted the boy – I didn't think now he had been her victim. Perhaps she'd only desired the meal and he had provided it. But he wouldn't have known that. *He'd* have wanted more – at first. Had she met him in the town that day? Or perhaps in one of the churches, where the burned claw marks of devil dogs striped the ancient doors? She'd intrigued him, I thought. He'd approached her, confident because he was handsome. He had asked her out for dinner. She'd certainly enjoyed the food and – now it seemed obvious to me – had only taken an interest in her companion when it became clear he hadn't intended to stay for dessert.

Back in my hotel room, I dug out a paperback of local folklore I'd picked up in a second-hand bookshop earlier in the day. Leafing through it, I found a plethora of hauntings and demonic attacks, and a couple of tales of fresh-water mermaids who'd lure people into pools at night, but nothing about the deities of the fens. This I found odd. There would have been plenty – for wherever people had lived in earlier centuries and raised their communities, they'd brought their gods and goddesses with them. The author clearly had no interest in that aspect of the past. I wasn't intrigued by stories of headless ghosts – I wanted to know what powers had once ruled the hearts and souls of humans here. Who had they worshipped and how? But then… I had only to imagine it.

History sank into the boggy earth and the ocean deeps, along with towns and graveyards – and also murder victims and sacrifices. Perhaps history rose from the elements sometimes too.

The following day, the fog called locally a fret rolled in from the sea. When I opened my bedroom window, the fret came insouciantly inside, as if it had the right. Fingers of air.

The town looked unearthly within this damp shroud and I was eager to walk in it, find more stories waiting for me to record them. I had a full breakfast beforehand – because the food at *The Tall Ship* was so good, no meal should be missed.

I decided I'd walk along the harbour, go to the pier where I could have coffee and watch the crowds or – and perhaps better – the vague outlines of them, since the sea fret was thickening across the town.

When I reached the beach before the harbour, the water was almost invisible within the fog, but for the cresting of docile, high-tide waves. The sea was dozing, I thought. The shingle seethed in understated agitation as the waves flopped over it. Groynes haunted the beach, their posts barely visible, standing like phantoms in the water.

Jetties came into view, slowly, falling out of the mist. The air was at one moment very hot, then piercingly cold. It felt deliciously unnatural, as if I'd stepped into another world.

Eventually, the pier loomed out of the curdled air and, as I approached it, I discovered holiday makers had not been discouraged by the eerie weather. The tables outside the cafes were fully occupied, but I managed to find one free on the very edge – a perfect vantage point for viewing.

It was here I saw the girl again.

She was seated at a table nearby, with a group of people but not part of them. Perhaps they couldn't even see her at the boundary of their crowd. She was eating daintily, with a long-handled spoon, an elaborate ice cream sundae from a tall glass. Today, her hair was tied back, once again pure white, as was her skin. Her legs were concealed beneath a long cream dress that left her arms bare. She wore silver, flat-heeled strappy sandals. I saw that her toenails were painted, a shade so pale I couldn't discern its underlying colour. I was astonished to see her and must have stared openly. She became aware of this and turned her head in my direction. She smiled.

I smiled back.

She returned to consuming her ice cream.

There was something almost catlike about her.

I finished my coffee, and she put down her spoon beside the empty sundae glass. She stood up and lifted a shoulder bag from the floor by her feet. She glanced at me.

I waited a few seconds before leaving my table and following her. I had no idea how this encounter might end, or even if it *was* an encounter. She might simply go up to a police officer, if we passed any, and complain a strange woman was stalking her.

I didn't think, though, that would be the end of our story.

She walked along the sea front, away from the pier and out towards where the town ceased, and the beach took dominion. There were a few small wharfs running into the fog, but eventually even these dwindled away and there was only the girl, the sea, the dense air and me.

I realised my heartbeat had increased and began to wonder if I was afraid or in danger. I felt strangely numb, so it was hard to tell.

She walked off the boardwalk and down onto the sand, of which there was a fairly narrow band before the shingle began. The fog swirled around her, so that sometimes she became clearly visible, sometimes was no more than the suggestion of a figure. She was heading towards the sea.

I didn't want to draw too close, sensed it would be foolish to do so.

She let down her hair, stood with her feet in the water, her back to me, unmoving.

I couldn't say anything to her, for what was there to say?

She was no ghost, and there was no sense of tragedy about her. I didn't think she was a drowned creature. Like me, perhaps, she was merely a visitor. People would not know her now, because her time had been forgotten, sucked down into depths of land and sea. This, I realised, would give her freedom of a kind.

The fog caressed her, stroked her, enfolded her. Visible, then not visible: her skirt – wet now to the knees – was moulded to her calves.

*Here's a story*, she seemed to say, not with words but with silence and stillness. *We come to land, we go back. Sometimes.*

Perhaps she was glad of me, amused, even. For I had recognised her.

The next time the fog enwrapped her she did not appear again.

# VIOLET'S HOUSE

# OR SONGS THE MARTYRS SANG

*Story History:*

This story isn't based upon anyone's particular anecdote or history. The characters aren't drawn – however remotely – from life. But what is real about this piece is mourning for lost youth, something I've discussed with writer friends, especially in respect of the otherworldly and mysterious. This mourning is not for the younger physical body but for the younger mind – the way we experienced things: what we saw, what we felt, what we believed. In early years, all children are story-spinners, imaginative and full of curiosity. Only the lucky few retain those precious faculties intact into adulthood. My tale concerns the moment when the magical world of the child shifts into the harsh mundane world of the adult, when wonder begins to die, and the ghosts of lost innocence haunt the high summer landscape – that most magical time of all. The story was written for "Splinters of Truth" the collection of my work published by NewCon Press and edited by Ian Whates in 2016.

I will always remember Aunt Violet, standing there in the drawing room of Herons, with evening sunlight pouring in like treacle at the tall narrow windows, saying, "But my dears, forget your Halloweens and dark nights of winter, the truth is the ghostliest time of year is high summer. If you don't know that yet, you will find it out, because this house is a haven for ghosts."

Violet was tall, given to shawls and draperies. She was something of an anachronism, in her late 40s, smoking cigarettes in a tortoiseshell holder, speaking in the tones of a vanished era, rather like a ghost herself, I suppose. And her beautiful house, the oaken chest of my dearest childhood memories, was in its very bricks extraordinary.

It was the custom of that time for children to be farmed out for the convenience of parents whenever possible – children, that is, of fairly well-to-do families. As Aunt Violet possessed Herons, a crumbling family inheritance that nobody else wanted, "out in the middle of nowhere" – as my own parents were fond of saying – with spacious rooms and sprawling gardens, it was an ideal summertime venue where Violet's siblings could deposit their offspring. Violet did not mind. She said she liked young people around – although for the two months we stayed at Heron's, her own rather louche crowd of bright young things were kept at bay. She had a moralistic thread within her that considered children must be protected from certain aspects of life. I doubt we ever saw the "real her" and I do wonder what that was like.

Sometimes there were four of us, but usually only three: Felicity and Nancy, daughters of my father's sister, and occasionally Beatrice, who was the child of my father's brother, and then me – Katherine, or Kitty as I'm known. Felicity and Nancy were always called Fliss and Nan. Bea wasn't quite like the rest of us – we found her rather dull – and we were always glad when it was just the three of us. Generally, Bea would appear for weekends, while Fliss, Nan and I would gorge ourselves on freedom for the two whole months of July and August. I was the youngest at fourteen, Fliss was fifteen and Nan, regarded as a mysterious beauty, was teetering on the brink of womanhood at sixteen, her toes still curled about the cliff edge of childhood, but her arms outflung, her head thrown back, waiting to fall into life.

Summers were hot back then, or my memories of them are, but I can remember only few rainy days and even then I wonder if I changed the weather to fit my memories because grey light is more apt for sadder times. We knew little sadness at Violet's house.

That one Sunday, only two days after we'd arrived at Herons, I remember Fliss hanging tiny bells in the rowan tree near the fish pond. They were Christmas decorations, I believe, and as this was in the days before wind chimes were popular and easy to find, the bells were the nearest we could get to the air playing music to us.

We lay on our backs on the grass in a row, sinewy blonde Fliss, black-haired Nan and me with my red curls and annoyingly-freckled pale skin, listening to the almost inaudible tinkle.

"This is the start of our summer," said Fliss, stretching contentedly, flexing her bare toes in the grass, "and that is the sound of it."

The house was built halfway up Mere Hill and the gardens gave a spectacular view of the landscape – soft ancient hills and blurry forests. The mere lay at the bottom of the hill and extended a large way round it, surrounded by spindly trees. Beyond that, a strange backbone of rock stuck up from The Climb, one of the nearby hills, and crawled across a valley to Stag's Top; we imagined this crag as the petrified body of a dinosaur. If you narrowed your eyes and stared for long enough, you could see curious shapes within it. Sometimes, I imagined it as a huge saurian, which had died upon its knees, its great head lying sideways on the earth. That day, squinting across the valleys, I fancied a bent and crooked castle was built into the side of the crag, where the dinosaur's hips would be. Its towers looked down over a great drop and I pictured at once the unfortunates who might have been thrown to their deaths from there. "There's a castle in Rookstone Ridge this year," I said.

Fliss and Nan half-closed their eyes, followed my gaze. "So there is," said Nan.

"That's where the bells are," said Fliss softly, "can you hear them ringing?"

"Why would a castle have bells?" Nan asked, although in a dreamy tone.

Fliss was silent for a moment. "It's... I think it's a kind of monastery, or used to be."

"Yes, it was... It's not now, though."

"No."

"But the bells still ring," I said.

We listened. Small bells nearby or the distant clamour of far-off chimes? To us, the choice was obvious.

"Girls! Girls!" came a cry and a clapping of hands from the house, which was Aunt Violet calling us like cats to our tea. We leapt eagerly to our feet and ran, hair flying behind us.

I always think of Herons as a purple house, because this was the colour that dominated it in various shades, and of course the name of its mistress occupied that band of the spectrum. Wanton swags of wisteria clung to its old grey walls, obscuring several of the upper windows. Within, lilac drapes framed the windows and in the drawing-room there was always a bowl of wilting violets, petals on the table around it. There was a library with half empty shelves and old leather chairs, where the walls were a dusty imperial purple, which complemented beautifully the faded gilt of picture frames between the bookshelves. The pictures were of dim landscapes like dreams. There was a bay window in this room, where an old round dining-table had rooted; late afternoon light always fell over its tired yet satiny surface. Here we would consume our tea because we liked the room so much, and Violet let us eat where we pleased. She approved of even the slightest hint of eccentricity.

We ate salty egg and cress sandwiches and slabs of creamy Madeira cake, sipping strong and very sweet tea from enormous china cups, patterned with purple irises and sitting on plate-sized saucers. As I chewed, in utter sensual contentment, I fancied I could still hear the bells blown on the breeze. This sounded almost like many people singing, a long distance away. I sat with my back to the window and opposite me was Fliss, ethereal in the golden light, the edges of her hair transparent and glowing like a waist-length halo. She was always thinking of 'other things' and in fact became quite a famous novelist later on. Fliss started the dreams and adventures for us, but I'd caught some of that imagination from her; it was remarkably infectious when we were at Herons. "Can you still hear it?" I asked her, waiting somewhat breathlessly for her reply and thus her confirmation of my fancies. She would never deny an idea, but she might embellish the details a little.

She nodded, took a dainty nibble of cake. "Yes – I told you: it's the sound for this year."

And there always was, every year, or rather it was more than sounds, also scents and tastes, and an overall ambience or emotion that was beyond human capacity to describe.

"Something is waiting to happen," Nan said. She rested her elbows on the table, her chin in her cupped hands. This made me think of praying for some strange reason. "It's shimmering all around us."

"This year feels really good," I said.

Nan half closed her eyes and smiled at me warmly.

Fliss said, "yes," her head bent towards her plate, since crumbs were spilling from the last bite of her cake.

That evening, as I took my bath before bed-time, submerged in lilac-scented foam, I could still hear the soft tinkle of bells from the garden, through the open window. I slithered down beneath the water, imagining myself as some river creature, with weed for hair. And down there, in visualised depths of green shadows and hidden currents, I fancied the bells became voices singing again, but so far away I could barely hear them. I could make out neither words nor tune, just the susurrating rise and fall of tones. There was a sadness to the song, though. In my mind I swam towards it, undulating like a fish, but could draw no closer. I pressed my cheek against the smooth enamel of the bath, and it seemed the voices were louder then – almost too strident and too near. Unnerved, I rose up from the water, flinging my arms high, as I imagined a Nereid might when she emerged from her element. In the dry air there were no sounds at all.

While I was an imaginative child, who adored mysteries and make-believe, I was also a very practical creature. As I towelled myself dry, I thought that the sounds must have been caused by the plumbing in this aged domain; all the wheezing and coughing of furred-up pipes. Knowing this, I would be happy to *imagine* what I'd heard was a ghostly choir, chanting at the boundaries of hearing.

I was so tired that night that I fell asleep almost instantly, cocooned in the most comfortable of beds, and slept the whole night through.

At breakfast the following morning, Nan seemed a little distracted – her raven hair wilder than usual. "They were singing all night," she said, "*all night!*"

I glanced at Fliss to see what her reaction would be. "Your room faces the ridge," she said, as if this was obvious.

"Who was singing?" I asked.

Nan waved a hand in the air. "Oh, the people in the castle, whoever they are. We must see."

"I heard singing when I was in the bath," I said, "if I put my head underwater." I didn't think I should mention my theory concerning the pipes. "And even when we were eating tea, as if the bells had changed to voices."

"They sing when the bells call them," Fliss said, buttering a piece of toast. "They're not monks or nuns, though. They sing for a different reason."

I waited for Fliss to elaborate, but she did not, thoughtfully munching her toast. Perhaps she didn't have the right idea yet.

"We should go to Rookstone," Nan said.

My first instinctive reaction was to say "no!", but I didn't voice it. I was surprised at the sudden frisson of fear that gripped my mind. We didn't travel that far alone when we were at Herons. The grounds, the mere and the surrounding woodlands were large enough to accommodate our adventures and, even after visiting the house annually for around seven years now, there were still places we hadn't fully explored or claimed for our own. I wasn't sure Aunt Violet would want us going so far, especially when the danger of injury – or worse – was a possibility. There would be many places where we might fall on that sheer bone of rock. And yet I didn't want to be the one to spoil the game, to voice such practical thoughts. I pleaded silently for Fliss to say something similar, but in keeping with the game. She said nothing but had a determined look on her face. Pushing her chair away from the table, she got to her feet and sauntered to the nearest library shelf, running her hands over the faded spines of the books. And then it was in her hands *Follies of the County*, with a worn colour cover showing three pictures of broken stones – a tumbled arch, a roofless summerhouse and the ridge.

Nearly a hundred years before, a rich man named Benjamin Caldwell had lived in a house below the ridge. He had not inherited it; he had bought it. The house was gone now, lost in a fire when no one was at home. Not a creepy, meaningful fire; just an accident. No one had died or even been harmed. The damage had been considered too great for the place to be resurrected, so the remains were dismantled. Rookstone Ridge was part of the estate and Caldwell had found it inspiring; upon its wide flat backbone he'd built follies – three towers, a tumble down chapel, two pagan temples dedicated to vague idols such as "the winds" and "the seasons". He'd even created the foundations of a small Roman town, which pretended to be genuine remains, and above them, jutting out from a cliff – the dinosaur's hips – the ruins of a castle.

While Fliss read these details to us, and showed us cloudy old photographs from the book, I felt light-headed. We invented dreams all the time, but not once had any of them proved real. They were our imaginings, safely untrue. I'd said there was a castle and now there was – and, more than that, it had been there all the time.

Neither Fliss nor Nan appeared to find this astounding or unusual – to them it seemed only fitting my observation had been based on fact. It was at this point I realised they believed in our games more than I did.

"Let's go today," Nan said, the book open on the table, her fingers resting on one of the photographs.

"We should ask Aunt Violet," I said, blushing immediately. My cousins gave me catlike stares. "Well, it's quite far. Won't we need to take a picnic? And we should tell someone where we're going... really... shouldn't we?"

Nan nodded and closed the book. "You're right."

"It's less of an adventure that way," Fliss argued. "We could smuggle food out if we wanted to. It's not as if anyone would notice."

True, Violet's staff were all as wafty and dreamy as she was. The housekeeper, Mrs Barr, seemed hardly worthy of the title and spent much of her day sitting in the kitchen, talking with Violet. The two girls who helped Mrs Barr with the house appeared half asleep most of the time.

"We *should* tell her," Nan insisted and glanced out of the window, a peculiar half-smile on her face. I saw Mitch, the gardener, strolling away from the house. He was new to us that summer, although he'd been taken on by Violet at the end of the season the previous year. A flurry of irritation went through me. At the time, I didn't know why.

As one, we went to our aunt, who always took her breakfast alone in a small airy room near the kitchens. She had told us on our very first visit she was a bear first thing in the mornings and not fit to be in company, but we considered our mission worth the risk of confronting this perhaps fearsome animal. Violet was wrapped in a fringed shawl of purple silk, reading a newspaper. She didn't

Storm Constantine

appear to be angry when we knocked on the door and walked in on her.

"Well, what's this?" she asked, smiling, perhaps sensing an adventure.

We told her, not about the bells or the singing, or any of our imaginings, but just an interest in visiting Rookstone.

Aunt Violet pursed her lips. "Well, it's private land," she said, "but I'm sure Alex Caldwell – who owns the land – wouldn't mind you girls going over there. He's a friend of mine." She paused. "It *could* be dangerous, though, all sorts of drops hidden among the shrubs, and those towers... a lad once broke his back climbing out at the top of one. The wind blew him down."

"We'd be careful," Nan said, in her most sensible tone.

"We wouldn't climb the towers," Fliss said.

Violet hesitated. "Well, I don't know. The place has run wild since Alex's grandfather landscaped it – half the hazards must be hidden now. I think someone should go with you, at least."

"You?" I asked, hopefully.

She laughed. "Oh, I've never been much of a hiker. I'll ask Mitch to take you over. It's going to be a glorious day."

"Can we take a picnic?" I asked.

Violet reached out to muss my hair. "A day out is not a day out without a picnic! Go and talk to Mrs Barr. I'll have a word with Mitch."

Arrangements were made, and before noon we were ready to depart. Fliss and I weren't happy we were to be escorted by the gardener, although Nan didn't seem to mind. Fliss rolled her eyes at me, grimaced. "Don't be dopey," she told her sister as we put on our shoes in the dim hallway.

"It was supposed to be just us," I complained, in a tone whiney even to my own ears. "How can it be the same if he's there, getting in the way?"

Nan shrugged. "He seems nice," she said. "It's better than not going at all, isn't it?"

I was the last to leave the house because I'd forgotten my hat. Violet was insistent our heads were covered, or we'd faint from the heat. As I ran down the drive, to where the others were waiting by the lion-guarded gateway, I was compelled to pause and look back at the house. There was someone in Nan's

52

bedroom, looking down at me. In fact, I realised, it was Nan herself. Had she changed her mind about the trip? She looked strangely young and childlike and rather sad. I waved at her. She raised a single hand, pressed the palm against the glass, then turned away. How odd. Perhaps womanly afflictions were upon her – I had yet to be visited by The Curse – and she'd been forced to stay indoors. No wonder she looked sad, I thought.

And then I turned a curve in the drive and could see them ahead of me: Fliss, Mitch – and Nan. I stopped, looked back – there was no one at the window. The girl had looked so much like Nan, and yet it must've been one of Violet's droopy house staff.

"What is it?" Fliss asked, when I reached them.

"I saw Nan at the window," I said, pointing back, "or thought I did."

"No, I'm here, *marvellously*," said Nan and stretched out her arms.

Looking back, I can see easily that Mitch was a dangerous sort, a certain archetype of a man. He was handsome in an indolent, boneless sort of way, with dark hair falling over his eyes. His lips were sensual and rarely out of a smile. He was watchful, particularly in respect of Nan. As for her, that day she burst open like a bud into a spreading exotic flower. She pranced around, she flung her hair about, she flirted. Mitch smiled at it all, but he was, as she had suggested "nice". He joked with us, treated us as if we were younger male friends of his, and didn't expect us to flounder over stiles or be helped up steep hills with treacherous stones underfoot. Grudgingly, I liked that about him.

We walked across fields spiky with the first mowing and Rookstone became larger before us. There was majesty to it, a feeling of great age. In those days no fence surrounded it and we passed simply from the sunlight of a hay meadow into the shadow of ancient rhododendrons that had grown so huge and wild they were like prehistoric trees. The blossoms had gone from them by July and, as we clambered up a narrow trail through them, I wondered what they would look like in full bloom – a blaze of colour on the cragside.

We had quite a walk to reach the place where the castle folly stood, or what remained of it. Once we'd negotiated the steep slope to a more level area, we found a patch of sunshine on a lawn among the trees, and here decided to eat our lunch. Nan opened the hamper, which Mitch had carried and had now laid on the ground. She spread out the blue checkered tablecloth within, began extracting sandwiches.

"What're you wanting to come up here for?" Mitch asked us. "Thought girls like you would want the town, shopping and that."

Fliss directed the most scornful glance she could muster upon him. "We're interested in local history," she said primly. "There are follies up here, castles and temples."

"Not much to see now," Mitch said. "Caldwell's let it go."

"You know about this place?" Nan said in a bright voice.

He shrugged. "A bit. Used to play up here as a lad."

"Not that long ago, then," said Fliss sharply.

He eyed her guardedly. "No, not really, but it feels as if it was." He lit a cigarette and the smell of tobacco enfolded us. "You'll feel the same one day, look back to this afternoon and think it was a century ago, yet it'll only be five years at most."

I could see Nan approved of this thoughtfulness, perhaps an indication of him having depth and character.

"Do you know about the castle?" she asked.

"We thought it was real when we were kids." He said nothing more on the subject – then.

After we'd eaten most of the sandwiches and slaked our thirst with the lemonade Mrs Barr had provided for us, we pressed on. Mitch picked up the hamper again, slung its strap over his shoulder. He handed his cigarette to Nan. "Want some?"

"No, thank you," she said. "I don't."

He shrugged. "Suit yourself."

We didn't talk much on the final steep climb to the castle, concentrating more on not slipping and sliding back down the slope. The sun, where it pierced the tree canopy of ancient oaks and beeches, was hot on my head, despite the hat. I could hear the bells now, and the singing; faint tidelike swells in my mind. Nan began to hum tunelessly beneath her breath.

We came to the shadow of the castle wall and here we could see it was constructed of large stones, but also some parts of it were common brick, weathered and crumbling, powdered with moss and lichen. A broken metal railing poked threateningly from a walkway overhead, its bars twisted and cruel.

"There's more to see from the other side," Mitch told us. "In its day, old Caldwell used to stay here overnight – he had proper rooms built and a hall where there were parties."

"Did anyone ever die?" I asked. "Did they fall?"

"There are always stories like that," Mitch said, "kids like to make things up." He shaded his eyes and smiled up at the dark walls. "When you play in a place like this, you can't help thinking of scary things that might've happened, ghosts that might've walked."

Again, I noticed Nan's wide and increasingly adoring smile of approval, as Mitch proved himself to be imaginative as well as thoughtful. He led us round the side of the building until we came to a ramp partially obstructed by fallen masonry that led into a courtyard. Half-fallen towers surrounded this space and below them a colonnade ran round the inner wall, draped in shadow. Proprietorial rooks complained about our intrusion, filling our ears with a more hectic kind of music. I couldn't hear the bells here, nor any singing.

"How wild it is," Nan said in a voice hardly more than a sigh. She took off her wide-brimmed hat, shook out her mane of rook-feather hair. The wind caught this in its fingerless grip, pulled it over her face, so she had to hold it back with both hands. I half expected the birds to come wheeling around her head, to pluck strands of her hair for their nests.

Mitch showed us to some narrow damp steps that led to the back of the castle, where the original owner had had his recreational rooms constructed. To reach this area, we'd have to negotiate the walkway that girdled the folly. It was dangerous on the sheer side, and here the wind felt malicious, but the safety railing was still intact and Mitch said that if we kept close to the wall on our left then we'd not be in danger of falling. If we'd leaned upon those railings, they probably would not have been as solid as they appeared. I felt strangely light-headed and a little sick as we negotiated that narrow trail. I couldn't help thinking of leaning upon the railings, for the iron to be rusted and rotted through at the base, for one or all of us to be flung out into the air, uttering thin screams before our bodies shattered upon the rocks below. All I could hear was the wind and screeching rooks, as if we'd emerged from the quiet summer element into a realm more fierce and dangerous. The thought occurred to me: were the castle and its guardians angry that we were here? Presumably, the folly had been molested by children for generations, some of whom had no doubt contributed towards its physical decline, yet I had the feeling few visited it now. The air was desolate.

Mitch led us round to the ruinous main hall, which was in shadow. The roof was still there in places – spiky broken beams, and in one quarter a number of roof tiles. I could hear pigeons now, their soft 'croo croo'. Bright green weeds grew between the bricks and among the remaining tiles.

"This is a brooding place," Nan said.

"It feels as if people died here," Fliss added with relish. She rubbed her arms. "Dark and damp, yet full of ashes."

"If you want to believe the castle is real, perhaps that's possible," Mitch said.

A light came into Fliss's eyes and I saw her estimation of Mitch rise instantly; he was prepared to share the game. "Were there not ruins Caldwell built on?"

Mitch shrugged. "It would've been a good spot to build a castle." He grinned. "And perhaps there was a siege, or it was set on fire. The house in the valley below burned, you know, a long time ago."

"Perhaps this too came alight at exactly the same moment," Fliss said.

As I peered at the walls, I thought they did look blackened, as if by a fire.

"This way," said Mitch.

We followed him into a short, lightless stone tunnel that led to an unpainted wooden door. He glanced back at us, grinned, then knocked upon the door. He put his ear to the wood, raised his eyebrows, then pushed on the door so it opened. "My lady's chamber," he said.

Nan was the first into the room. The windows were still whole, miraculously, and light and heat streamed in through them. The air at first smelled musty but also faintly sweet, as if of flowers or incense.

"Marvellous!" Nan breathed.

Fliss entered the room behind her. "It's intact," she said. "Perhaps someone still cares for it."

I stood at the threshold, frozen. I couldn't enter that room. The smell in there had turned repugnant, still sweet yet also somehow bloody. I couldn't describe it, but I felt close to gagging. This was a dreadful room. Without saying anything, I backed away. The others didn't appear to notice I'd not followed them.

Stumbling – dizzy and nauseous – I found my way back to the dank, gutted hall, where the pigeons still made their soft song. I felt I'd emerged into a different place to where we'd been before. The hall now smelled strongly of excrement and rot and I saw the lower walls were slimy. *No one ever came here to do any good*, I thought. Desperate for clean air, for light, I inched back along the walkway and down into the sunny courtyard, where the rooks still wheeled and squawked. This was not how the day had been supposed to proceed. Somehow, I had been cast out of the adventure, perhaps didn't exist anymore for those still wrapped within it. I couldn't even hear their voices now. Then a susurrus of song came to me, the same as I'd heard beneath my bath water, faint on the breeze, hardly there at all. It came from everywhere at once and yet nowhere. For a moment it swelled loudly, and I felt that if I gazed up at the high walkway I'd see the singers, ranged in a line, chanting into the wild air. But when I did turn, there were no figures outlined against the sky, and further concentration on the song transformed it simply into the wind whispering through old stones, mingling with the croak of the rooks and the more distant murmur of pigeons. These components had always made the song, I thought. There were no ghostly choirs around. Nature herself was the ghost.

After some minutes, while I calmed down and unpleasant sensations subsided, I became angry my cousins hadn't come after me or asked what was wrong. So, I'd just go home without them, then. Eventually, they'd have to worry.

Tense with resentment, my head aching with it, I retraced our steps to the outside of the castle. The place seemed tawdry to me now; no enchanted realm, but a folly of disintegrating bricks stuck onto a crude skeleton of corroded iron. There was nothing to be scared of, but equally nothing to be awed by. The forest below it was more beautiful, the fields beyond more fragrant.

By the time I reached Herons, I was beginning to feel guilty for storming home on my own. I felt Aunt Violet would be disappointed in me, so didn't go into the house. Instead, I wandered to a favourite spot by the mere, where the willows rinsed their lush tresses in the still, mosquito-kissed waters. I sat down on the prickly grass, my heart thumping. The place didn't feel the same without Nan and Fliss beside me. Usually, to our imaginations, this was the haunt of lissom water maidens, of whom we yearned in vain to catch sight. Now it was simply a forlorn and empty place, where the stagnant waters reeked foully in the heat of the day. Miserably, I put my face against my raised knees and curled my arms over my head. When would it be safe to go back to Herons? I wanted to run there now, to hear Violet's warm voice, to be embraced by the colours, the scents of home. How could I explain my behaviour? The answer came to me, and in a flood of relief, I jumped to my feet and ran up the hill to the house.

Later that day, in the early evening, Fliss and Nan came to my room, where I lay in bed, attempting to appear delicate and worthy of sympathy. "Why didn't you *say*, you silly thing?" Nan said in concern, sitting down on the coverlet.

"You were having fun," I answered awkwardly. "I didn't want to spoil it."

"This illness came on very quickly," Fliss said, a note of suspicion in her voice. It was – and still is – very difficult to deceive Fliss.

I shrugged, wouldn't meet her eyes. "I just had to get out because I needed to be sick. I didn't want Mitch to see that."

My excuses were all plausible; there was no reason to disbelieve them. The truth was I actually *did* feel ill now, slightly feverish.

That night, I had a dream, of which even to this day I can remember every detail. I was walking round the garden of Herons in moonlight, barefoot. The grass beneath my feet was slightly damp, yet warm, and where I trod the shorn blades released a green scent. I came to a place where usually there was a stone fountain fashioned of grey, lichened urns. Now, this spot was occupied by a rhododendron bush in full bloom. Even in the moonlight, I could see its flowers were a deep violet colour, with pink hearts that emitted a rosy glow. Around the bush, motes of muted light floated and spun, like down or feathers, almost grey in colour but occasionally lighting up in pin-pricks of brilliance. I had never seen anything so beautiful and went towards the bush, which was twice my height at least. As I drew close to it, I could smell that the blooms were scented, which was unusual for a rhododendron. I wanted to bury my face in those magical, fragrant blooms and reached out to touch them. But the merest contact of my fingers made the whole bush shudder. In horror, I watched every single flower fall down simultaneously to pile upon the stones beneath my feet. The strange motes of light swarmed up and flew away. Then it was over. I didn't wake up, but moved to some other dream that I don't remember.

The following day, Aunt Violet told me to keep to my bed. I had a temperature. Despite this, I no longer felt ill and was restless. I couldn't hear my cousins and imagined darkly they'd gone off with that Mitch again, on some other adventure. All day, I either read or dozed, simmering with jealousy but also disappointment I was being excluded from the day's activities. The only person who came to see me was Anne, one of Violet's staff, who brought me lemon barley water and some biscuits, since I didn't feel like eating anything more filling.

Around tea-time Violet put her head round the door to see how I was. I insisted I felt much better and was hungry. She allowed me to dress and go downstairs. The thought of food still made me feel slightly bilious, but I was determined to hide this, to think myself well. The illness wasn't real after all, so it would just have to accept that and go away.

Downstairs, I found Fliss in the library, curled up with the book we'd been looking at the day before. She glanced up when she heard me enter the room. "Hello, feeling better now?"

"A bit," I said. "Have you been out?"

Fliss shook her head. "No. I've been helping Mrs Barr with the baking."

"Why didn't you come to see me?"

"Violet said to let you rest." She smiled. "Anyway, you're up now."

"Where's Nan?" I demanded.

Fliss shrugged. "I don't know. She didn't want to do any baking and went off by herself."

These activities were so far removed from our usual habits, I felt unnerved. If we did ever go to the kitchen, it was all together and only to beg for left over cake mix or lumps of icing, rather than actually involve ourselves in culinary tasks. None of us ever went "off alone" either.

"Something's wrong," I blurted.

Fliss raised her eyebrows at me. "What do you mean?"

"It started yesterday in that awful place," I began, then lost confidence to continue. I could see that Fliss and I were in different fields, an ocean of grass between us. There was no immediate empathy as there usually was between us.

"Awful place?" Fliss put down her book. "Kitty, what's the matter with you?"

I turned away from her. She'd not felt a thing. My eyes grew hot with tears that could not fall. "Nothing," I said. "I think the heat got to me yesterday, or there was something in the sandwiches disagreed with me."

"Poor you," she said. "You do look a bit odd."

"You didn't come after me," I said plaintively, still unable to look at her.

"We thought you were behind us," Fliss said. "And when we were ready to leave, you'd just gone. I'm *sorry* we're not psychic. You should've said something." Her voice now was sharp.

At that moment, a stranger walked in through the French windows – a stranger wearing the body of my cousin Nan. She had on her wide-brimmed hat as before, but also a more formal blue polka dot dress with a full skirt. When she took off her hat and laid it on the table by the window, I saw her lips were crimson with lipstick that had clearly been recently applied. She also appeared to have aged around ten years overnight. I could only stare at this apparition in dismay.

She laughed at me. "Seen a ghost, Kit?"

"Where've you been?" I asked.

She touched her hair – which was neatly brushed and ribboned into a ponytail – in a grotesquely adult way. "Oh, just the village."

"What were you doing *there*?"

She shrugged, laughed. "You're so *nosy*, aren't you? I went to the tea rooms, actually."

I knew then she'd been with Mitch.

Saying nothing more, I went out into the garden. What was the point now? To me, our summer world had simply… gone.

I went to where we'd strung our bells in the rowan tree; the air was achingly still so they didn't chime. Here I lay on the grass in the shadow of the branches, almost witless with a grief I couldn't explain or understand. Somehow, we'd *made* this terribly estrangement between us happen. I pawed back through my memories. Had I started it with that talk of the castle on the ridge? Maybe the ruin hadn't been real at all before I'd dreamed it up. Now it was a monster, warped and disgusting and stinking. The ethereal voices had been silenced.

*No*, I told myself sternly, *no. You can't invent a building of bricks and stone. That's just stupid. It* was *in that book, after all.*

What had been in that room? I wondered. That was the moment, surely? Until then, the day had been fine – more or less – but for Nan and Mitch, with their absurd mutual attraction waiting to happen. I wished he didn't exist, that he could in fact be wished away. If only we could get back to normal, but how could I make this happen?

When dinner was ready, Nan came out into the garden to find me. She put an arm around my shoulders and said quietly, "Everything's all right, Kit. You *do* know that, don't you?"

Looking at her, I saw she'd wiped off her lipstick and had changed into shorts and shirt: *our* Nan, not that other one. I shook my head. "I felt ill. I'm fine now."

Nan kissed my hair. "There, then. We'll do our usual things tomorrow, I promise."

Looking back, I can see that Nan did try to keep things together as they'd always been, but it was like trying to shore up a building where the foundations had gone. Perhaps Herons, like me, was suspicious, even frightened, of change. Or perhaps I became more sensitive. I can't be sure. But I remember how I heard the house creaking all the time, as if stretching its bones in discomfort. When I mentioned this to Fliss and Nan they immediately thought up some far-fetched reason for this – something to do with a walled-up girl and clanking chains. Even our make believe had changed somehow, become a parody of itself. I joined in as I'd always done, but it was as if part of me now was simply an observer looking on from a distance. Also, we had to share Nan with Mitch, who became to me obnoxious. I felt he was sly and feckless, with a satyr's face, and a satyr's disregard for people's feelings. Nan was careful to divide her time between us all, and Fliss didn't seem to mind. In fact, they now had whispered conversations apart from me that involved a lot of high-pitched shrieks and giggling.

Consequently, I spent time alone, but I wasn't unhappy. In just a week or so I became used to my own company and began to prefer it to that mockery of intimacy that waited for me in Fliss and Nan's presence. With Violet's encouragement I started painting in water colours – scenes of the mere and house, but always peopled with supernatural creatures – secret faces looking out here and there. Violet praised my work. I knew she was aware I was hurt by the change in my relationship with my cousins, but she didn't talk to me about it, perhaps waiting for me to bring the subject up myself. Sometimes, I saw her look at me in a certain way and felt she knew everything about me.

Once I heard Violet speaking to Nan in the sitting room, while I was rummaging around outside in the shrubbery near the house. The long windows were open. I remained very silent and still so they wouldn't realise I was near. All I caught of the conversation was Violet saying, "You will be *careful*, sweetie, won't you? I'm sure you know what I mean."

*I* didn't, but I intuited it must involve the vile Mitch.

"Violet!" Nan squealed, laughing in what could have been embarrassment or delight. "You're terrible!"

"Not at all," Violet replied smoothly. "I know well enough that prohibitions and rules don't work in the hearts and minds of young people, who are naturally wilful. Best to give them advice on how to sail the dangerous waters than try and keep them to shore, since even if you tied up all the boats, or scuppered them, the young would simply swim away regardless."

"I can sail, *and* I can swim," Nan said proudly.

"I hope so," Violet said. "Come, I have some dresses I think you might like."

They moved away from me then, Nan talking swiftly but quietly. I heard Violet's low, comforting voice responding to her.

After we'd been at Herons for nearly three weeks, Beatrice came to stay for a week. I was surprised to find I was glad to see her. She seemed a solid piece of dependability, standing legs apart in the hallway, booming, "Hello, everyone."

Bea too had grown and changed since I'd last seen her. I realised she was becoming attractive. She was somewhat masculine, so I suppose the word to describe her is handsome rather than pretty. There was an open honesty to Bea that I felt no longer existed in Fliss and Nan, if it had even been there in the first place.

I offered to help carry her two suitcases to her bedroom. Here, she said bluntly, "What's up with the ballerinas?"

I realised she must be referring to Fliss and Nan. "Why? What do you mean?" Before this summer, I would have been outraged if Bea had referred to my cousins in a sarcastic way and would at the very least have snubbed her. Now, I felt slightly satisfied. This, I knew, was a contemptible reaction, but it still felt cosy.

"You three were always thick as thieves. Not so now, is it?" That Bea could have picked this up from the scant ten minutes she'd been with us all in the hall was astounding, if not a little frightening to me. "Had a barny?" Bea enquired relentlessly.

"Well…" I wondered then if I could tell Bea everything, but decided against it. "There's this boy," I said.

"Oh, is *that* it?" Bea said. "Let them get on with it, then. Nothing you can do about that."

That evening, I saw Nan sitting in the garden beneath the rowan tree. There was something about her posture that impelled me to go to her; I felt she was sad. She had her back to me, gazing down at the mere where the shadows were clustering thickly, preparing for night. Was she remembering previous summers? Did she mourn for them as I did? I felt that now was the time to talk frankly with her, try and reclaim our friendship. But as I drew closer, I realised it wasn't Nan at all. In fact, there was no one there beneath the rowan, just the shadow of gently-moving boughs.

I dreamed again of the violet rhododendron in the place where a fountain should be. This time, I was crying as I stood before the naked tree. I was scooping up the fallen petals, which I could see were already turning brown. I was attempting to attach them once more their branches. I woke from the dream to my moonlit bedroom, and I knew then that the rhododendron was the past and that I couldn't make it come back.

From that time, I often caught sight of Nan-who-wasn't-there around the house and gardens, always a distance from me. I'd see her walk past the sitting-room windows, or spot her disappearing round a corner in the corridors of the house. I wasn't sure if what I glimpsed so fleetingly was a ghost or a figment of my imagination. I'd wanted so desperately for ghosts to be real, for the supernatural to be real, but faced with a situation that might possibly *be* supernatural, I didn't feel the level of excitement I was sure I *should* feel. I couldn't discuss it with anyone because Nan and Fliss felt so apart from me now, even though we maintained an act of close camaraderie. I believed they'd think I was making it up to get attention.

While Bea was with us, we all played tennis and badminton, and if bad weather confined us to the house we played cards and Monopoly. Once I saw the non-Nan standing by the door of the library while we sat round the table, laughing and chattering. She was there for only a moment, and I thought she'd been looking at herself – wanly, sadly. This was a younger version of Nan, so it couldn't possibly be a ghost. Nan was very much alive, more present in the world than any of us.

Later that day, as Bea and I had moments alone together before dinner, Bea said, "what spooked you earlier?"

I took more notice of her now and had learned she was an observant person, who could interpret the words and actions of others quite accurately. There was no point denying it, because clearly she'd seen me stare at the doorway for some moments, no doubt with mouth open or a blanched face, or other typical symptoms of seeing something odd. I looked at Bea for a moment, then said, "you wouldn't believe me if I told you."

"If you believe it, that's good enough for me," Bea said. "Doesn't mean I have to believe it myself, of course, but that doesn't matter. Tell me."

And so I did. I didn't mention that I thought I'd somehow *created* the castle. I emphasised Nan's flirtation with Mitch, and then somewhat more reluctantly told Bea of the phantom I saw so often. "Our visit to Rookstone changed everything," I said miserably. "I wish I could take back what I said. I wish I'd never seen that castle in the stone."

Bea drew in a breath. "Kitty... you can't stop Nan growing up, and that's what you're describing. I've seen it at school. People seem to change overnight sometimes, even people you care about, who you think you know." Her face was sad, and I knew she'd lost someone to adulthood too.

However, this rather dampening explanation did not satisfy me. "But the ghost…"

"You know what I think?" Bea announced, brightening, stamping her memories down. "You need to go back to that place. I'll go with you."

"Why? Why go back?"

"Face your ghost," she said.

"But I didn't see it there… It was here."

"Things turned the moment you entered that room in the castle," Bea said. "You said the smell changed and then you had to escape."

"Bea… do you believe there's something *unnatural* about what's happening?" I was actually aghast she might think that.

"I really don't know," she replied, "but I think that's what you should do."

I considered. Perhaps I shouldn't have run away that day. Perhaps returning *was* appropriate. "Do we go with the others?"

Bea shook her head. "No, let's just go together."

It was not difficult to escape Fliss and Nan. While Nan gave us her time most days of the week, on the remaining days she'd be off in the village, presumably with Mitch and his friends. She sometimes smelled of cigarettes, and I believed she'd taken up smoking herself. When Nan was absent, Fliss spent much more time with Mrs Barr and her assistants. Bea remarked rather scathingly that while Nan had taken a shine to boys, Fliss had turned to the skills of home-making. "She'll be a wife not a lover," Bea said. Sometimes, she could come out with what seemed to me extraordinarily adult statements. I wondered where she heard such things.

Thursday gave us our opportunity. We didn't bother taking food with us or attempt to make the visit to Rookstone anything but an essential task. We'd go there, see what happened, come home. No one would know.

As we left Herons, I turned to glance back at the house, see if the ghost-Nan was in the window again. She wasn't.

The day was dappled – mostly fine but sometimes clouds muffled up the sun. Bea did not dawdle, so it took far less time to reach the shade of the rhododendron forest than it had on my first visit.

I felt no trepidation as I led the way to the hall and the room beyond it. Disgust for the place had left me; it was just a ruin. I wondered in fact why I'd even bothered to come. What had happened was within Nan, Fliss and me, not something external. Bea was right – time alone was changing us all. We couldn't remain children for ever. That in itself was a shock, but of course for everyone there comes that moment when we realise this. The moment had in fact passed for me.

At the entrance to the hall, with its dank, dirty smell, I turned to Bea behind me and said, "Is there any point to this?"

"Don't you want to go on?"

"I'm not bothered. Do you want to see it?"

"Yes."

We stepped into the green shadow of the hall. As before, pigeons hummed above us, but the smell was not as bad as I remembered. Still, it was an unwelcoming place. As we made our way to what I now called 'the hidden chamber', I heard a noise that halted my steps. "What's that?" I murmured.

It was a series of noises, a song perhaps, but nothing like the ethereal choir I'd once imagined I'd heard. Grunts, cries, rhythmic – almost tribal. The sounds appeared to be coming from the room ahead of us; its door was closed.

"Kitty..." Bea said in an uncertain tone, "I don't think..."

No, I had to find out. If there *was* something supernatural here, I was compelled to open the door on it. I had Bea with me, who was strong and fearless, so I wasn't afraid either.

I put my hand upon the round knob of the door, which was warm, as if someone had recently held it for a long time.

I thought he was killing her – the sounds were dreadful. She was lying on the floor, her skirt up around her waist, her legs spread wide. He was lying on top of her with his trousers round his knees, bouncing up and down on her. Disgusting!

"Nan!" I yelled and hurtled into the room, throwing myself on top of that vile youth, beating at him with my fists. "Get off her, you beast!"

"Kitty, no!" Bea cried behind me, then I felt her hands on my shoulders, pulling me back. I struggled, but she was stronger than I was.

I saw Nan's face, horrified, staring madly at me over Mitch's shoulder. Her mouth was open, lipstick smeared over her lower face. She didn't seem to recognise me.

Mitch's head was turned to me, his face furious. "Fuck off you, stupid brats," he spat. "Just fuck off."

Bea dragged me protesting to the door. She closed it, leaned upon it, held me close. I'd begun to cry. "Come on," Bea said, "let's go."

She led me, arm around my shoulders, back to the hall. I felt dazed, as if I'd fallen and hit my head. What had I seen? Once we'd made our way to the courtyard, Bea produced a handkerchief, which she held out to me. I took it and wiped my eyes, blew my nose. "What was he *doing* to her?" I asked. "We should stop it. We can't just…"

"She doesn't want us to stop it," Bea said.

That night, I awoke from a dream I couldn't recall. My room was lit faintly by moonlight. I was compelled to get out of bed and go to the window, which I opened wide to let in the scent of the dark. I saw the phantom Nan standing under the rowan tree. She was gazing up at me, and from that distance I couldn't see her expression. She was a true ghost, though; white, almost transparent, very beautiful. I didn't have to shout, because I knew that she'd hear me. "Go away," I whispered. "You must go away now. You're dead."

I realised some years later how lucky Nan had been to avoid a teenage pregnancy, which would have been a far more traumatic situation then than it is today. I'm quite sure now that all she'd had to protect her was Violet's mild warning. Our summers inevitably changed. Nan in fact did not come to Violet's house again for the holidays, and Fliss only for one more year. That last summer when we'd been together, after the incident in the castle, and Bea's rather embarrassed explanation to me back home, Nan underwent another change. Perhaps Mitch had been spooked by being caught, or he'd had what he'd been after and wanted nothing more, but he turned cold on her. He gave up the job as Violet's gardener. Nan no longer went to the village or put on her lipstick. She cried a lot, and didn't sleep very well, becoming a lot like the little ghost I'd seen of her. First love – a tsunami of pain we have to survive. She didn't share any of it with me. She blamed me, I think, for Mitch dumping her. I never told on her, didn't even tell Fliss, although I believe Nan confided in her sister, because Fliss too withdrew from me. The rest of the summer passed uneasily, although Bea wrote to her parents and asked to stay for longer. I was grateful to her for that.

Once we were all women, engrossed in new lives, my cousins and I became close again – in a different way to how we had been before. We never talked of that summer. It left a scar on Nan. She became a brittle, sharp creature, and the years only honed the blade of her. She was always very witty but had a series of disastrous relationships with unsuitable men, including three marriages, which culminated with her early death at the age of 35. At the funeral, Fliss said to me, "She'll be happier now." I wanted to believe the potential for what she became had been in her all the time, and it hadn't been Mitch who'd turned her that way. Because, if it had been, we might've helped her, stopped it. But if any of us were remotely responsible, it was Violet. She should have sent Nan away the moment she realised what was happening.

Bea and I continued to visit Violet in the summer times, through the remainder of our childhood, through our college years, through relationships – in my case, marriage – break ups, career moves and house purchases. We kept on visiting right up until her death, and that was a good many years, for she was ninety-six when she died. During her final illness I stayed with her a lot, taking my work with me, since I was freelance and could work where I liked. The modern age had come. I could work on my computer in the old library, surrounded by childhood memories.

One evening, as we sat drinking gin cocktails in the dusk of a perfect summer day, I told Violet all about that *other* summer, even up to stumbling upon Nan and Mitch at Rookstone, and how I'd foolishly believed I'd conjured up the castle and made it all happen.

Violet had smiled at that. "You know," she said, "there might be something in it."

I grinned. "Oh, come on! What do you mean?"

"That castle you describe – I never saw it as a girl, and I went to Rookstone quite regularly. And that book you found in the library – I can't recall ever seeing that either, and I *did* know the books in there quite well."

Violet was very old by then. Her memories often became confused with dreams. It's likely she was mistaken.

# DOWN INTO SILENCE

*Story History*

This story was written for *What October Brings: A Lovecraftian Celebration of Halloween*, edited by Douglas Draa, and published by Caeleno Press in 2018. I've always loved H. P. Lovecraft's work, and leap at the chance to delve about in his mythos. I've written several stories in this vein. I'm also fascinated by fact and fiction colliding – such as when you visit a meaningful site and find things there totally in accord with what you might be researching at the time. That happens a lot to me – and I love it. I've never had the privilege to visit the state of Maine in the States, but I can visualise clearly – with all senses – what it's like. How lucky the protagonist is, to find what she does – a strange female who appears to walk straight out of the pages of a Lovecraft story, and also the ability to bring a character invented by Lovecraft to life.

Sometimes, places are more beautiful in decay, no matter how elegant and grand they might have been in their prime. Gone the straight lines of walls and roofs, gone the smooth roadways, the tidy gardens. The mellow light of October gilds the ancient stone, the defiant spires still standing. The sun falls down the cloud-flecked sky, robed in the colours of harvest. The palette of Fall roars against the dark hills, the trees still clothed in finery, hanging on, perhaps, for the ball, the festival: All Hallows'' Eve. Gazing upon such a scene, you cannot help but feel melancholy, grieving for a world you never knew, but which you know is lost forever and cannot truly be restored or replicated, even as a theme park. That lost world was somehow greater than what has come to replace it.

There are few hidden places now, few uncovered secrets –

*anywhere.* We know the secrets of Innsmouth, or what the alleged witnesses told us were true so long ago. Nearly a hundred years has passed. The way the town draws her skirts around the truth is clever; those who *did* witness, *if* they did, lost a degree of sanity, could never be thought of as entirely reliable again. Maybe *none* of it was true. The surviving records sound like witch trials to me, more imagination than fact.

And yet, standing here on the bridge over the tumbling River Manuxet, gazing out to sea, I wonder. The fact is, I *want* it to be true, all of it.

I went to Innsmouth to capture the spirit of the town in pictures – this is my hobby, not my job. I visit places of ill or unusual reputation and post the results of my captures on a blog. Halloween seemed an appropriate time of year to visit this allegedly blighted spot. So – I'm on holiday, shooting the memory of monsters, but not with a gun.

I've already begun to compose the text that will accompany my pictures. I think the old stories are *based* on fact but have been exaggerated over the years. The only person who revealed the 'truth' was Zadok Allen in the 1920s, and he was hardly a reliable source, being an aged and raddled alcoholic. Robert Olmstead, who collected and revealed Allen's ramblings, proved to be equally unreliable. Claiming to be a "descendent" of the famed Marsh family, he ended his life in an asylum. Records state that a tumour on the brain altered his behaviour and made him prey to delusions. Most historians interested in the town believe Allen and Olmstead concocted the most outrageous of the stories between them. Allen, immersed in inebriated fantasies fuelled by paranoia and plain lunacy, found in Olmstead an eager and gullible listener, who egged him on, drawing ever more dubious tales from the old drunk.

When I first arrived in town, like everyone I suppose, I began hunting for the "Innsmouth Look" in the faces of the inhabitants – traces of a batrachian ancestry, beasts from the sea and their hybrid offspring. But it soon became clear that the majority of the modern population came from somewhere else. There is plenty of work here now. Innsmouth is up there with Salem and Arkham as a tourist destination. There's a huge welcome sign on the main road in, sporting a cheerful fish man waving at new arrivals with webbed hands, claiming "Welcome to the Darkest Corner of New England". I forced myself not to buy a luridly-green, batrachian plushie *thing* from the gift shop I passed, even though I could imagine the toy sitting on my work station and how well it would go with my other fetishes. But regardless of the kitsch appeal, I felt it was more of an abomination than anything that might have happened here in the past. Yet despite the gift shop and the welcome sign, the place is still recognisable as the town that fell to ruin early in the 20th century. The famous old landmarks remain, even if a couple more cafés have been added to the main square. *The Gilman House Hotel*, the largest hostelry in town, has been renovated to a state of shabby chic – it's now fit to house guests. Those who run Innsmouth must be aware that the greater part of the town's allure – and therefore their livelihoods – derives from what it *was* and that must not be obliterated.

Of course, I *had* to stay at *The Gilman House*. Even though other guest houses in the area had interesting names, *Obed's Rest*, *Sumatry* and *Eliza Orne's Cottage*, I doubted the people who worked in them were natives to the area.

I registered in the lobby, which was hung with plaited ropes of dwarf corn cobs dyed different shades of red, orange and gold. Before the desk was a pile of plump pumpkins carved into grimacing faces.

When I entered my room, it smelled of spiced soup and candy, undoubtedly courtesy of a seasonally-themed air freshener.

Now, I gaze out of the window. Innsmouth is quite beautiful in the light of the fading day. I wish, though, I was closer to the sea. I'll eat dinner in the hotel, and afterwards will take my initial steps into the town, without baggage; the true start of my exploration. I prefer to absorb the atmosphere of a place, attune to it with my senses, before capturing its soul through my camera. Sniper shots on my phone, however, are allowed.

*The Gilman House* lies on the Town Square and my first pictures are taken from my window. There's a fountain in the middle of the square now, with wooden benches around it. Children are playing there. Immense stone fishes with mad eyes vomit water into the wide, sea-shell bowl.

The old families of Innsmouth were supposed to have died

out or been killed, but over the years off-shoots of these lines have appeared from other, often distant places. Perhaps they are charlatans, but they have reclaimed their ancestral homes with the blessing of the town council. They too are now part of the tourist industry, even if their eyes don't bulge, and they have discernible chins, the necks beneath disappointingly lacking gills.

According to Olmstead, when he visited this town, he eventually had to escape it, pursued by monstrous inhabitants. I suppose he *could* have been driven out of town, but surely only because the community was closed, undoubtedly inbred, and resented outsiders poking about. It's likely many of them had been deformed because of their heritage. Maybe the legendary sea captain Obed Marsh *did* bring strange ideas back with him from his voyages to Polynesia. But had the inhabitants of Innsmouth bred with fish people? Much as the idea is appealing for someone who loves mystery and strangeness, I don't think so. I accept it's possible they worshipped gods of the sea and believed the agents of those gods were fishlike beings that could come onto the land. The Esoteric Order of Dagon, whose temple still stands, was undoubtedly an offshoot of Freemasonry that embraced the new religion Marsh brought to the town. The people believed in it and their town – particularly their fishing – flourished; the power of suggestion is a powerful thing. Believe something hard enough and you can make it true.

There's no doubt that something shady went on that inspired the government to raid the town in 1927. The official report claims this was bootlegging and no doubt it was. The bootleggers fought back, and many were killed. Perhaps they hid some of their booty beneath the sea, which accounts for the explosions that allegedly took place near Devil's Reef.

There *is* truth there, I'm sure, but also fantasy and wishful thinking.

Still, I must open myself to all possibilities and search. I'll expose myself to the ambience of Innsmouth, sniff out its soul.

The elegant dining room of the *Gilman House Hotel* is Edwardian in theme. The staff are quiet yet pleasant. The dinner they bring me is seafood, exquisitely cooked. I wonder what the ghost of Robert Olmstead would think if he was sitting here with me, observing this lovingly reimagined building. It's easy to picture him there, opposite me. He appears somewhat surly in a shabby dark suit.

"You see, Robert," I tell him silently, "all your efforts did no good. The town did not sink into the sea. The notoriety you enhanced has made it *this*. The food is very good."

Remembered as being an ascetic, if not a miserly man, he no doubt disapproves of the luxurious fare.

I often create invented beings to accompany me on my travels. I see them as tendrils from the deepest pools of my mind that are able to communicate with me. I decide to take this *idea* of Robert with me on my walks. I'll allow him to talk to me, see what comes out of my imagination.

We take the main road across the river, Federal Street, which has the largest bridge. Below us, towards the harbour, the waters throw themselves over the lip of the falls, eager for the sea. The air is full of mist and the perfume of the land – water, wet rock, the tang of salt.

On the bridge across the Manuxet, which feels flimsy above the rowdy waters, I pause to take in the scene. I take a few shots on my phone, place-markers for the future.

Robert is uncomfortable, perhaps afraid.

"It was a long time ago," I tell him. "Nothing can harm you now, not even memory."

It's recorded that, when he died, Robert Olmstead firmly believed he was living in a palace beneath the ocean, so perhaps my *tulpa* of him fears the recent changes in Innsmouth more than its history.

On the other side of the Manuxet, we turn east into River Street and follow this until we reach Water Street and the harbour. Everything looks ancient and faded, but not derelict – a deliberate effect. The tide is in, and the fishing boats rub against one another in the docks. I wonder whether they are still used for fishing or merely for ferrying tourists, perhaps not even that. Along the sea front, there are cafés and fish restaurants, yet more gift shops, and a small maritime museum. There are piles of pumpkins here too, most of them for sale, heaped outside the small shops. Their smell soaks the air, mingling with the aroma of the sea. Seagulls hang in the air, uttering cries that conjure inexorably the boundless summers of childhood. Families stroll up and down the harbour. A child skips by me, wearing a witch's hat and holding a green balloon with a picture of a fishy face on it.

In the water, a few heads of corn are bobbing – an accidental spill from a shop crate or a local custom? I photograph the scene on my phone.

The harbour is constructed around a cup-shaped cape, with the open side to my right. A spit of land can just be discerned across the water. Beyond that, the ocean will be wild, untamed, unlike this waterfront calm. Perhaps the far side will be more like the original Innsmouth. As I stare at it, the place exudes a greater sense of desolation.

As the night draws in and the temperature drops, a grey veil of mist rises from the prowling sea, but I think I can just about make out the dark smudges of the reef emerging from the far waters to the northeast of the cape, the smash of waves against them.

Robert is being stubborn. When I invite him to talk all he can repeat in my head is "I cannot be made to shoot myself."

Perhaps I should discard him as a companion for a while.

Leaving him to mutter at the water, I head back across the bridge towards the old wharfs, which are picturesquely decayed. A mass of brightly-painted small boats cluster around them, rising and falling restlessly on the high tide, like gulls waiting to be fed. But then I see they are chained together and held to the land with locks and keys. According to a painted sign on the boardwalk, again with cartoon representations of cheery fish people, these vessels can be hired by tourists. In addition, organised trips in larger boats will ferry people out to Devil Reef, where you may peer into the waves and hope to see something scary peering back. I might go there tomorrow.

I find the wharfs beautiful. They have not been overly 'prettified' and their sagging boards feel restful rather than an unsettling reminder of inevitable decay.

I wander along the boardwalk, soaking up the atmosphere, taking a few shots on the phone now and again. There are few other people here, as most tourists no doubt prefer the attractions of the harbour and the centre of town.

Eventually the boardwalk sinks into gritty sand, tufted with coarse dune grass. There is a strong salty smell. The twilight comes down and I see there is a figure at the water's edge. It wears a long bulky coat and appears to be poking around in the rock pools. This person is awkward somehow, their movements those of a self-conscious teenager not yet at home in their skin.

The figure pauses as I approach, and I sense within them an urge to flee.

"Hi," I say – not too enthusiastically, hardly more than a sigh, really.

I see it's a woman before me; as yet I can't determine her age, but she doesn't *feel* old to me. She grunts and sidles away. All I see is the gleam of an eye through the lank dark hair that hangs over her face. She's different. She's wary. What's she doing out here?

"Do you live here?" I ask her.

She straightens up and stares at me. She has huge round eyes in a long face, but her jaw is firm and well-sculpted, her lips somewhat thin. She is young, perhaps in her early twenties. She doesn't have the 'look', as it's described, yet to me she's... *other*. Her long coat hangs open revealing a fisherman's jumper and trousers tucked into waterproof boots. She carries over her arm a basket filled with shells and stones. "What do you want?" she says in a heavy accent that has a foreign lilt to it.

"I'm a photographer, and I'd like to take your picture."

She coughs out a short laugh then. She knows my sort, doesn't have to say so. She's not conventionally photogenic, so my reasons for capturing her must be voyeuristic in a sense other than sexual. *Freak*.

But she's not hideous. If anything, she's striking: her long hair drifting like strands of seaweed on the breeze, her gaze steady and dark. I can see her in a picture, and it would be a good one. It wouldn't be a picture of a freak.

"My name is Maisie Horne." I fish out a card from my jacket pocket. It's turned to felt at the edges from living in my coat too long, but I hold it out to her.

She looks at it without moving.

"When I photograph a place, I seek its inner life, its soul, if you like. I look for interesting people who have stories in their faces..."

I trail off. It sounds ridiculous.

The woman takes the card from me, holds it close to her eyes to study it. "Do you pay?" she asks.

"Yes," I answer at once, even though my funds aren't that healthy at the moment. "I pay $25 for a few shots."

She sniffs. "50. Take it or leave it."

I can tell she won't negotiate, but the price is still cheap, of course. I nod. "OK. I can stretch to that if you give me a full hour. Tomorrow?"

She puts my card in her pocket. "Has to be morning. Early. Around 7. Have things to do."

"That's fine." I pause. "Would you let me have your name?"

"Kezia."

I'm itching to point my phone at her, but sense this is not part of our agreement; it would seem too eager.

"I'm staying at *The Gilman*. Would you meet me there?"

"I'll be outside at 7," she says and turns her back to me.

I stand there for some moments, because although our scene has ended, we're both still standing in it. It's awkward. I'll go and look for Robert. "Goodbye," I say, but she doesn't respond.

I find Robert sitting on a memorial bench at the harbour. He's staring moodily out to sea. I've seen photos from his medical records, but the man before me now is shape-shifting, perhaps becoming more like what I find interesting rather than what he really was. He's dark, ascetic-looking, but attractive in a gaunt, Gothic way. No one would believe his anguished stories. He's tragic.

"Let's go back to the Hotel," I say to him. "You must sit downstairs in the bar alone, but you have plenty of money and can drink there."

When I'm creating imaginary people, I try to give them some autonomy, the permission to exist when I'm not there. Whether this is effective or not, I of course have no idea.

I meet Robert at breakfast. He's sitting at one of the tables and appears to have been waiting for some time. He's irritated. I sit down and say good morning. A waitress comes to take my order – no buffet meals here. Today is the Eve of the Hallows, the day when the veil between the worlds of the living and the dead is reputedly thin. Perhaps this is true. Robert is vivid across the table from me.

"I'm going to take photographs of a young woman this morning," I tell him. In my mind, I'm talking aloud, but naturally it's not advisable to talk to invisible people in public. Our conversations must remain private, silent. "I want you to come with me and tell me what you think about her."

Robert doesn't speak but stares at me, blinks once.

"I want to believe she's a descendent of an original inhabitant," I say. "Perhaps you'll have more idea about this than me."

He shrugs, then says, "Why do you keep me here?"

"Because you're a witness. You can help me. I'm here for two days, then you can go."

He looks at me with contempt, so I visualise the waitress bringing him a breakfast and he has to eat it. His miserliness won't allow him to let the food go to waste.

After our meal, when we go outside, Kezia is standing hunched on the hotel porch, her hands thrust into the pockets of her coat, which hangs open and looks somewhat damp and mildewy, as does the long black woollen dress she wears beneath it. Her feet are encased in workman's boots. "Can I have my money?" she asks.

"When I've taken the pictures," I reply, then add, "I need to go to the bank. I have no cash."

"Where you want to go?"

"Well, let's just walk, shall we? You must know the streets that are least touched by… change."

I notice she glances to the side of me, where Robert is standing. For a moment I think she can see him, then realise she must be looking into the hotel lobby, which is no doubt a place she's never been.

She jerks her head to indicate I should follow her.

After calling at the bank, where she waits outside for me, we head down to the waterfront, but not to the harbour. We traverse one of the six bridges across the river into a residential area. There are fewer tourists here, even though a fair percentage of the buildings are now guest houses. The decorations on the doors are traditional – woven dried grasses, elaborate wreaths of foliage and dried fruit, with the inevitable cackling pumpkins squatting on the porches.

"This town is lucky, in a way," I say to Kezia. We have walked most of the way in silence, with her only occasionally pointing out areas of interest to me.

"How do you figure that?" she asks.

"Well, because of its history, for a long time it was… shunned. This means it wasn't gutted and mauled by town planners. What remains has been renovated with at least some dignity or left alone completely. Have you lived here all your life?"

"It's my home."

"Let's take some shots here."

I position her before the tall, gambrelled buildings of Washington Street, but she doesn't look comfortable. This isn't her area; at one time it was affluent, before it was abandoned, and now it's affluent again. I realise I'm imagining she's lived here since the 1920s, which is clearly not the case. She's no ghost, and if she were really that old, she would've transformed into a denizen of the sea, as the elderly Innsmouth inhabitants were said to do. "Isn't that right, Robert?" I ask silently.

"That's what happened," he says. He's oddly unmoved by Kezia. I was hoping for fear, surprise… something.

"If you were to be photographed in the place you felt you most belonged, where would it be?" I ask her.

"Out by the sea," she says.

"The wharfs?"

"The place I love is the far side of the cape. It's wild. No one goes there."

"Sounds perfect," I say.

"It's a long walk."

"That's OK."

On the way, I take pictures of the houses and occasional shots of Kezia when she's not aware. She feels increasingly to me like a teenager who wants to appear rebellious or different. She's not told me her surname and I realise I'm not going to ask for it; I'll imagine it's Marsh, Waite or Eliot, or another belonging to one of the old families, not a name from somewhere else, somewhere new.

We walk down Martin Street towards the sea and eventually come to Water Street, which follows the harbour all the way round the inner rim of the cape. Gradually the buildings become fewer and shops and cafes are no longer to be seen. As we reach the farthest side, the quays are more widely-spaced, and the boats moored there are mostly dilapidated. Sheds huddle in exhausted groups. A cold wind blows over the land, which is flat and sandy, but for the rise of dunes on the seaward side, and covered in a dry kind of grass that is almost colourless. The only trees are bent and spiny like hunched crones, maledictory branches pointing like fingers. Water Street persists, but is now a sodden boardwalk, occasionally covered by sand. Bleached wooden picket fencing staggers beside it, almost upright in places, but mostly fallen, with grass growing over it.

"Stand still," Kezia says to me. "Listen."

The wind is singing, or perhaps hidden within it is a voice calling from the deeps. Melancholia steals over me. I'm overwhelmed by a feeling of reverence.

"This is the best spot to hear the song of the wind and sea," Kezia tells me.

I realise she's opening up slowly, if not exactly warming to me. "I can see why you love it here," I say. I notice Robert has wandered off towards the open ocean to the east. He's of course drawn mournfully to what he believes lies beneath the waves.

Kezia and I walk in the same direction. The smell of salt and fish is overpoweringly strong. We climb a rise of dunes and, once at the apex, gaze down a stone-littered sandy slope towards the sea. To our left a tall, sagging lifeguard's chair still stands, if leaning dangerously towards the ground. It's hard to imagine that once people spent summer days here, children running in and out of the waves, women lying down on the sand wearing sunglasses. Now, the beach lies desolate and abandoned, as if we've walked into the far future of the world and no one is left alive, anywhere. But what kind of people once came here?

As the wind grabs handfuls of Kezia's hair, I photograph her against the backdrop of the open ocean. Devil's Reef is clearer now, the suggestion of land upon the horizon. If we drew closer to it, we'd be able to see it is jagged and deadly.

The Deep Ones come from below, it's said, to cavort upon the sharp rocks, to take the sacrifices offered to them. Here is the sea priestess, ready to preside over the festival of death. She's disguised in dingy clothes, but her eyes are on fire and her smile fierce. She gives herself to the air, at one point throwing out her arms, her head flung back, a laugh pealing from her. Robert stands behind her, some distance off, a thin black shape amid the dune grass.

In Kezia's moments of joy, it's hard to credit she's a native of this place. Surliness is a documented accessory to the Innsmouth

Look. She's in love with the town and its landscape certainly, fascinated by it, perhaps obsessed, but is she that different to me? Has she moved here to live or, when she told me Innsmouth was her home, was that only her dream?

"Have you ever seen the ocean glow?" I ask her.

She glances at me suspiciously, then answers guardedly, dropping back to sullenness. "Sometimes it does."

There's a silence, then I say, "This place is precious. We should be glad people are taking care of it, even if they don't fully realise what it is they're looking after."

"Shouldn't be this way," Kezia snaps angrily, loudly. Her sudden mood change is unsettling. "One man killed old Innsmouth... just one man. Couldn't leave it alone."

I glance somewhat nervously at Robert and say gently, "If it hadn't been him, then it would have been someone else, Kezia. Innsmouth couldn't have stayed hidden for ever. The modern world doesn't allow that. If Innsmouth had – or has – an enemy it is time, the changes in society, not merely the word of one man."

"He was bitter," Kezia says, in a voice craving for vengeance. "He wanted to be here, he was one of them, but he ruined it. They chased him out and then, like a mean little boy, he told tales."

Her impassioned words make her sound more ordinary – rooted in the mundane world – and yet at the same time more credible as the opposite. I realised her summary is accurate. In no single account did anyone ever wonder if the people of Innsmouth had been frightened, could perceive the potential of their own fate in this meddling, damaged man.

"She's right, isn't she?" I say to Robert, not even sure if I've bothered to keep the words silent.

He stares at me mulishly. "I want to go home."

The crossing is easy, of course, at this time of year.

Kezia has also fixed me with a stare. "Can you take him?" I ask her. "He was never quite himself, you know."

Her eyes are fathomless, and she is so still, like a picture. Then she turns to where Robert is standing. I raise the camera before my face but close my eyes as I take the shot.

I remain like that for some time, and when I lower the camera, I'm alone. I leave 50 dollars on the grass and hold down the notes with a stone.

# In the Speed of Their Wings Keep Pace

*Story History:*

This is another piece that was commissioned by an editor but was never published because the collection was cancelled. Happens all too often, sadly. I was asked to write a folklore story, but a science fiction piece, which was a fascinating mix. I chose the subject of harpies – the half bird women of Greek mythology – which are being investigated by a loner scientist on a distant, lonely world. The protagonist has no love of human company, and even refuses to allow her sophisticated AIs the ability to demonstrate feelings and sociability. The story concerns how the harpies change her life, and the innocence of a fledgling scientist, bring insight into the human condition.

The harpies come to roost each evening, funnelling down over the mountains Layna has named The Long Teeth of the World. Invariably, by that time, the sky will be bruised with heavy clouds that soak the black peaks but only rarely carry their dripping skirts to the endless lakes below.

Layna awaits the onset of night and the return of the harpies. They will assemble in the immense trees that grow from the flat water, its dreaming surface reflecting the honeyed sky. Layna has named these trees 'roost spires'; this is not their official classification.

The flock will come through the murk to the west, not gradually materialising but bursting suddenly, as if tearing a skin from another reality, in a mess of sound and movement. Their cries will be exuberant, triumphant, as if their return to the roost marks a victory. Layna still doesn't know whether they are as aware of her as she is of them. They will cavort round her, steal anything shiny or edible nearby, then soar and cartwheel up to the high branches and the vast yet delicate nests they have made there.

She has named the flying creatures harpies because they remind her of pictures from a story long ago; half bird, half woman, only they are not with gender in the way humans understand it. They have arms that become wings from the mid-bicep, and long bird-legs trousered with feathers. In the distance they appear black, but close to they are oil slicks of colour. Their crests resemble floating downy hair, forever being raised, fanned or flattened, most likely a component of their communication. Their faces are beaked, but their eyes are weirdly similar to a human's, even if they do pass over Layna without much interest.

Above the Long Teeth a crooked needle of jade lightning stitches the sky. The harpies scream before the storm, rushing home. Layna sees them flare in the near distance like an immense black flower with a spiralling stem, dancing in the air, weaving their sacred geometries. She has never for one moment regarded them as alien; this is their world – she the outsider.

Planets are often named by those who first set foot on them. This is Paget's World. Sometimes they are named for a child, as in the case of Suzie Prime. Or they will be given, by the more imaginative, a literary or mythological name. Layna once visited a solar system where the worlds were siblings to those that circle the Earth's sun: Zeus, Aphrodite, Ares, Hades, Hermes and Gaia. She has also spent time on Asmodan and Belial – which were, as to be expected, somewhat inhospitable environments. A world called Strawberry mimicked the whimsical nature of the one who named it – it was indeed red and weirdly soft. Layna liked it. She has mixed feelings for Paget. Shortly after arriving, and a brief exploration a hundred miles in each direction, Layna chose this spot for her settlement. The landscape is wild and harshly beautiful, and this area resembles a hot wilderness of ancient Earth, being similarly unwelcoming. Cloudless days are stifling, rains too heavy, nights either too clammy or too cold. Nearly every plant has a sting, and all examples of fauna – mostly insects and tiny reptiles – are disposed to bite, or shoot quills and irritating hairs. Rocks are uncongenially friable in some areas, like brittle meringue. Yet when broken their shards cut like splintered glass. Layna has sacrificed her blood to the landscape on countless occasions. She doesn't expect Paget to become her friend; its personality is crotchety, even petty at times. Yet why should any living thing conform to what she considers agreeable? If anything, she respects Paget more for its quirks, but she cannot love it. She doesn't believe love exists beyond a chemical and biological response.

The silvery habitation-pod of the set, and its carbuncle growths of extensions, covers a fairly large area; it appears vulnerable beneath the towering spires. The landscape of Paget is huge wherever you go, yet here Layna feels particularly small, a microbe beside the endless shimmering flats of water, the massed piles of clouds in the pale-peach sky, and the severe mountains that block the horizon on all sides, monstrous and eternal. This immensity amazes and unnerves her in the most pleasurable way. The world is a nature reserve for now, which simply means the colonial corporations haven't yet got round to deciding how best to ruin it in the name of settlement. Perhaps Paget senses this, resents it, and thus resents Layna, even though she thinks its virgin landscapes will be irretrievably polluted if touched by humankind – not in the old rapacious way, (they have learned their lesson about that), but simply by their very presence, their bacterial spread. Layna doesn't like other humans. This is why she's perfect for her job and vice versa. She catalogues the natural history of distant worlds, far from the hub of human hiving, yet she never fears being alone. The universe is her companion, unravelling before her in whichever direction she travels, always full of secrets, beguiling, sometimes frustrating and perverse, but never dull. And its cruelties, when they are revealed, are without spite. She will travel within it until she dies and her atoms melt into the endless dark, travelling still.

Today, the rains follow the harpies, but without much conviction. The misty deluge dulls the shine of Layna's viridian land-sphere, which she likes to keep polished. The harpies avoid the sphere, which is a blessing as their droppings are highly corrosive and would dapple the sheen of the vehicle even if they couldn't actually harm it.

When she goes into the set, the house-bot says in its soft female voice, "There's a comm for you, Layna."

Unlike many of her calling, Layna doesn't anthropomorphise her robots. While they pretend to intimacy, she knows it's not real and can't fool herself otherwise. She refuses humanoid housings for her robotic staff, considering that delusional.

"Would you like to take it now?" continues the bot, a smooth insistence in its tone.

"Play," Layna says, taking a towel from the floor; old, worn thin, purchased from an antiques bazaar some time ago. With this, she rubs her hair, which she keeps conveniently short.

A screen unwraps upon the wall opposite to her. She glimpses a young female face, framed by curtains of limp brown hair, and turns away. "You're through to Layna Hart," she says.

"Hello…" The voice betrays nervousness, shyness. "This is Murne Evison. An advance notice. I'll be arriving on Paget's World in two days, your time."

Layna doesn't stop rubbing with the towel. "Why?"

"I'm studying for a Specialist Accolade in comparative astrobiology and want to make a snap-study of the *johnsonerii*."

She means the harpies, which inevitably some explorer naturalist named after themselves.

The girl pushes on into Layna's lack of response. "I know it's short notice, but I have a permit from the Lyceum in Robel City on Chard. Would you like to check my authentication code?"

"The bot will have it already. I take it you intend to use my facilities."

A moment's silence. "I won't intrude."

Layna is used to this; it's happened before. On the rare occasions she meets up with other naturalists, their conversations generally revolve around the foolishness of those they've at times had to accommodate. "All sets are designed to quarter extra personnel," Layna says. "You'll have your own space. The bots will see to landing. If you should require anything, put your requests to them."

"Thank you. See you soon, then."

"Goodbye." Layna sighs, throws down the towel, gestures at the screen to end the communication. "Mara!" She must use this name to get the house-bot's attention.

"What is it, Layna?"

"Take care of this new arrival and ensure privacy for both parties."

"Of course. Would you like data on the visitor?"

"No. That is all."

At dawn, the harpies lift in a smoke of wings and fluting calls, and billow towards the Long Teeth. All that is left behind is the occasional feather floating down and a faint musky scent. Layna has catalogued everything about her immediate environment, yet is continually drawn to the harpies, to write about them. Her land-sphere can transport her to far corners of the world, but mostly she directs it to scout alone, only venturing further afield herself when something unusual turns up on the feed that she feels compelled to experience first-hand. She sends the sphere out before breakfast, then has time to herself until it returns later in the day, when she interprets the feed and dictates her findings to Mara. Mornings are reserved for her book on the harpies, which she writes by hand, albeit with a stylus on her script-tab. She enjoys the act of shaping letters. Most people can't write with pens anymore, and the use of paper for anything other than a component of art or architecture is regarded as ecological negligence. Few even use keyboards to type. Most authors dictate their stories and ideas to an electronic amanuensis. Eventually, Layna imagines, humans will share only thoughts winnowed direct from the brain by a machine. Will this be more authentic than the laborious recording of words by hand?

*The harpies would think so… Collective noun: a scorn of harpies… Communication direct, meaning immediate and clear…*

There is no advancing species like humanity here; the harpies are the nearest to that, and like modern humans they do not write, but use only their voices to communicate. The difference is they never *could* write, have never built or created anything, except the beautifully complex platforms of their woven nests. They never stop jabbering or singing or screaming, except for when they sleep, and even then soft murmurs can be heard from the high roost, the dreams of harpies. From the moment they emerge from the egg-clusters carried in their parents" chest-pouches, they begin to make sound. Layna doesn't think they are communicating ideas or thoughts, other than "I'm here. We're fine. We're all here." Or they might warn of danger, or announce a good foraging spot. In the breeding season, they all scream in the same raw tone, which mimics uncannily the words, "Take me! Take me!" Sometimes they squabble like human children – this sounds bizarrely like name-calling – but such altercations are swiftly forgotten. They are intelligent in their way, and from the evidence of their complicated and beautiful nests Layna suspects they *could* build if they had a mind to, they *could* create. They simply choose not to; perhaps life itself is art to them. They rejoice loudly until they die, when funerals, of a type, are held. The harpies do not eat their dead but carry them to a place where carrion-eating reptiles live. While the dead are devoured by these slow, stately beasts, the harpies sing. The voices then are softer, not sad, but the song a mother might croon to a child who has to make a journey away from home, alone. "Don't be afraid. The roost will always be here. And one day you will return…"

No, she was being fanciful, imposing fictional ideas on the creatures. They could not possibly believe in reincarnation. Do *you?* Layna wrote.

*Humans are communal creatures like the harpies, and we are rarely truly alone, estranged from the flock. If you live in isolation on a settled world, you have the knowledge, always, that others of your kind inhabit that world. You are still connected, even if you believe yourself a solitary creature. We have left the original roost, the Earth, and are driven to create noisy colonies wherever we roam. I am the outcast bird, disconnected, inhuman in that I never feel alone.*

She pauses in her writing, not sure what she's trying to express. Is it that, despite her choices, she never *can* be alone? Some people might consider themselves loners, retreating to hidden corners, but it's not real – they fool themselves, because at some level they are still linked to everyone else on their world, the human roost. Her robots are designed to be fake people, giving the illusion of community to those who work in the farthest reaches, in the dark. Should she shut off the voices, see what happens? Will she go mad, but not realise it?

Murne Evison arrives late in the afternoon, when the lakes are smouldering mirrors and the scents of their flora make the air narcotic. Layna watches from the high branch of a spire she has climbed. The bark of the giant limb is hot and slightly damp beneath her. She is surrounded by a halo of gauzy insects, whose wings beat their own drowsy song. Murne steps forth from the lander, which then leaves with almost insulting haste. An ignition. A blast of light. Gone. She stands motionless, looking around herself uncertainly, a white gear capsule at her feet. She is dressed plainly, in soft grey trousers and shirt, covered by a long coat of flimsy black fabric. She looks, Layna thinks, *deposited*. What a forlorn, frail creature she is.

Layna swings down from her perch and can't help but be gratified by Murne Evison's startled spasm. "I'm Layna Hart," she says.

The girl laughs. "Made me jump. I'm Murne." She holds out her hand in a quaint, old-fashioned manner.

Layna stares at it for some seconds before clasping it briefly. "The house-bot is Mara," she says. "It'll check you in."

Murne nods and disappears into the set.

Layna supposes that she should offer to take refreshment with the girl, be polite. She's slightly annoyed that she wouldn't mind doing that. She doesn't want company. Is she simply curious about this other person? She is, after all, here to study the harpies.

Murne is interviewing Layna, gathering initial information for her task. Mara has provided refreshment, which Layna has to fetch from a serving-hatch.

"Must be annoying the bot doesn't have a sim," Murne observes, smiling. She's more relaxed now. "Doesn't your agency provide such things?"

"Two steps across a room is hardly inconvenience, is it?" Layna responds, setting down a tray. "I have to survive in harsh environments. Being mollycoddled by machines that look like nursemaids is hardly the best practice for someone like me. What if they were destroyed? What then?" She knows her words are too defensive. "It's my choice," she adds.

Murne nods. "I see your point. Still, they can be company, can't they?"

"Fake company."

Murne clearly realises the subject should be dropped. She sips her hot drink.

After some further minutes of questions, during which Layna

reports reluctantly and with scant detail on her observations of the harpies, Murne says, "Why do you call them that? Harpies."

Layna stares at her for a moment. "It's from an ancient legend. Harpies were vicious monsters who were half bird, half woman. They were servants of creatures called the Erinyes, spirits of vengeance."

Murne covers a smile. "You can't see your AIs as anything but lifeless robots and yet you give the *johnsonerii* the face of mythical beasts, agents of vengeance. Is that how you see *them*?"

Layna delivers a hard stare. "In the past," she says, "the word harpy could be applied to an unpleasant or annoying woman. Someone who didn't watch her mouth."

Murne's smile fades. "I'm sorry. I didn't mean to be rude. The name is apt. They do look half human from a distance."

The girl's presence makes Layna's skin itch. Even when she's some distance away, it's as if she's intruding on Layna's personal space. Murne is not an abrasive sort of person, in fact rather too much the opposite, but she's alive and human. The connection is there and to Layna it's not pleasant.

Murne spends the first few days wading through the shallows of the nearest lake, videoing harpy spawn. She spends minutes at a time staring up at the roost, occasionally filming it. She hums to herself, slightly out of tune. When the harpies leave and return to the roost, Murne squats at the lakeshore, her knees up, rather like a bird in posture herself. She remains absolutely motionless.

One evening, around a week after her arrival, Murne again perches on the shore, waiting for the harpies to return to the roost. Layna is watching her covertly, pretending to fiddle with equipment near the land-sphere. Suddenly, the girl gets to her feet and raises her arms to the sky, her head thrown back.

The abrupt movement after minutes of stillness makes Layna jump. *What is she doing?*

A twister of harpies manifests from the air, spiralling nearer. Their noise becomes riotous; the clatter of wings, the strident cacophony of competing squawks and croaks. Then Murne begins to call in the same way, mimicking the raucous tones. The harpies do not pause, but funnel over her so she's all but lost to sight in the whirling black.

Layna watches, stunned, for a few seconds, then calls,

"Murne! Get down, you idiot! Cover your face!"

Through the maelstrom of feathers and bodies, Layna sees Murne turn towards her. She thinks the girl is smiling, but it's hard to tell. She doesn't move or cry out, and a few moments later the harpies lift as one, then scatter in small groups, like strands of hair, to seek their high nests.

Layna runs over to the girl. "Have you lost your mind?" she yells, but in a cold, low tone.

Murne runs her fingers over her face. "No. They wouldn't hurt me. Why would you think that? I simply mimicked the homing call."

"You fool," Layna says. "They're not human. They could have taken you for an enemy and killed you. Predators mimic their prey here. It's common. I'd have thought you'd know that."

"It would be a very stupid predator to try that on with so many prey around," Murne said, somewhat sullenly, adding archly, "don't you think?"

"What were you trying to prove?"

The girl shrugged. "Nothing. Just getting them to accept me."

"And do alien species accept you often?" Layna asks.

Murne ignores the sarcasm and answers as if the question is sincere. "Not all, no, and with some I wouldn't try, because they are predators with little reason to communicate beyond their own kind, and only then at certain stages in the life cycle. For me, it's a question of determining the *type* of creature. Communication is very much the same wherever you go. Similar protocols for social interaction apply, and through close attention differences can be identified, allowing for modified strategies."

Unspoken, but perceivable in Murne's expression, are the words: *but I'd have thought you'd know that – given your occupation.*

"Sounds like wishful thinking to me," Layna says. "Not very scientific, is it? Imagining all living things think and feel as we do."

"It's a starting point," Murne says. "Eventually, I hope to be an inter-species communicator. At present, I'm experimenting, researching."

"I see. Well, be careful. I don't want to have to explain anything messy to your department. It's my duty to warn you, and I must make a record of this with the house-bot. You must also confirm you received this warning."

"Understood."

The harpies always have sentinels stationed at the perimeters of the roost. Layna notices that two of them have moved to lower branches of their spire. They appear to be watching the humans below them.

The following morning, Murne asks to use the land-sphere.

"What for?" Layna demands. "This is irregular."

Murne frowns. "I wasn't led to think so. If you look at my official request, which Mara should have…"

"Just tell me why you want to use it," Layna snaps. Educational departments with which Layna's agency is in partnership are sometimes given leave to make use of all equipment. She doesn't approve of such arrangements but can't oppose them.

Murne adopts an assertive posture. "I want to follow the harpies when they leave the roost, see where they feed and so on. They might meet with other communities."

"Well, I can't let you take the sphere alone." Layna pauses. "I'll have to go with you." She doesn't trust the girl not to do something stupid and put the sphere in danger.

Outside, the harpies are screeching loudly to one another.

"Listen, they're preparing for their day," Murne says.

Layna says nothing, passes her left hand over the sphere's portal sensors. Its skin peels back to provide a door, and the women climb inside. The sphere's AI greets Layna warmly. "How nice to see you."

"Just get on with it, Bode," Layna says, strapping herself into a seat, and indicating Murne should do likewise.

"What is your wish today?" Bode asks.

"Follow the harpies when…"

"The *johnsonerii*?" Bode interrupts.

"Yes. They'll be leaving the roost presently. Keep a discreet distance."

"Certainly."

"Bode," Murne asks, "how do you determine a discreet distance?"

"Such a distance was decided upon some time ago," Bode replies. "Layna and I have worked together for nearly six years."

"Ah!" Murne laughs, while Layna seethes quietly the girl has the nerve to question her machine.

They have to wait for some minutes, Layna not speaking. Murne appears uncomfortable, perhaps emanating enough uneasiness to alert the sphere's empathy sensors and prompt a platitude designed to soothe nervous humans. "Nice to have company for a change," it says.

"Don't you ever?" Murne asks.

"No. Layna generally sends me out alone."

"Oh..."

"Harpy lift off," Layna says. "Time to go."

The scorn of harpies is pouring towards the mountain in a spiral formation. They fly swiftly. "May we have sound please, Bode?" Murne asks.

The raucous chatter of the harpies fills the sphere. "Is that too loud?" asks Bode.

"No, fine. Thank you." Murne settles back in her seat. "Are you recording?"

"Yes, Murne."

"I'll work with Mara later to analyse the data. Feel free to tune in, if it will be helpful for your research."

"I will. Thank you, Murne."

"You're welcome, Bode."

Layna can't help thinking that Murne is taking liberties with her equipment, which she knows is a ridiculous way to feel. She realises, though, that Murne's treatment of the AIs, chatting with them as if they were human, gets on her nerves. She wonders if the girl's doing it deliberately to annoy her. *Harpy.*

Although the Long Teeth appear as a solid mass on the horizon, as the land-sphere draws close it's possible to see variety in the landscape – small bundles of hills, deep chasms, blue mountain lawns, long slopes of treacherous scree. Waterfalls cascade from impossible heights, making clouds around the lakes they nourish.

"How beautiful it is," Murne murmurs.

The scorn of harpies billows ahead of them, clearly intent on a particular destination. Layna has followed them before, noting their feeding sites. They spend their day eating and flying. In the afternoons they tend to rest, rousing themselves for a final feed before heading back to the roost. Layna had hoped initially that harpy secrets would be revealed, but their behaviour wasn't unusual or different to how they were back at the lakes. They are simple creatures, yet still bizarrely fascinating, perhaps because they look the way they do.

The harpies funnel into a valley where water streams down the rock into a series of pools. These waterfalls are narrow, so the air is fairly clear of spray. When the women emerge from the sphere, Murne comments excitedly about the different scents in the air.

Layna doesn't respond. She finds a lichened rock on which to sit, while Murne sets out her research equipment. Layna intends to write, perhaps jot down mordant impressions of her companion. Her book is about more than harpies; she can't kid herself otherwise. It's about her life.

Some distance away, near the pools, the harpies tumble over the grass-like, ink blue ground cover, tearing at it with their claws, exclaiming in triumph when wriggling invertebrates are yanked through the surface. Tart earthy aromas become stronger in the blended perfume of the air.

"Why don't you travel?" Murne asks, making adjustments to her video pad.

"Me?" Layna responds.

Murne shrugs, but aims the pad at her for a few seconds.

Layna winces, turns her face away. "I did at first, but now it's more efficient to send the sphere out to gather data. I can work back at the set while it's away."

Murne turns round, aiming her pad at the landscape. A single tone, like that of a piano key, advises her she's taken a single frame picture. She turns towards the pools, utters "Oh!"

Layna is looking at her tab, scrolling through notes she's made. She glances up. A harpy is standing around ten feet in front of them, motionless, its head to one side.

Murne utters a harpy-mimicking call.

Layna can't speak.

The harpy minces forward slowly, not with caution exactly but as if it's not sure whether to bother.

Layna has never seen one this close other than in video enlargements. If they should alight near to her at the set they move so quickly they're hardly more than a blur. She would never consider it right to try and approach an alien species, impose herself on it. And yet Murne does so casually. It's strange just how much like a bird and how much like a human the harpy is, close up. This one is about four feet tall and could almost be a woman in an ornate costume.

Murne moves very slowly to retrieve an item from her carry-case. Layna sees it's part of a bread roll from breakfast. Murne sniffs this, shows it to the harpy, then tosses it carefully about five feet in front of her.

Layna holds her breath, waiting for the harpy's reaction.

After some moments of consideration, and the raising and flattening of its crest, the harpy darts forward and picks up the fragment with its beak. Then it lifts off and returns to the scorn. The fragment is deposited and several other harpies gather round to examine it. After a minute or so, they drift away. Layna can see the white crust lying on the ground.

"Be thankful they didn't bring you a grub in return," she says.

Murne laughs. "I've eaten vile things on more than occasion," she says. "It's worth it. Hospitality, the sharing of food, is a most important aspect of establishing communication. To refuse hospitality implies a lack of interest or respect, or worse – can be seen as an indication of hostility. You should never refuse it."

"The harpies usually help themselves," Layna says. "From my recycling tank."

"But you permit that, don't you? They might see the leftovers as a gift."

Layna shifts uncomfortably on the rock. "Well now you know they won't eat bread," she says. "They prefer rotting trash."

"The gift was accepted; that means something."

Layna isn't sure if it's her imagination or not – given what's just occurred – but the harpies do seem more relaxed than usual. It's almost as if they put on a show for her before, or rather concealed themselves. Today, they groom one another, and spend time immersed in what looks like conversation. There are certain repetitive croaks that sound like laughter, and once a shriek expressing shock.

Layna writes on her tab. *Murne Evison seeks to anthropomorphise the harpies, and I wonder if her passion has infected me. Did I all along – secretly – want to perceive human characteristics in these creatures? Is this the human drive to connect? Till now, they've exhibited no interest in me; the only thing at the set they examine is the recycling. Have Evison's overtures affected their instincts to avoid us? Is this a good thing? Has she deceived the harpies, tricked them? Are her actions simply human arrogance, human imposition, yet again?*

Layna's thoughts are broken, by the soft touch of Murne's fingers on her left arm. "Layna," she murmurs. "Look."

While she's been writing, more harpies have arrived in the meadow. Layna thinks there must be tens of thousands of them. They have clustered thickly in the trees, and others have formed a circle on the ground. These are alpha harpies, with elaborate crests, the elders of the scorns. The crests can be seen clearly, even from a distance, because they are raised and fanned, as if importantly. Head-dresses of rank.

"I want to film them," Murne whispers, "but don't think I should. They've given us permission to be here…"

"What are they doing?"

"It's a parliament," Murne whispers.

"What?"

The girl grins. "An old collective term for birds known as rooks. People thought that when they gathered together, sometimes they seemed to be in parliament. That's what this looks like to me."

Five harpies have glided down from the trees, and appear to be guiding another pair into the middle of the circle. There are some harsh calls from the onlookers above. The pair, who could easily be imagined as criminals on trial, huddle in the centre. Their crests are flat but occasionally they screech, as if to proclaim innocence. The alpha harpies engage in a loud and rowdy discussion. Some flatten their crests as if in disgruntlement. Others fan their tails to make themselves larger, perhaps to emphasise a point.

"This is amazing," Murne says. "Have you ever seen anything like this?"

"No," Layna answers.

The trial, if such it is, goes on for around ten minutes. The accused aren't given opportunity to speak, at least not in attentive silence. At the end of this time, one of the alphas rears high and extends its wings fully, fans out its tail and crest to their limits, utters one long squawk. After this, silence, but only for a few moments. Then chaos.

Thousands of harpies descend, screeching and cawing. The

pair in the circle vanishes beneath a maelstrom of wings, claws and stabbing beaks. At the end, once the scorns lift once more to the trees, nothing is left on the ground, except the crust from Murne's breakfast. Feathers float in the air.

The women sit in silence, stunned at what they've witnessed, for once completely of one mind.

The harpies, it seems, are now resting, recovering from the drama of the day.

Eventually, Layna says, "We just witnessed an execution... didn't we?"

"I think so," Murne murmurs.

"Why?"

Murne is hugging herself, as if cold. "I don't know. An infraction of some kind. But we were allowed to see it."

"A warning?"

"I don't think so. An *inclusion*."

Layna utters a cold laugh. "Wishful thinking. It could mean anything."

Murne gets to her feet and discreetly films for a few seconds, although now there is little to see, as the thick foliage of the trees hides the scorns. She begins to pack away her equipment.

"You want to go back?" Layna asks.

Murne is subdued; clearly, the scene has affected her deeply. She nods. "Yes." She looks Layna in the eye. "They could have done that to you – me – at any time – attacked, *devoured*."

Layna stares back, thinking *well, I did warn you the other day*, but an unfamiliar feeling within her prompts the words: "They had no reason to."

Murne is close to tears. "Didn't they? Just by being here we might've given them a reason."

Layna gets to her feet, pats Murne's shoulder awkwardly. "I'm sure Mx Johnson, who named them, was quite convinced by evidence that wouldn't be the case."

Murne shrugs miserably and heads towards the sphere. Layna follows.

The journey back to the set takes place in silence, even Bode doesn't break it. Layna is surprised Murne seems so affected by what they've witnessed. As the girl said, it could be regarded as a privilege the harpies behaved that way in front of them. Layna has never felt threatened by her local scorn, but then the harpies have never paid her any attention, and she kept her distance. They existed easily with one another. Perhaps now she should speak to Mara about heightening defences at the set, just in case.

Once home, Murne disappears into her sleeping-chamber and emerges only briefly in the early evening to fetch food from the kitchen area. Layna leaves the girl alone, poring through her notes. She falls asleep on the sofa and dreams of flying with the harpies. In her dream, she remembers she's done this before and that she'll most likely forget it again upon waking. But then she's snatched from her sleep abruptly, so much so that for a moment she tries to flap her wings in alarm.

A harpy is in the room with her, standing some distance away, its crest half raised, staring right at her.

"Mara," Layna says, her tone neutral, not too loud.

"Yes, Layna?"

"We have intrusion. Assess risk."

Mara would have observed the harpy enter the set; its entrance is never secured at night. After a couple of seconds, during which the AI would have operated her pheromone scanning procedure, Mara says, "I can perceive no risk, Layna."

The harpy shifts from foot to foot, utters a soft burring call. Is it calling its roost mates?

"Mara," Layna says. "What's happening outside?"

"Nothing to be concerned about," Mara replies. "This is the only harpy down from the roost."

The creature doesn't appear to be hostile, but Layna is aware it could attack at any moment. "Put defences on high alert, Mara."

"I have already done so, Layna."

Woman and harpy stare at each other for long moments. Why is it here? Curiosity alone, and a new courage engendered by Murne's behaviour?

The harpy leans forward, stretching its wings backward. It shakes its head, so its quills rattle.

"What do you want?" Layna asks, thinking aloud rather than trying to communicate. She lays her hands on her thighs, palm upwards. The showing of empty hands is advised when dealing with alien species. This is another universal gesture. *I have no weapons, and my claws aren't flexed.*

The harpy draws itself erect and begins to strut around the

set, apparently pausing to examine items of interest. Layna remains quiet, allows this inspection, but she is tense. Eventually the harpy returns to Layna and turns its head to regard what lies on the low table by the sofa. Layna's tab. With a brief glance at her, it leans forward and gently places the tip of its beak on the glossy surface, then taps once. The screen blooms with blue light. The harpy flinches back, its head drawn into its chest, but appears surprised rather than afraid.

"It's all right," Layna says. She reaches out with one hand and picks up the tab, touches its screen. Images bloom across it, mostly text, but she finds an image of the roost she has captured. She turns the device around so the harpy can see it.

"Your home," she says. "See?"

The creature can't possibly understand her and yet she feels this doesn't matter. Have the harpies watched Murne and her using their equipment? She places the tab on the table once more, taps the screen to change the image.

The harpy utters a caw, then flies from the set so quickly Layna barely sees it leave.

For a moment, she is silent, then says, "Mara... what just happened?"

"The harpy was curious," Mara says in a soothing tone. "My conclusion is the creature felt there was no danger in entering the set to satisfy that curiosity."

"It's not good the harpies see our technology close up," Layna says, realising even as she says this that her concern comes far too late. "It risks... contamination."

"They have seen it since we arrived. And before that, during the initial survey." There is a short, pulsing silence, then Mara says, "Everything changes. Always. For all creatures. That is the nature of creation. Don't worry about your impulse to show the harpy your tab, Layna. There is nothing to blame yourself for."

*She knows me*, Layna thinks, but why be surprised? The AIs have had several years of observation, analysis and interpretation. Even the fact she doesn't converse with them will have told them much about her. Now, in this surreal moment, she wants the contact of another being like herself, but not Murne. She doesn't want to wake Murne. The girl will have to be informed about what's happened, of course, but tomorrow. "We should make a report to the agency," Layna says. "The harpies aren't listed officially as being open to communicating with humans."

"You have this in common with them," Mara says. Was that a trace of dry humour in the tone, perfectly emulated?

Layna ignores the remark. "Close the set," she says. "I need to sleep and this precaution must be taken."

"Of course. And I will make the report."

Asleep in her bed, Layna dreams of Earth, although she has never visited it, the home roost. She is one of a clamour of rooks that funnels up into the sunset, dark wings stretched against the deepening magenta of the sky. The clamour is rowdy, flying higher, so high the world becomes the memory of a jewel. They wing their way far from home, too far to be imagined, cawing to each other through the spangled night: *I'm here. We're all here. We're fine.*

# Spirit of Place

*Story History:*

This tale also appeared in "Splinters of Truth", published by NewCon Press in 2016. It was a very old piece I decided to work on and polish up for publication. It began life as the start of a novel, many years ago. A friend of mine told me stories of her grandparents" house, where she'd spent a lot of time as a child. She remembered apparently supernatural events in the house, including the chimney incident described here. Her memories were hazy as to what happened after that, but I saw it as a good place to start a supernatural novel. Nothing happened to my friend that was anywhere near as traumatic as what the girl in this tale has to endure. She just remembered strange phenomena, which she didn't like particularly but which never threatened her, and eventually, I suppose, she grew up and such episodes no longer happened. She was happy for me to write about it and – of course, as it's a fictional tale – embellish greatly upon her experiences. The family, incidentally, are entirely made up, as are the dreams and the climax to the story. The garage and garden are based upon my paternal grandparents" home, where I used to spend weekends as a child – although I was never scared there. Unfortunately, the book never got to be written, as other projects took precedence, and its opening scenes languished in the backwaters of my computer for many years. Then recently, when I was browsing my half-finished works, I felt I wanted to finish this piece. I chopped it down considerably and added some new paragraphs. It's no longer a first chapter but just its terrible self.

The house went on and on and on.

Mia could not remember the first time she went there, because she'd been a baby when her mother had carried her over the threshold. Neither could Mia recall when the house *became* for her and assumed an identity of its own. Even when she began to get scared was impossible to determine: to Mia the frightening times had always happened. No-one listened to her, of course, although her grandmother now allowed her a night-light when she came to stay – a small concession to a child's fears. Sitting up in bed, dry-sobbing after having screamed for her Grandma to come to her, lights ablaze everywhere, Grandma in the bathroom running palliative water into a tumbler, she once heard an aunt's voice in the corridor outside, saying, "She's such an *imaginative* girl!"

The house was very long and dark, an end terrace in the city that was so big its original owners must've had servants. To Mia, it seemed all the corridors were endless and disproportionately high. So dark. In some rooms, lights were turned on even in the daytime, even in summer. No light from outside could find its way in. And the darkness resounded with the ticking of her grandfather's clocks – one in every room. At night, they ticked louder, echoing down the stretching corridors.

There were numerous bedrooms on two floors above the ground storey. Not all of them were used, but those that weren't were ready stiffly to receive guests, distant relatives who might appear at Christmas or other family social occasions. Some of these rooms were more frightening than others. A few were so dark and still the air in them was almost unbreathable. The bedroom Mia had to occupy wasn't the worst one. She was glad of that.

Downstairs, there were three large reception rooms leading from a wide, tiled hall. Then, there was the big kitchen, where the family often shared their meals, followed by the smaller kitchen, where the sinister mangle stood. Beyond stretched the conservatory, a brief realm of light, although its panes were covered by mats of basking ivy, making that light green and watery. Here, Mia's grandparents, along with any of their children who happened to be at home, would sit on Sunday evenings in the summer to read the papers. Mia would spread out her crayons and paper on the floor, and lie on her stomach drawing pictures, waiting to be picked up and taken home by her parents. Sunday evenings were the best times in the house. Whatever watched her in the tall rooms and passages of the main building lingered in the small kitchen, avoiding the slanted rays of late sunlight. It could not cross the threshold of the green conservatory: at least, not on summer days. In winter, in darker times, it extended its territory, and Mia would have to recite her small ritual of protection as she crossed the bare flagstones beneath the glass roof. "Mammy, Gammy, Gammio. I'm in-vizzy-billy-oh!" She kept her fingers crossed during this rite.

Beyond the conservatory, a short corridor with windows down one side led to the garage, giving access also to a small sliver of a room, which was the second toilet. Mia particularly hated that room and would not use it. She felt the place had its own occupant, a separate thing entirely from what scared her in the main house. This thing lived in the pipework, and for obvious reasons use of the toilet was unthinkable.

Just before the narrow door to the garage was another little room, where her grandmother kept bottles of pickles, home-made jams and old mops. Perhaps it was supposed to be a coal house. The garage itself was shadowy, and pungent with oil and metal and weed killer. Tools covered the walls and there was oiled sawdust on the floor. A high wooden bench stood at the end, old and scarred, where Mia's grandfather did his mysterious 'jobs'. Mia never knew what these were but accepted they were 'men's things', involving metal, wood, hammers and nails. She liked the grinding wheel attached to the table and would spend hours turning the handle to make it go faster and faster. Above the bench was a fly-blown window that looked out over the small patch of concrete beside the high double gates that led onto an alley, which allowed Mia's grandfather to manoeuvre and park his slow, stately car in the garage.

Beyond the concrete lay the garden. This too was long, and in two halves, with the first half, nearest the house, lawned and bordered with flowers and shrubs. An overgrown fishpond sat in one corner, where black tench lurked, once caught by one of Mia's uncles. The top garden was walled by privet hedges, neatly trimmed, and a path through the tight leaves led to the orchard, and the gooseberry bushes, and the thick, fleshy rhubarb. There was a stream at the bottom of the path, which actually bubbled up through the earth – from an ancient grate – at the right hand corner of the garden. Sometimes, it was mysteriously dry. The first half of the garden was innocent, empty. Playing there, Mia would feel light, so light, as if she could just float away. Only the presence of the brooding house, which she would not face, kept her anchored to the earth.

There were watchers in the second half of the garden, and in the stream-bed, but to Mia these creatures were less threatening than what walked in the house. Not friendly, certainly, but distant, disinterested in tormenting her. She often thought they liked her being there, although she was never unwary. When she ventured into the thick, rooty-smelling patch of rhubarb, which she felt was a place of power, her ritual words for the watchers were, "The garden is lovely, jubbly, zubbly, ubbly!" This she felt appeased the unseen occupants, although in her heart she wished she had stronger words, and that if she had, there would be something to gain. She could not think what, though.

Whatever might live in the lower garden, Mia loved to play there, enfolded by the greeny-black shadows and the high grass. She would run around pretending to be a horse or a lion, or she'd imagine herself a princess or a witch. "Never, never, shall you see the sun again!" she would cry, entombing her enemies in lightless dungeons or magical caves. She swept, her eyes flashing, among the palace towers that were the trees, and beside the great river where majestic ships plied, which was the tiny stream.

Then, in the midst of her happy daydreams, a call would come. Her Grandma. Time for tea. And the day would close behind her like a fist.

At home, Mia was often alone in the front room, the kitchen, the bathroom, or her bedroom, but she was never frightened there. At her grandparents" house, there always seemed to be a lot of people around, but their presence did nothing to dispel the aura of gloom and threat. Mia's mother had three brothers and two sisters, all of whom were younger than her, and four of which still lived at home when Mia was very young. The uncles and aunts were mostly young and carefree, slamming in and out of the house with loud voices and groups of friends, but sometimes it seemed as if they lived in a completely different world to Mia. They used the house, but in some peculiar way they were not part of it. Neither did they seem a part of Mia. The house ignored them and they, for the most part, ignored Mia. Occasionally, one of them, in a moment of boredom, might be moved to play with her, but this was rare, and happened mainly at Christmas, when they'd been drinking. Mia often wondered whether her uncles and aunts could actually see her. The house saw her though, and it watched her continuously.

Mia is five years old, staying with her grandparents for the weekend. It is autumn-time and Mia has been sent to bed in the dark. The night-light is on, and Mia's Grandma has just finished reading her a story. It was about a little girl and her kitten; happy and shadowless. All Mia's bedtime stories are carefully chosen. Mia's Grandma does not want to have to get out of bed in the middle of the night to attend to the screams of the child. Mia has been drinking a hot, malted-milk drink, and her Grandma wipes her mouth with a tissue. "There now! Sleepy-byes!"

Mia feels tired. The story has soothed her. Her Grandma is good at mimicking funny voices, and Mia liked the voice of the cat. It has been a good day. All the uncles and aunts are away for the weekend, and their absence has brought a strange peace, almost as if the house doesn't feel so mean when they're not there. Mia hasn't been frightened today, and the clocks have ticked evenly in the still rooms of the house. The sheets are crisp and fragrant beneath her chin. Her toes wiggle comfortably in the cosy depths of the bed. Tomorrow is Sunday, and her Grandpa has promised a day out in the car. Away from the house.

Grandma kisses Mia on the forehead. "Night, night, sleepy-head." Her voice is kind and calm. It always is. Mia knows her Grandma has never been frightened in this house, but tonight she does not think about it.

The door clicks shut.

Mia lies on her side and stares at the night-light on the table beside her bed until her eyes water. She holds her breath waiting for some fear to come, but it doesn't. Sometimes, she can go for weeks without being scared, and can even forget about the bad feelings, but just as she's nearly forgotten them completely, they come back. They pounce. Almost as if they have been waiting deliberately until she feels safe. Nobody else in the family believes in her fears, because none of them have ever been frightened here. Mia's mother has told her that she simply frightens herself by thinking too much. Her favourite picture book, a very old one handed down from her father's side of the family called *Myths from Other Lands*, has been consigned to the attic in a box until she's grown out of her childish terrors. Mia's family believe that books like that encourage her silly ideas, with their tales of deadly wild woods, cruel witches and creatures partial to child flesh.

Mia can hear a clock ticking. It sounds as if it's just outside her bedroom door, but she knows it's echoing down the corridor from the top of the stairs, where there is a spindly-legged table on which resides an aspidistra plant and a carriage clock. If Mia listens too hard to the ticking, it sounds as if it's actually in the room with her. Angry with herself, she pulls the blankets over her ears and hums softly beneath her breath to shut out the sound. It's been a good day. She mustn't spoil it.

Gradually, the child's breathing becomes soft and slow as she is carried into sleep. She dreams of playing in the garden, dancing with a black kitten who sings in a funny voice. The kitten is the same size as she is and capers about on its hind legs.

"Round and round and round and round, we run, run, run!" it sings.

Mia laughs, holding its front paws. She has a taste of lemonade in her mouth and her feet are bare. The grass is warm and moist beneath her toes. There are women in bright, flower-patterned summer dresses sitting on seats round the edge of the lawn. These are her relatives, although they are wearing different faces to the ones she knows. They smile and clap at the antics of the kitten and the girl.

Then a noise comes from the dark bulk of the house. A rustle and a crack. All the women turn their faces quickly towards it. Their hands freeze in mid-air. In her dream, Mia feels the dark bricks leaning over her, but refuses to stop dancing, refuses to look.

"Oh no!" says the kitten. Dropping onto all fours, it shrinks in size and scampers off towards the bottom garden.

"Don't leave me!" Mia calls after it.

Then she wakes. Breathless and hot. For a moment, the dream is still with her; she feels confused, and then she realises she is afraid. "Oh no!" Her whisper echoes the last words of the dream-kitten.

The night-light is behaving queerly, flickering. Mia feels a cry building up within her. When she releases it, her Grandma will come, as she always does. She must let the sound go. And yet, it feels trapped somewhere, as if she's grown a kink in her chest. The cry can't get out. The walls of the room seem very far away, lost in a brown shadow. Mia can't even move to hide beneath the bed-clothes again. She wants to go to the toilet. She feels sick. Then the sound comes again. This was the sound that woke her, that pushed into her happy dream.

A rustle, a crack, a tumble of stones. It's coming from the fireplace.

Mia has never actually *seen* anything frightening in the house, yet even so wishes she could stop herself looking at the high, slate mantle, the dark hole beneath. There is smoke coming out, as if dust has been dislodged. Birds in the chimney; she's heard of that. A bird. Dust falls again, and stones clatter onto the empty fire-basket. There *is* something there, and it must be something real. She gets ready to call for her Grandma, sure the sound will come out now, because whatever is happening is a real thing. Then she sees a flash of movement.

In a moment of absolute stillness, before feeling or reaction can seize her, she sees the red boots coming down the chimney, sees them hanging there above the grate. One foot kicks spasmodically, as if whoever is wearing the boots is stuck. Mia is frozen by utter incredulity at what she sees. They are women's boots, high-heeled and laced. Then they begin to shudder, to vibrate, and the first scream seeps out of her in a thin trail. She can almost see it winding from her mouth and into the room; a bright, silvery colour. The boots kick and thrash. More stones come. The fireplace shakes. Whatever it is, it's coming in! The scream comes on like a train, like a steam-train shooting out of her. She can smell smoke, hear the high whistle, the rumble of wheels on metal. The house shakes. She will scream for ever.

Lights on. Voices murmuring. The slap of slippered feet on carpet. The door to Mia's bedroom is flung open and both Grandma and Grandpa hurry into the room.

"What a racket!" says Grandpa gruffly, and then Grandma sucks in her breath sharply, cries, "Mia!"

Even when they slap her, the child will not stop screaming, her eyes bulging from her head, staring at the fireplace. Her face is brick-red, and she is surrounded by the ammonia reek of urine.

Grandpa carries her rigid body from the bed. They take her downstairs. "It's a convulsion," says Grandma, and phone calls are made.

The doctor comes in the middle of the night. Parents are summoned. "A fever, a juvenile fever," says the doctor, shaking his thermometer. He has silenced the child with an injection, but her little body is still rigid and trembling, wrapped in blankets on the sofa, her eyes unfocused, but staring. They are waiting for the parents to come, to take the child away.

"It must have been a terrible nightmare!" says Grandma, glancing fearfully at her grand-daughter.

"Delirium," corrects the doctor. "Not as uncommon as you'd think."

A couple of days later, at home, recovering from her fever, Mia listens to her mother telling her she had horrible dream, which had been caused by her illness. She tells her mother what she saw in the fireplace. "Do I have to go back there?" she dares to ask.

Her mother laughs and ruffles Mia's hair. "Don't be silly, darling! It was only a dream. You were poorly, but you're better now. You must be a good, grown-up girl for your Mummy." She and Mia's father have a full social life that takes up all their time at the weekends. Boating trips, parties, the races. Mia's father's parents are often with them. It is more convenient to have the child stay with the mother's parents at the weekend.

"I don't like that house, Mum," Mia says.

"I grew up there, darling," Mia's mother replies in a gentle voice, trying to soothe her. "I was never frightened. There's nothing there to be frightened of."

They will never believe her.

They will send her back there.

And they do.

# WHEN HE COMES HOME THROUGH THE SNOW

*Story History*

This piece was submitted to a Christmas themed anthology in the States, (on the suggestion of an acquaintance, who had read the story and thought it was suitable for a collection she knew was in progress). Unfortunately, the story met with quite an abrupt – almost rude – response from the editor, who decided it was based on "Germanic" beliefs, which didn't sit comfortably in his world view. Actually, it is simply based on traditional paganism – I had no thought in mind from which particular country it might have derived. I simply love writing about folklore and paganism. Anyway, I included it in an anthology I was compiling that year – *The Darkest Midnight in December,* Immanion Press, 2017 – but wanted it to be in the latest collection of my short works as well. It's a simple piece, based upon a dwindling bloodline in a traditionally pagan family.

A Yule tree does not live until it has taken blood, or so my father said. He and my brothers, Jermyn and Locke, would go out into the forest every year, observing the proper rituals. They would select for us a festival tree, cut it down, and bring it into the house. When they came home, their hands were always bloody from the cutting.

Of all the seasonal celebrations, Yule is primarily for family. There is a certain feeling, an ambience, that cannot be described, but you can sense it early in the month of December, taking root and beginning to grow. The light begins to change, the evenings redden earlier in the day, and already there are scents upon the air that conjure years gone by; the aromas of spiced baking, cut greenery, wood smoke, hot wine. And yet the true spirit of Yule is beyond the senses, a bringing together of those who are kin, drawn back from all corners of the world to stand around the tree and gaze upon one another in candlelight. A sense of imminence for what will come. I think my family would be aware of this strange pull, and find their feet heading for home, even if they lived in some hot, humid land and had forgotten what time of year it was. There are other festivals, but the family does not gather for those as they do at Yule. The season of snow is sacred, eternal.

As a child, I adored the whole ceremony of this time of year. I loved its build up, from the first of December, when my sisters and I began making presents for the family, to the second week when the baking began. Our mother would sacrifice three blackbirds at the greenhouse shrine, one for the birth of the sun, one for the departing year, and one, (out of respect for other people's beliefs), for the birth of the Christ child, although he was not ours.

As the solstice drew close, other relatives would begin to arrive at our house on the hill at the edge of the forest. Rooms that were silent and sleeping all year would be opened up and woken. Shutters were thrown back to let in the low winter light. Voices would echo along corridors normally silent, and the patter of young feet, the trill of childish laughter. Two days before Solstice Eve, my brothers would go to the attics and carry down the oak chest in which all of our seasonal decorations were stored, wrapped in tissue and sprigs of rosemary to keep them fresh. And while I, my sisters and female cousins, unpacked excitedly all the ornaments and trinkets we'd seen every year yet seemed forever new, the men went to find the tree. They would capture and cut it, bring it back, where it would perish slowly in our house, while bringing joy to its inhabitants. This was a symbol of the god of the end year, who must die to make way for the child of the sun. The old god would pass away in the embrace of our love. The women of the family would robe the tree in its ritual garb, the bright glass orbs that represent the stars and the planets, the winding, shining tinsel that is the star path to the heavens, ascending to the top of the tree where the glittery, spiky ornament is placed: the star at the centre of the sky.

By the time of the tree-dressing – and from a very early age – my heart would have become winged in the cage of my chest, fluttering against the bars. This was because soon my cousin Gage would be here. He was the same age as me and I'd always loved him, even before we were too young to know what love was. I never knew what he did all year, with whom he played. To me, he existed solely in that glorious fortnight of the festival. He was as pretty as a girl, with his long, thick hair and wide luminous eyes. Later, when we reached our teenage years and beyond, I knew he had another life, that might include other women, but I could shut those notions away and ignore them, because at Yule he was always mine. Our relationship was platonic, but I never gave up hope. He looked at me in a certain way and smiled at me in a certain way; he was biding his time, I was sure. In the early days he would come with his guardian, for his parents were dead, but as we grew older he came alone.

As a girl, I'd known when his feet approached, even before he could be seen. I'd be curled in the drawing room window-seat, with only the light of the fire for company, the great tree behind me, its shuttered candles yet unlit. There would be snow coming down, great soft flakes, and this made the world visible, even in darkness. I would watch the gate and the driveway, waiting for his shape to become distinct through the snow. Then I would see him, and a light would bloom within me, and also a terrible ache that was at once the greatest pleasure.

On Christmas morning, a few days after the solstice, we would all go to the church in the village below the hill. The priest would be dressed in his red vestments, which my mother said represented the hide of the recently-slaughtered king stag, bloodied side out. The priest spoke of the Christ child but also, without knowing it, the older ways beneath the modern stories. Gage would sit in a different row of pews to me, but we'd steal glances at one another, pull faces to show how bored we were, desperate to get out into the daylight, for the days of the solstice were always sunny then, the snow shining like crystal, hares in their white winter coats pelting across the fields and us running after them.

Yuletide was the same every year, familiar and comfortable.

Whatever troubled us in other months was put aside at this magical time, when our senses gorged on the season and that indescribable feeling of unity and hope filled us all. Our rituals of feasting, our traditions, never varied. And over us all, the light, the soft winter light, as the old sun died, red across the snow; silhouettes of pines against the sky on the horizon and the wide-winged owls sailing on the night.

At the end of the festival, just before everyone went home, and the fortnight had grown old, the tree was disrobed and taken to its pyre at the edge of the forest. Here it was burned. Gage and I stood together in the light of the flames, certain of our meeting again next Yule.

Now, as I tidy the hall in preparation, I can hear my sister Lettie calling from the kitchen. The family are coming home. We still see a few children, but they are rare now and very shy, scampering unseen in the less-frequented areas. Yule is not the same as it was; how can it be? Yet the feeling remains unchanged. The house still smells of spice and greenery, and I still build the fire in the great hearth, from holly and oak. It is Solstice Eve and they are all here, each attending to that part of the celebration that is their long-appointed task.

I go out to the gardens for my walk, as I always do when the daylight dies, and wander to the greenhouse. I find the blackbirds there, dead upon the little altar, a bright-bladed knife beside them, patched rusty with blood. I catch a ghost of my mother's scent that she has left behind; she has only just walked away.

Standing behind the ancient glass, that is misty now with lichen around the edges of the panes, I look back at the house and see the shadows in the firelight of the drawing room – my cousin Amy putting the last touches to the tree, the taller shape of my father watching on. Slowly, I walk back to the house savouring the cold spice of the air. Snow has begun to fall, as it always does – but late this year. The long, sloping lawn is beginning to whiten. From the village I hear singing, the voices of children. I look down the hill and see the windows of the houses emitting a gentle, buttery glow. Every family is in its nest, taking pleasure in the familiar activities that are created anew each year.

Whatever happens, Yule draws us close. Tragedy strikes, lives are battered and shaken, but always the light of home in winter is a sanctuary, a place where troubles are left by the door with snow-damp coats and boots. There are more of them arriving at the house now. I can hear them as I draw near to the door – stamping at the threshold to shake off the packed snow, laughing and shouting greetings. "Good season to you, cousin!"

But *he* is yet to arrive.

When I enter the house, the hall has become quiet and still, yet I hear activity all around me in other rooms. I feel a little weary this evening, but of course I am no longer a girl. I go to the drawing room, which is dark but for the fire, and drink the globe of fiery brandy I've left out for myself. If I close my eyes, the past comes back, splashing over me, *through* me – all those years, those joys. Now we are quieter in our pleasures. I open my eyes and for an instant the years are laid over each other – flashes of colour, of smiles and jewels and gowns, swift shapes flitting across my memory. I sigh and the house sighs with me. One day, I will simply melt right into it and that time will be at Yule.

I put down my brandy glass and prepare to take my place at the window seat, even though curling up there has become difficult. My limbs are stiffer than they used to be.

But now there is a knocking at the front door. Have I lingered too long over my thoughts? Has he come already and I missed him walking through the snow? Am I ready for him? Have I powdered my face, brushed my hair? I can't remember. I hope he does not mind how different I am, but he must have grown used to it over the years. To me, he is always beautiful.

I open the door. Once again, in my heart, I'm a girl, with welcome in my smile, my breath. But it's not Gage standing there – it's a woman. She's looking at me with an expression of enquiry and – loathsomely – pity.

"Yes?" I snap. I know I shouldn't be rude at Yuletide, but she's not meant to be here. She's not family. She's interrupting.

"Miss Harford?"

"Yes. Can I help you?"

"Well, really, it's more about me helping you." She smiles and extends a hand, which I do not take. "I'm Sarah Coombe." She gestures down the hill. "From the village."

She's wearing a coat and hat that look like fur but isn't. It has no smell, and the snow does not cling to it. I wait for her to state her purpose.

"I'm on the Parish Committee, and We're reaching out to people in our community at this time of year, in the spirit of the season. We know you're alone up here, and I'd like to invite you to my home for Christmas dinner this year. I hope it's not too short notice, but..." Again she smiles, peering round me into the hall. "May I come in?"

"I'm afraid not," I say. "I'm expecting someone, and you're wrong. I'm not alone. My family come home at Yule."

She frowns a little. "But Miss Harford, it's so cold and dark here. Are you ready for guests? It's such a big old house. Might I help you?"

Help me? Those are hands that never cut wood, nor lit a fire, nor made a spirit of a blackbird. She's not one of us. "We're fine," I say and try to shut the door on her. "Thank you, but We're fine."

"Miss Harford..."

I wish my sisters or mother would come and tell this woman to leave, but they've all retreated deep into the house. They don't like strangers, never have. She's tough, this one. As she stands there, I feel the season dying around me. She can do that, bringing with her the harsh present moment, brash and meaningless. I *am* cold – perhaps I didn't light the fire after all. And it is very dark. The sun has sunk while I was patrolling the gardens and the greenhouse. This woman, she intends to step over my threshold, and when she does...

Then I see the tall dark shape approaching behind her. Gage! He'll get rid of her, tell her to mind her own business.

"You don't look well," she says, but I'm gazing past her now. I see him tall and strong, his beautiful face. He'll always be mine. *Save me, Gage.* He puts a long white finger to his pale lips, blinks at me. And now he stands behind her, the snow upon his long red hair. Yet it was never red in life.

# COLIN'S COUGH

*Story History:*

This piece first appeared in *"Splinters of Truth"* through NewCon Press in 2017. I knew someone who was in the situation of having a relative they found very difficult to be around. My friend felt really bad about this, because the relative concerned had "problems". Being repelled by such a person seemed a horribly cruel and selfish reaction, but they just couldn't help themselves. While stories of their encounters with the unfortunate relative were often quite funny, there was an underlying pathos to them. In writing this tale, again with all serial numbers rubbed off that connects it to real people and situations, I wanted to portray that – to conjure the occasional smile as well as sympathy.

The characters of Annie, James and Heather came to me all of a piece, as it were. As soon as I began writing, I felt as if I knew them, even though they are entirely fictional. They are people who might once have been termed "yuppies", somewhat ill-equipped to deal with the situation when the supernatural creeps in.

How quickly short stories become period pieces! When I wrote this a few years ago, *Top Gear* was still on the BBC. I haven't changed any details like that to keep the tale current. It's a snapshot of its time.

The worst part of having Cousin Colin to stay was that he was repulsive. Annie could barely stand to look at him – not because his features were ugly particularly, or even in the slightest deformed, but just somehow creepy, discomforting. He was thirty-eight, going on fifteen – a child in a grown-up body; small of stature, thin, somewhat bent of spine and while he had a good set of teeth in his small face, seemed toothless. Even his name – to her – sounded like a cough filled up with mucus. He talked to himself obsessively – along with manifesting a host of other OCDs – and whenever he caught sight of her cats went into a frenzy of conversation that frightened the poor creatures into the deepest, darkest corners of the house.

"Here darlin', here, oooh lovely darlin', aren't you looovely, ooh sweeties, c'mere. You're all right, all right, lovely, aren't you darlin'. Oooh…"

And so on, to the accompaniment of skittering paws, bellies close to floor as they ran. This in fact made Annie feel rather sad. If he'd had some cruel streak that made it possible he might harm an animal, fair enough, but he merely wanted to be liked, by human and beast both, and unfortunately nature had cursed him to be utterly repellent.

So, Easter time, with the month of April in a good mood, flowers billowing forth, blue skies kissed with perfect little clouds. And Cousin Colin for the weekend. It was her turn. They all had turns – her brother James, her cousin Heather and Annie. The parents had all done their bit years ago and it was clear they felt this responsibility should now be passed on. They never said so; it was simply known among the family. So, while it would have been bliss to have a weekend alone for once, to lie on her very comfortable recliner on the lawn, to read lazily, drink wine, eat sumptuous foods, surrounded by her cats, instead Annie would have Colin, with his incessant chatter, his vampiric drain on the life force of any living creature. Wasn't his fault, of course – he'd been born that way, and left orphaned in his twenties. The family looked out for him, admired his ability to maintain a household and hold down a menial job, despite his disabilities. He was kind-hearted, loved people, and she knew it was really very bad of her to feel so sickened by the thought of having him around. *It's not his fault.* They all had to remind themselves of that, even when they were growing up and summers had been spent together, sun-drenched beaches, buckets and spades, escapades – and Colin. Then it was the parents saying, "Now, take Colin with you, children", even though, for Annie at least, the prospect was filled with dread. The unpleasantness in him wasn't the fact he was 'a bit simple', as people would say in those days, but something else.

She couldn't say what then and still couldn't now. It was as if he was an affront to all the senses.

Colin's first words when he arrived, before Annie had even opened the door to him, were "Oooh, hello Annie, how are you? Did you sleep well? How are the cats? I've got some presents…" His thin silhouette bobbed about behind the pastel stained-glass of the door. Sighing, she opened it. There he was, despite the balmy weather, trussed up in a beige anorak.

"Hello, Colin. I'm fine thanks, and you?"

She ushered him into the kitchen where he unloaded all his gifts from a series of supermarket bags. A pang went through her – he bought her things she liked; special French cheeses, sticky liqueurs, expensive chocolate and a bottle of very fine single malt. "That's thoughtful of you, Colin, thank you," she said. She should smother the irritation he conjured in her, be a *better* person. "But really, you shouldn't. You always spend so much!"

"Well if I can't spoil my favourite cousin, who can I spoil?" He grinned at her, and she could see in his eyes the weekend spread before him – the comfort of her old but airy house, its carefully furnished guest bedroom, her immense TV and Blu Ray player, her cats, her company. She knew that for him these prospects were as wonderful as an ocean cruise on the most luxurious liner in the world.

"I'll make you a nice cup of tea," he said, making a determined bee-line to the kettle.

"Well, okay…" She had wine out already but as he *did* make a good cup of tea – her cousin Heather had taught him carefully many years ago – she might as well drink it.

As he bustled about her kitchen, the air was filled with the cheap, flowery women's perfume he always wore, which perhaps on an elderly lady would have been fine, but not on him. It smelled musty, weirdly ancient, dead, and tended to fill the house like a creeping mist during his visits. Annie knew he would soon decamp to the bathroom, where he'd arrange his toiletries for the weekend – equally grandmotherly in nature – scented talc that she was sure you could no longer buy in the metal tins he somehow managed to find, a plastic vanity bag with various creams inside, toothbrush and toothpaste, a pink plastic hair brush, and his one concession to masculinity – a disposable razor. It didn't add to his appeal that he was so inordinately *hairy*, having to shave at least twice a day, and usually ending up bloodied from it, which he never bothered to wash off, despite apparent fastidiousness in other aspects of his toilet. She remembered that one time on a previous visit he'd surprised her in her small office, his face looming over her shoulder as she worked at her computer. She'd turned and had been faced at close quarters with the thick smears of dried blood and patches of unshaved whiskers on his gnomelike face. She had cried at him, "For God's sake, Colin, go and wash yourself, wash all that blood off!" The image had been hideous, and she'd never forgotten it. He was effeminate in a strangely asexual way and yet thick black hair covered him, spurting from the neck of his shirt, mossing the backs of his hands. She shuddered to think what his clothes concealed. If he fell over from a heart attack, or started choking, Annie wondered if she could bear to touch him. Perhaps that was why she always felt a little tingle of relief when she learned her neighbours would be at home on the weekends Colin came to stay. They were only a garden away.

"I've got some films for later," she told him as he menaced the teapot. "Two new horrors."

This was a love they shared, both adoring of haunted houses and terror conjured through atmosphere and sound rather than gouts of red or spilling innards. When they talked about films, he was almost normal; she could forget about the rest. This was perhaps the only thing that made the visits bearable.

While they sat watching the first of the films in the flickering light of the TV screen, the garden quiet and dark beyond the long windows, Annie noticed Colin was still coughing badly – a smoker's cough. In February, after phone consultations with Heather, Annie had bought Colin an electronic cigarette starter kit for his birthday – a rather expensive one. None of the family approved of Colin's chain-smoking habit, nor the fact that the cheap cigarettes he smoked seemed inordinately pungent and stale-smelling. Despite the fact they put up with nearly all of Colin's quirks, the family had to put their foot down about the smoking in their houses. Weirdly, even if he went outside to smoke in a porch, conservatory or garden, the smell fingered its way inside. It was Colin's business what he did at home, but all of them – Annie particularly – detested the rank stench his cigarette smoke had left behind in their rooms.

Colin had appeared to adjust to the electronic cigarette quite quickly. Annie taught him how to maintain it, and he now brought it with him on the weekends he came to stay, smoking continuously whenever they sat to watch films. And yet... he still had that smoker's cough. As an ex-smoker herself, who had used e-cigarettes to overcome the habit, Annie knew the cough should be gone by now.

"Still getting on okay with the e-cig?" she asked, after the first film was finished.

"Oooh yes, can't thank you enough for getting me into them," Colin said, waving said artefact before his face. "Saving me so much money as well. Real bargain."

She sensed then, with a tired sinking feeling, he was still smoking as much as before in his own home. That was another thing about him that wound her up – his lying. He would say what people wanted to hear, always. You could never be sure any of his anecdotes, however minor, were authentic.

That night, when she got into bed, she lay in the darkness listening to Colin coughing two rooms away, accompanied by his doglike snuffling. This was going to be a long weekend.

A week later, before Colin arrived for the weekend, Heather had to pick up Henry from his karate class and collect Winona from ballet. God, she could do without Colin this weekend! So much going on. She had half a dozen cakes to bake for various customers, including a large decorative one, Rob needed help with his invoices, and they'd promised to pop over to see his mother on Sunday. Taking Colin along was always a trial, because Mary – Rob's mother – was not blood family so wasn't as forgiving of Colin's traits as she might be. She was too polite to say anything direct, but her lips would disappear for the afternoon, and whenever Colin passed close by, she seemed to draw up her limbs like a spider feigning death.

Driving with unsafe speed, Heather threw her car around town, yanking offspring into it with barely a pause, careering back home with minutes to spare. They had a large old town house in the centre of the city, three stories high. Heather adored her home. She and Rob had restored it lovingly and it *was* a home, not a sterile show piece. You could tell a family lived there – untidy yet comfortable rooms, clutter on every surface, the delicious smell of cooking lingering like incense in the air, boots and shoes thrown around in the hall. Heather knew the house was haunted but felt the unseen ghost's personality was that of a loving mother; it too was not terribly fond of Colin, though.

"Winnie, I'm super busy at the mo'," Heather called over her shoulder as she ran to the kitchen. "When Colin comes could you make him some tea and take him in to watch telly for a bit?"

Winona rolled her limpid fourteen-year-old eyes, and taking the pins from her bunned hair, tossed back her glorious blonde mane. "God, Mum, do I have to?"

"Winnie!"

"Why is it always me? Let the boy share some of the 'fun'!" She pantomimed drawing commas round the word 'fun'.

"He's a *boy*, Win. 'Nough said. You know he can't cope with Colin."

"Like *I* can!" Winona grumbled, prancing off to the living room to turn on the TV.

She could, though. Henry was simply terrified of Colin, as were their two collies – the three of them, boy and dogs alike, were usually romping bundles of energy, yet hid whining behind furniture when Colin was here. She really *had* heard her son utter a soft whine once, cuddling the shivering dogs.

Heather heard the doorbell ring and Winona's haunting sigh echo loudly round the hall, her dragging steps. Before the door was open, having spied the girl through the frosted glass, Colin was crying, "Ooooh, hello Winnie. Did you sleep well? How are the dogs? I've brought some presents."

"Great. Let's watch some TV while Mum gets dinner," Winona said in the voice of a girl being led to the scaffold.

It was the snuffling that got to Heather the most. Colin breathed in and out through his nose very loudly and made this odd, doglike sound with it. He always drew in an even bigger breath after just having uttered one of his 'witticisms', pursing his lips in a proud smile at the same time, waiting for laughter. They always laughed, no matter how unfunny the words. Heather had trained her family well. When both children were old enough to understand, she had explained Colin's 'difference' and that they had to be patient with him. "Just think, that could be you," she said. "Imagine being in his shoes for a day."

Never had a bogey-man so dire been conjured. The thought made the more sensitive Henry cry, but then he had only been seven at the time. Winona, at nine and a half was twice as worldly as her mother had been at that age. "He's not *my* cousin," she'd complained.

"No," Heather said briskly, "he's your second cousin, and believe me, when the time comes, you'll be having your turn with him too."

"I *so* won't!"

Heather had left it at that. Her daughter *so* would!

Colin's noises and smells grated on Heather's nerves like a fairy chainsaw – invisible to the naked eye yet deathly sharp. Thank god, she and Annie had stopped the smoking between them, but that godawful perfume he wore – ack! It turned her stomach. She'd once bought him some decent aftershave as a birthday present, but if he had ever worn it, had never done so in her presence. She suspected it was still in its box, somewhere deep in the ragged squalor of his home.

After Colin's parents had died, within eighteen months of each other from mercifully swift-acting diseases, the parents of Heather, Annie and her brother James, had gutted Colin's house. Two skipfuls of rubbish and tat – curtains, carpets and beds that had to be burned, so sinister was their condition. But even so, despite what they'd tried to accomplish, the old bungalow was still dank and dark, fraying at the seams. And Colin ever since had been committed to filling the place with junk again. His parents, Ken and Fiona, (the mother being the blood relation), had been somewhat 'different' themselves, outsiders from the mainstream family, hoarders, who lived in a twilight world of curtains closed and slowly-crumbling lives. No wonder Colin was as he was. When she thought about it, Heather experienced brief spasms of anger against the ineffectual humans who had created and raised Colin. They had cursed him from the start. Cruel, terrible. She swallowed her disgust at him because he had been dealt such a rotten hand by life.

After dinner, a small argument broke out around the table. Heather, exhausted and feeling that because she had to deal with

Colin deserved to get her own way tonight, wanted to watch several episodes of her favourite soaps she'd been saving up on the Tivo. Winona wanted to watch a new horror film because it had one of her favourite actors in it. She'd bought the DVD earlier that day. "Mum! You know how long I've been waiting for this to be released."

"Colin doesn't like ghost films, Win," Heather said firmly.

"Oooh no, give me the willies," Colin confirmed. "Can't be doing with ghost films. Nice soaps, that's what I like."

Heather gave her daughter a triumphant stare over the rim of her wine glass.

"Most of my friends have their own Blu Ray players, *in their rooms*!" Winona announced, before flouncing out of the door.

At the head of the table, Rob sighed. He would soon retreat to his workshop and build a cabinet or something, holing up there for most of the weekend, no doubt with Henry and the dogs huddled somewhere near him, behind some lumber.

As if the misery of her children, husband and pets wasn't bad enough, the house had also begun to act up. Since Colin had arrived two hours earlier, tap washers had given up the ghost in unison, light bulbs had blown in three rooms, two items of crockery had fallen from the dresser for no apparent reason, and the stairs creaked twice as loudly and on *every step*, as opposed to the three or four steps that usually liked to groan. Doors refused to remain shut or open, depending on how a human had last left them. Clearing up after dinner, Heather put her hands into her hair and mimed a silent scream. "Don't you start too!" she told the house. "It's not like I *want* to inflict this on you all."

As if in grim reminder, the house allowed a whiff of Colin's perfume to sidle across the kitchen.

"For fuck's sake!" Heather growled and poured herself half a pint of red wine into a very large glass.

Annie was set to have a wonderful weekend. The last vestiges of Colin's perfume had faded from her rooms and the atmosphere within them was serene. Planning to see her lover tomorrow night, Friday had been allocated for feminine pastimes – washing her hair, painting her nails, some TV, then reading the new ghost story collection she'd downloaded onto her Kindle. There had been a jarring moment in the bathroom when she'd discovered the plug-hole in the sink was matted with a clump of thick, black hair – from which part of Colin's body this had derived she dared not think, and was not prepared to prod and unravel it to discover its nature. Could he possibly shave his armpits? She wouldn't put it past him. But how had she not noticed this during the week? Using toilet paper, she gouged out the hair and then flushed it down the loo.

Later, before going to bed, Annie found more remains of Colin in the bathroom – a wanton dusting of his sickly rose-scented talcum powder over the grey slate floor tiles. Of course, it *must* have been there earlier, she'd just not noticed it, so preoccupied had she been with disposing of the hair. But how had she missed it *all* week? Admittedly she had used the downstairs loo and shower a lot, because they were close to her office and she'd been working so hard, but surely she'd been up here at least once? Why couldn't she remember? Unnerved, she mopped up the powder with the sponge she reserved for cleaning the sink and bath, and then felt compelled to throw the sponge into the waste basket. She washed her hands thoroughly, as if she'd touched something poisonous. As a final flourish, she sprayed some air freshener into the room, then gagged; it smelled just like Colin's awful perfume and she could *taste* it in the back of her throat, chemical yet cloying. She opened the window swiftly, batting the air frantically with her hands, then scooped a couple of handfuls of water from the sink cold tap to rid herself of the taste. She went to her bed feeling somewhat anxious.

The following Friday, Colin was due to visit James, who lived alone in a relentlessly modern bachelor apartment.

"Hello, chap!" James greeted Colin at the door to his flat. Of he, Annie and Heather, James was the least affected by Colin's visits, simply because he refused to acknowledge oddness in anyone. He didn't have pets to be traumatised, or a current partner to be irritated, so he treated Colin as he'd treat any other male friend. As Colin dithered in the hallway, chattering about presents and had James slept well, James simply thrust a can of beer into Colin's hairy hand, saying loudly, "Come on in, mate. Take your coat off. Just watching *Top Gear* on iPlayer."

For the entire weekend, Colin would be carted around the venues of James' pleasures. He would watch James play paintball on Saturday and football on Sunday, an eerie spectre at the side-lines, among jovial, ordinary men. He would be taken to the pub. To offset any curiosity in his friends, James had explained to them that Colin was 'a bit special', making a twirling gesture at the side of his head with the fingers of one hand. Female friends took care of Colin for him, mostly because they recognised the fact James was entirely unsuitable to look after anyone. If given the job in rotation, James had found the women were less inclined to become annoyed or despairing. Most felt sorry for Colin and this emotion could last years if they were exposed to him in small doses.

James did not notice unpleasant smells or noises emanating from Colin and was oblivious to his aesthetic deficiencies. Colin's chatter passed over James's head like white noise. He could say "Yeah, mate, yeah," or "what a bummer", or laugh at appropriate points, without really listening at all. This was partly why he tended not to retain romantic partners for very long. But despite James's laddishness, he didn't find Colin's visits a trial – they were just something he did, once every couple of months or so, a small blip in his social calendar when he had to cart 'someone a bit special' around with him. He didn't resent this at all. After all, Colin was happy to sit with the wives and girlfriends, spinning them a load of bullshit – James was not ignorant of the fact Colin spoke mainly in fiction – so there was no skin off anyone's nose.

And yet, following Colin's visit, something didn't feel right to James – a bit as if there was still someone else in the flat, but always in another room. Yet it was more than that... As James lacked the vocabulary to describe his uneasiness, he put it down to 'bad prawns' from the Chinese takeaway he and Colin had eaten on the Sunday night. He felt grumpy at work all day Tuesday, and when he went to bed that night heard the sounds of coughing and snuffling, seeming to emanate from the guest room. That was impossible, of course. It must be some bloke out in the street below. His excuse for not going to investigate was that he was too comfortable in bed and couldn't be bothered.

Next morning, his mug of coffee tasted weird – it reminded him of Colin's perfume, a smell that had become a taste, filling his throat and nose. Must be the milk. But the milk, when he sniffed it, was perfectly fresh. When he went to the bathroom to finish getting ready for work, he found that Colin had left his cheap pink toothbrush – almost child-size, balding and caked with old toothpaste – next to James's own, in the stylish stone pot he kept on the rim of his pristine basin. Also, a nasty little turquoise plastic razor – rimed with old soap – lay in a seeding of minute whisker fragments and scummy grey liquid next to the stone pot. James actually gagged and realised for perhaps the first time that part of him was actually nauseated by Colin. "Man, this blows," he said to himself, somewhat reluctant to pick up the toothbrush and razor to dispose of them. It occurred to him he'd not noticed these items on the Tuesday morning, or indeed as he'd brushed his teeth before bed the previous night.

While he might be unimaginative, when James was faced with the inexplicable, he simply accepted it and was actually curious. At work, the first thing he did was phone his sister, Annie. He realised it might be a bit early for her, since she worked at home, so rose later than those condemned to nine to five existences, but she answered quickly enough, even if she sounded a little sleepy. "Hey, Jimbo," she said to him affectionately.

"Annie, there's something weird about Colin."

She laughed. "You don't say!"

"No, I mean it. I've found things of his in the flat that have just well... to be honest, they've just *appeared*."

"What do you mean?"

"Stuff of his that deffo wasn't there when he left Monday morning. A fucking horrible toothbrush, and a razor."

Annie paused for a moment. "Any... um... *smells*?"

"No, but I tasted his perfume in my coffee this morning and last night... Well I heard that coughing and snuffling he does. Thought it was outside but now... not so sure. Is this possible? What the fuck does it mean?"

"I've found stuff too," Annie said. "He was with me a couple of weeks ago, and the first week after I found the most putrid lump of black hair in my sink, and then his talc all over my bathroom floor. Like you, I didn't see these things straight away. They seemed to appear *after* Colin had gone. And I've heard the cough."

"Bloody hell!" said James. "It's like he's a fucking ghost, haunting us! This is just crazy. What can we do? Will it go away? And why now, after all these years?"

"Good point," Annie said. She hesitated, then said, "James, we have to look at the most obvious explanation first: i.e. he's actually creeping back into our homes and putting these things there."

"Aww, come on, do I have to look for a recording of a cough in my spare room? He's not capable of stuff like that, Annie. I really don't believe he is."

"We need to look at that before a supernatural alternative," Annie said. She laughed. "This is weird. I feel it should be *you* saying that to *me*. I'm the artist, you're the... Well, you're the least likely to be spooked."

"Call Heather today," James said. "See if anything's happened to her."

Annie waited until she thought Heather's kids would be at school, then phoned her. Heather answered quickly, and there was a dreadful row in the background, as if builders were tearing the house apart. "Just stop it!" Heather yelled angrily, away from the receiver. "I'm on the bloody phone!"

The row abated.

"My god," said Annie, "what the hell was that noise?"

Heather sighed down the phone. "Don't ask. Really... don't."

"I think I might have to," Annie said. "James and I have had some weird things happen... to do with Colin. It's why I'm calling you."

"What kind of weird things?"

"In a nutshell, it's as if he's not leaving us, or he's leaving bits of himself behind when he goes."

Heather uttered a mournful laugh. "Don't tell me – his smells. Cigarette smoke, disgusting perfume..."

"Not so much smells with me, but *hair*... in my sink... and the cough. James heard the cough too, and he tasted Colin's perfume in his coffee. You've had things too, haven't you?"

Heather sighed. "You could say that. You know we live in a haunted house, right?"

"Er..."

"We *do*, and the house is more upset than any of the rest of us. Colin's perfume will fill a room, then the house goes crazy."

"That was the noise just then, the house?"

"Yes, the bathroom got invaded by smell a few minutes ago, so she made her displeasure known by doing a Can-Can with the plumbing."

Annie laughed shakily. "Well, this is new. A haunting being haunted." She'd always known that Heather liked to believe she lived in a haunted house, but Annie herself had never felt anything unusual there, only a beautiful, homely atmosphere. And Annie had always longed to see a real ghost. "Heather, I do wonder – and this isn't a nice thought – if Colin is creeping around, doing these things himself. Let's be honest, he loves coming to stay with us all. Perhaps he doesn't want to leave."

"I don't think the house would get so cranky if it was that," Heather said. "She's like an animal, and senses things in the same way. The dogs are terrified of Colin. What about your cats?"

"Same."

"Have they been acting strangely?"

"Not that I've noticed, but they're out a lot now the weather is nicer. I'll keep an eye on them."

"We need a meeting," Heather said firmly. "Can you manage tomorrow evening? Would you ask James?"

"At yours? Wouldn't it be easier to meet at mine, since I'm sort of in the middle of you and James?"

"Well, I think the house should be in on the meeting."

"I'll get back to you," Annie said.

"The thing I don't understand," James said, sitting in Heather's capacious sitting-room the following evening, "is why this shit is starting to happen now? Or have we just been blind and not noticed before?"

"There could have been a trigger," Annie said. She shook her head. "Oh, I don't know. It *is* strange, though. What do you think, Heather?"

Heather sighed. "I did consider what you said, Annie – perhaps that Colin is planting things in our homes – but that explanation doesn't feel right to me. I just can't see him scaling the sides of buildings and squeezing in through windows. Unless, of course, he's had copies made of our keys."

There was a moment of horrified silence.

"I can't see that, though," Heather added hurriedly. "He's just not capable of planning in that way."

The conversation continued in circles, with no conclusion being reached. The three swapped stories of what it was like for them to host a Colin visit and decided it was abnormal, the strong effect he had on human and animal alike. And house. Apparently.

"He's not evil," Annie said, "quite the opposite and yet... all I can say is that I have a physical reaction to him, as if he floods my senses in a horrible way. Offensive to eye, ear, nose, hand and... I won't say tongue, but you know what I mean."

"And you feel twice as bad for thinking that because he's the way he is," Heather said.

Annie nodded.

"He's what... *backward*, right?" James said.

"I don't think we're supposed to call it that, nowadays," Heather said, "but essentially yes." She raked her hands through her hair. "I sometimes think our parents could have done more for Colin. There was a problem way back, but no one ever did anything. Fiona and Ken were not fit parents. Colin was neglected, which must have compounded his condition."

"And now it's too late," Annie said. "But that aside, what's going on? Is there a message here for us? Or is it simply Colin gets creepier as he gets older?"

"I think," said Heather, "that in two weeks' time, when it's your turn again, Annie, we're going to have to eliminate the most obvious answer – that Colin's doing everything himself. We need to be alert for clues. Perhaps James and I can visit you. We never see Colin when we're together."

"OK."

"Other than that..." Heather began, but never finished her sentence. At that moment, the whole building shook to what afterwards the cousins could only describe as a tremendous sigh of exasperation.

"Jesus!" James exclaimed, a mild expletive for him.

"What the...?" Annie glanced around fearfully.

Heather got to her feet. "What?" she said, her head raised as if to gaze through the ceiling. "Tell us."

There was a profound silence, as if all the normal sounds of the house, even human breathing, were suppressed. And then, from overhead, as if from a distant attic, the cousins heard an unmistakeable sound: a baby laughing, the free and innocent expression of happiness that rarely survives childhood.

"What?" Heather asked again, softly.

James and Annie were silent, staring at their cousin, holding hands.

There was another sound, as of fingers being dragged down a damp windowpane. Heather turned and walked to the front of the room, peered at the condensation in the glass. "Ask him," she murmured.

"What?" Annie and James got to their feet.

"That's what it says," Heather replied, pointing at the window.

They were like marks a child would make and yet, if you stared at them, the words were there: *ask him*.

After the regulation respite gap of two weeks, Colin's visits were set to start once more, beginning with Annie. Heather and James would call round on the Friday evening: the three of them had resolved to have a little talk with Colin. Heather's house seemed to think the solution was clear, although Heather had perhaps embellished the communication her haunting had offered. "It's to do with his childhood," she'd said. "Obvious now. And we ask him about it."

"If we can get the truth from him," Annie had said.

"We got a message," Heather had insisted, somewhat smugly. "We have to act on it."

Even James had refrained from mentioning mundane explanations such as faulty plumbing after the bizarre experience at Heather's house.

Annie felt slightly nervous as she waited for her doorbell to ring, and Colin's inevitable babble beyond the glass. She was still awed that a supernatural communication had apparently occurred, and that Heather's haunting had had something to impart about Colin. That seemed to imply the supernatural was at work in Colin too.

He arrived early as usual, bringing a chugging steam of chatter and perfume into her home. The cats scuttled off. While he asked her senseless questions about her work – about which he knew little and could have no real interest in knowing – Annie mustered her courage.

"Colin!" she said firmly, stemming the flow of words.

He froze at the kettle, appeared momentarily frightened.

"Colin," she said in a softer tone. "When you use the bathroom can you clean it properly, please? I found talc all over the place after the last time you visited, and the plughole up there was full of your hair."

"I *did* clean it," Colin said. He had a cornered look about him Annie had not seen before and uttered a couple of forlorn snuffles.

"Well, that's odd then, isn't it?" she said. "Come on, let's go into the garden. James and Heather are popping over later. We can get a pizza first, my treat."

She felt the ground had been prepared.

The jollity felt rather forced when Heather and James arrived – together, as James had given Heather a lift. Annie and Colin had eaten outdoors, but now Annie ushered everyone inside since the air had begun to cool. Annie wondered if Colin considered it odd – the four of them getting together like this. It hadn't happened since childhood or the occasional big family gatherings. Still, he didn't appear perturbed in any way, and the brief episode earlier seemed forgotten.

Heather curled up on the sofa, sipping from the large glass of wine Annie had given her. She was plainly in charge, and Annie was happy to let her be. She had no doubt James felt the same. Heather began by reminiscing about their childhood holidays, recounting amusing little tales. Colin had a remarkable memory and could remember things the others had forgotten; a particular lady who'd lodged nearby to them two years on the trot, the proprietor of the newsagents, where one of their grandfathers had always bought his paper every morning, accompanied by Colin. His childhood recollections were caught in amber, glowing beautifully. You could see it in his face. All those happy times spent with the extended family, over summers that had seemed endless. Even back then he'd been farmed out to relatives – mostly to grandparents in those days.

Ken and Fiona were but murky shadows, never part of mainstream family life. Fiona had succumbed early in years to mental illness and had met her future husband while in hospital. Colin did not speak of them, only his other relatives. And while he was speaking of the past he didn't cough, he didn't snuffle, nor – most bizarrely – could Annie smell his perfume as strongly. He was still that boy, she felt, had never grown up, and yet the world had expected him to.

"It must've been hard for you," Heather said gently, interrupting one of Colin's anecdotes about a neighbour. "What with your mum and dad being the way they were."

Colin hesitated, but not for long. "Yes, they could be a

bother," he said, "but I didn't take much notice. And the old lady used to care for me, even when I was a baby."

"Which old lady was this?" Heather asked. "A neighbour?"

Again, a slight hesitation. "No, it used to be her house... Where we lived. She sang to me at night when I was in my cot."

"You can remember that?"

"Yes. I never forget things. Sometimes, I was hungry, and she'd sing to me then. Jessie, who lives next door, she remembers her: Ada Jones. But Jessie's very old."

"Tell us about Ada," Heather said.

Colin laughed. "She said, 'Young man, I'll help you through life,' and she did..."

"Does?" suggested Heather.

Colin pursed his lips and a small snuffle emerged. "I... don't *see* her now. That was only when I was little. She said when I was sad I should have a ciggy and everything would be all right." He smiled wistfully. "That was how I knew she was there – or was coming – the smell of her cigarettes and her perfume."

"Jesus," James murmured softly, leaning forward in his chair. "Was she a ghost, mate?"

Colin nodded. "Yes. That's why I never talked about her. People wouldn't believe, although Mum heard her over the baby monitor sometimes. I heard them talking, but Dad put it down to her hearing things."

"So, Ada isn't around anymore?" Heather asked.

"She'll always be around," Colin answered, "just in a different way now. I can remember when she faded out – when I couldn't see her. It happened bit by bit. And then her voice disappeared too. The smells lasted for much longer, then they were gone as well. But I know she's never left me."

"No," said Heather, "I don't think she has."

"I can feel things," Colin said. He cast a guilty glance at Annie. "She didn't like me not smoking. She missed it. The e-cig's not in her world, you see. She can't smoke that."

"So, you let her have a cigarette at home," Annie said.

"Now and again. I can't really afford it now."

"Is she cross with us, Colin?" Heather asked.

"She was cross about the smoking," Colin said, "but I told her she'd have to put up with it, because you've got to respect people's houses."

"Were you cross about it too? Annie asked.

He shrugged. "Not really. I know you didn't like the smell. People don't anymore."

"Does she come to our houses with you?" Heather said.

"A bit of her does, I s'pose, because she's looking after me. But it's not like she's sitting here now."

"Glad to hear that!" James exclaimed with feeling, earning stern glances from the women.

"You wear her perfume, use her toiletries," Annie said. "Is that to keep her around you?"

"I just like them," Colin said.

"You'd live in the past, if you could, wouldn't you?" said Heather.

Colin's face lit up. "Yes. I'd live in the summer times," he said.

A tiny boy who'd needed help had reached out, Heather realised, perhaps through desperate screams in a darkened room, and someone had found him, come to his aid. While Colin's relatives ignored his plight, considered him as odd as his parents, the shade of Ada Jones had nurtured him, listened to him, given him advice on how to survive. And Colin *was* a survivor, existing in a world he found alien, trying to blend in, to be like others, but mostly lacking the tools to do so. Perhaps Ada, realising her power was diminishing in the modern world, had been trying to attract attention for a long time, make people *really* listen, smell and see, especially those who were able to take action. This is what Heather, James and Annie concluded. Whether Ada was real or had somehow been conjured by a desperate little boy hardly mattered. It had taken a haunted house to hear the message, to make a supreme effort to communicate in a manner that dense humans would understand.

Things would never change dramatically. No matter how much practical help she and the others gave him now, particularly in respect of renovating his home, Colin would still be himself, full of annoying quirks and habits. And if he was once again allowed to smoke the occasional real cigarette outdoors, and the smell might drift inside, if his perfume lingered cloyingly on the air, and his cough reverberated through guest room walls, it was a small price to pay. Cats and dogs might still run spooked, but Heather's house was peaceful. That was perhaps the strongest message of all – beyond human senses.

# When The Angels Came

*Story History:*

Hopefully, most of you reading this collection will be familiar with some of my work, and might even know that my novel, *"Burying the Shadow"*, is a reinvention of the vampire myth, influenced strongly by legends, from all over the world, of fallen angels.

The following fragments were written while I was researching *"Burying the Shadow"*, and were inspired by the stories of fallen angels gleaned from Enochian mythology (from the ancient text *"The Book of Enoch"*), Milton's *"Paradise Lost"* and ancient Sumerian legends. I had a vague idea that one day I might turn the short accounts into a novella, but once I got into the flow of writing *Shadow*, these fragments became a forgotten file on my computer, and were only rediscovered some years ago as I was browsing through my story notes.

A version of these fragments appeared in a chapbook to accompany my Guest of Honour appearance at the Birmingham SF convention, Novacon, in 1992.

I've always been fascinated by the idea of superior beings arriving – or appearing – among human communities in ancient times to impart knowledge; a possible real event that inspired the legends of angels, gods and all manner of other semi-divine beings. The Sumerian legends, as extravagantly and somewhat over-enthusiastically interpreted by Zecharia Sitchin in his book, *"The Twelfth Planet"*, held a particular interest for me as I was researching. Although the book suffers dramatically from Von Danikenism, (Sitchin''s ideas require a certain suspension of disbelief concerning alien visitors), he explores many of the ancient legends in depth, describing the apparently all too human in-fighting, scandals and power struggles of the gods, as they sought to colonise a new world. As a book on mythology, rather than a possible para-history, *"The Twelfth Planet"* was a great inspiration. As in the Judaeo-Christian legends, used by Milton for *"Paradise Lost"*, there were elements among the divine community that resented the authority of their superiors and sought to seize power of their own. While bemused human beings evolved from mere beasts of burden into intelligent creatures in their own right, the gods stampeded back and forth around them across the land, (in space rockets, Sitchin would have us believe!), quarrelling and destroying each other as their temperaments and rather hysterical politics saw fit.

In Enochian mythology, I found the rebels appeared to have a more altruistic motive for their rebellion; they desired to give humankind knowledge that the gods, (or God), kept jealously for themselves. The angelic teachers imparted to humanity information about magic, science and medicine. Their punishment for this crime was eternal damnation and torture. The Enochian angels were forced to watch all the children they had created with mortal women die.

The fragments that follow are first person narratives that describe what happens "when the angels came". I suppose they could be part of a prequel to *"Burying the Shadow"*. The fragments are raw, unpolished, but I resisted the urge to work on them further. As they stand, they capture (for me) the voices of the characters as they relate the events, the actual moment of narration.

### On the Marsh

These people, where did they come from? I heard talk they fell out of a low pass cloud, the kind with the bloody-brown fringes. Possible? Maybe. All I know is they strange as people can be. How do I know that? Well, you see this? Yes, you can touch it… One of them gave it to me. What is it? You tell me. Feels weird, doesn't it? Yes, it does get warm. What? Oh, they call it a show-stone. I want it to show me things, but I don't know how. It's too late now…

No, don't go. You talk to me. You talk to me, because I was

the first to see. You want to know, don't you?

I was out in the marsh, digging up mud lizards, when it happened. It was a misty day, shapes all around, but not spirits singing. I headed out early because Ma wanted the lizards quick. We ate the tails, but the rest went to the barter ground, out on the flat fields where the old trees are. I was poking around with my spike, waiting for the squish and squeak, which meant I'd spiked a lizard, when my gut started to tell me something. I remember standing up and noticing how quiet it had got. Nothing marshy moved at all. It was like everything was holding its breath; critters, water, mud and air. I got a feeling I was being belly-stalked by something bad, and all I had was a lizard spike. Some protection! I hunkered down in the tussocks and kept my lizard spike ready, thinking that maybe I was going to die. Weird things can happen on the marsh, but we don't talk about them much.

Then I saw a darkness in the mist. It looked like a man. *Was* a man, to my eyes. "Stranger," I said, standing up. We did not fear other men in those times. He did not say anything, and I was wondering whether he was lost. Very tall. I couldn't see much because of the mist, but I knew he was watching me. "You looking for something?" I said. He didn't move. I was starting to feel uneasy. Maybe he was sick, so I began to leap the tussocks to get to him. That's when he disappeared. I swear it. Just vanished. So weird. I went home pretty quick after that.

## The First Witch

She had terrible green eyes, you know; terrible. Her hair was the colour of wet blood, arterial blood, from somewhere deep anyhow, and she wore those clothes that were like moss. We were scared of her but interested. Know what I mean? She'd lived alone all her life up on the Cloudy Steeps, for as long as anyone can remember. When we heard the spirits singing to turn the world golden, she just spat at the grass and called it mud. On misty days, if you squinted up the Steeps, it seemed that tall figures were standing motionless around her shack. Later, we found out that the strangers had gone to talk with her – long before they talked to anyone else around here, but then she was strange herself, like she knew something we didn't, so perhaps she was just 'the one' for them.

Me and the other kids used to go up to her shack once in a while. She'd shout insults at us through the door rags, and then bring out a jug of that thick ale she brewed and a pipe of skerry moss to pass the time. She'd sit on a big round boulder outside her door, sit like a boy with her knees up, with her fierce hair, the pipe in her mouth.

"You killed anything yet, sonny?" she'd say and then flash her eyes like it was a joke.

I was aching for the day when I could say yes to that question, but some part of me knew it would never come.

Her hands were amazing, the fingers just a little too long and always seamed with moss juice. These hands, they would just hang there between her knees as she talked and sometimes the fingers would twitch as if they were waiting for something to grab at. Our kin never used to talk about us going up there – the girls never came – but we guessed the women were afraid of her. That is, they were afraid until they *had* to go visit her and then it was time to muffle up in a cloak, bend into the mist, and just melt away from the village. No, the women never talk about her, not even now.

## The Late Caller

My story is this. There was a wind outside, like a beast howling. It was night-time, very cold. Fire burning in the cottage, the smell of burning peat and oatcakes. I was burning my legs, so close to the fire. My back was chilled. I was listening to the sounds outside, sounds like furious hands pulling at the planks across the windows. I could hear my mother and my aunt chewing in their sleep on the platform at the back of the cottage. My place was always next to the fire. I had a pallet there. I never slept on the hair-filled couch, because things lived in the stuffing that made me itch. I didn't want to move, burning up my legs so close to the fire.

It was unusual for someone to come a-knocking so late, but not totally unlikely. My aunt waves hands over the dying, so she was sometimes needed at odd hours. I hoped whoever it was would just go away, and didn't get up at first, but they kept on knocking, so I knew it had to be serious.

The wind came in like a hungry dog and I said, "Don't just stand there!"

Then he came in.

I didn't know him, never seen him before. He was so tall I thought he had to be foreign, or something. I wondered what he wanted. Had he come for my aunt? He had a long black cloak on, and a wide-brimmed hat, both of which looked wet through, although I couldn't see him too well. He walked past me to the fire and put one hand on the hot bricks of the wall.

"What do you want?" I asked him. We didn't get too many foreigners coming to us, and when they did, it was generally to the barter grounds.

"Shelter," he answered. Just that. His voice sounded strange, but the request did not. It was a wild night outside.

"We've not much room. No beds."

He turned and looked at me, taking off his hat, smiling. "Doesn't matter." When his hat came off, all this hair tumbled down around his face. A stranger's face; none like it around here, highly boned and pale. His hair was the colour of veins in salty rock, dark, but like sunlight was trapped there.

"Who are you? Why are you here?" I wondered whether he had knocked upon other doors and been sent away, although that was unlikely.

"My name is Gadreel," he said. "As to why I'm here..." He shrugged and looked around the cottage. I suppose he was wondering about the answer to that himself.

"You've come to trade?"

He looked at me keenly, just for a moment too long, and then said, "Yes. Trade. Something like that." He took off his cloak and underneath it he was dressed in grey. The cloth too was wet. Only his hair was dry.

"A storm outside?" I asked him.

He glanced at the shuttered windows. "Yes." The question had been pointless, of course.

I went and dragged my blanket out from under the couch. "You can use this," I said. "Put your clothes by the fire."

As he undressed himself, I went into the cold room to fetch some milk. I would heat it in a pan for him. When I went back into the room, he was sitting in my mother's chair beside the hearth, the blanket wrapped round his waist. His body was thin, but so long, if you can understand that. I had never seen anyone so tall. It looked very odd. The room was small around him.

"Are you alone here?" he asked me.

I shook my head. "No. My mother and her sister are asleep up there."

"Yet you are still awake."

"The knocking woke me," I said.

"Then I disturbed you. Sorry, but I find the weather uncomfortable here."

"Where you come from?"

"Came down from the High Place. I had to find shelter. There was light beneath your door."

I poured the milk into a bowl for him. "Drink this," I said. He looked at the bowl uncertainly and then took it from my hands. He sniffed the liquid within and put his tongue into it. Then, he drank. "From the breast," he said.

"Milk from a goat," I replied.

Perhaps he was mad.

I told him he could share my warmth beside the fire, and he stretched out beside me. I turned my back on him, curling into the blanket. It was lucky it was so big, but even so, I think his feet were left uncovered. I tried to sleep, but all night I lay awake there, feeling his body tremble beside me.

In the morning my mother and aunt were surprised to find this big man in our cottage. I told them his name, and my mother gave him hers. Such is the custom. "What have you to trade?" she asked him.

Gadreel smiled his strange smile and tapped his head. "This," he said.

My mother laughed. "Your head? Your hair?"

"No. My knowledge."

My mother laughed again, her eyes sliding towards mine. She too thought him a little mad. "And what knowledge is this?"

"One part of a great whole," he said. "Others of my family will come after me. They will give you wonderful things."

"And the price?" This was my aunt, hanging over the edge of the sleeping platform like a great bat.

Gadreel looked up at her. "Less than the gift," he said. "To you."

He came with me when I went to feed the goats. Other people were about, and I felt proud to have him there. He was tall and good to look at, and no-one but me knew who he was. The storm had passed, but the ground was cold and muddy.

"Take me to the hills," Gadreel said. "There." He pointed at the green slopes, at the place where the trees were, on top.

"That is where we worship," I said.

"Take me there."

We climbed the damp, slippery slopes, me tugging at the grass with my hands. At the top, we sat down at the edge of the tree circle to catch our breath, and I said, "I don't think we have use for your knowledge, Gadreel, whatever it is."

He looked down at me and raised an eyebrow. "Oh, you think not?"

I shook my head. "No, but it doesn't matter."

"You are wrong."

"Then tell me the knowledge, so I can find out."

"My knowledge is of the bitter and the sweet," he said.

I frowned. "Taste."

"No. Not that."

"Then what?"

He sighed and wrapped his cloak around his knees. "It is too soon to demonstrate."

"How can you say that? You could die before you told us."

"How?"

"That tree behind could fall on you. The ground could shake and grab you. Anything. Tell me."

"You are very innocent here. Like animals," he said.

"Animals don't build houses," I said.

"Animals don't have love either. You have shuttered hearts, like animals."

I did not understand what he said.

"You have been kept in ignorance," he said. "Too long. And it is not innocence anymore, but stagnation. There are things you must know, to progress, to evolve, to become great..."

When he said these things, it was like the sun coming down to Earth. It made me feel that something indescribable but wonderful was about to happen, but I still didn't understand. Then, he did a very strange thing. He stretched out one hand and touched my face, ran his thumb down my cheek and pinched the flesh of my jaw.

"Why did you do that?" I asked him.

"Because I wanted to. Hold out your hand."

I did so, wondered what he would do next. He took hold of my fingers and traced a pattern on the palm. It was like being tickled by leaves.

"What does this make you think of?" he asked.

I told him.

Then he ran a finger up the inside of my arm. I could feel it in my shoulder-blade. It was very peculiar.

"You must learn to touch one another," he said.

"What for?"

He shook his head and dropped my hand, grinning to himself.

Something about his amusement annoyed me, so I pushed my hands against his face. He went very still. I could feel the muscles twisting, the outline of bone. He did not look at me, but kept staring, straight ahead. I kept my hands there until my arms began to ache. Why should we touch one another? What's to be gained from it?

"I could fall upon you like the sky," he said.

## The Watching

These people, they are not men. Something else, but wearing the skins of men, the eyes of men, their hands. We took to collecting the sound of them in our flesh, the aorisms of power, without substance yet entirely substance; an unexplored integrity of sound. In these waveforms of kelestic symmetry, we felt the remote passing into the definite. We saw the wings of change form within the ichor of their sound; a thick smoke, sweet upon the tongue, curling into unimagined shapes that suggested surrender, ecstasy, pain, renewal.

These people, they are not men. We learned their names: Semyaza, Kasday, Azazel, Salamiel, Penemue. These are the ancient names of their native land. In this place, on this Earth of now reality, the names are different, but the old cadences can still be uttered, chanted; they will still vitalise the call.

We stand together in the wildest places of the earth, and form a forest of hands against the sky, stretching up, reaching for what is ours to take and yet never to attain. Our bodies begin to pulsate to a subliminal rhythm, and we feel the imminence of contained energy, soon to be released. We dilate our throats to the air and resonate the ancient names.

We convoke them, and they come to us, these people who are not men...

## Forever Remain... A Myth

*"...the angels showed me, and from them I heard everything, and from them I understood as I saw, but not for this generation, but for a remote one which is to come..."*

The Book of Enoch

This is the last time you'll look out there, see that cityscape, take in the hot, breathing smell of the city, feel this flesh on your bones, too hot to wear, too damning to discard. Last time.

There are dreams in the clouded glass; not the silvered mirror, the harlot's tool, but the glass in your hand, the nepenthe-draught. Too much to recall. The bitter and the sweet. Swallow it all, a searing cataract of forgetfulness.

Think you can lose it all? The doing, the watching, the words that were heard? Too late. Done now, and the inevitable approaches. There is only one escape. Discard the knowledge. Hide. Tomorrow, wake reborn.

And the memories will sleep in the dark. Watching. Waiting. For the touch. For the summoning. To come through once more.

# LA TENEBREUSE

*Story History:*

This story was written for the anthology *The Alchemy Press Book of Horrors*, edited by Peter Coleburn and Jan Edwards, Alchemy Press, 2018, an anthology of weird tales. My story features a character who has appeared in a previous weird tale collection of mine. The story was called "The Secret Gallery", first published in *Dark in the Day*, Immanion Press, 2016. Alex is a mysterious character, who is trans-gender or androgynous, or even something else. They have strange abilities, a connection to the weird and unseen, and can usually handle any peculiar investigation thrown at them. But in this one they almost meet their match. I won't be surprised if Alex turns up again a story in the future. If they smell a good mystery, they'll be on their way to help me investigate it. The story was initially inspired by the opening sequence of the movie *The Ninth Gate*, showing a series of doors opening one after another, as an unseen viewer moves through them. It's spooky and unsettling, and I never forgot it, always wanting to include a version of it in a story. Here it is, hidden in this piece, straight from one of Alex's dreams.

I dreamed of the house before we visited it, but dreams are rarely very accurate. I was sauntering up a red-pebbled driveway towards a yellow building, which looked two-dimensional to me, like a cut-out. It reared backwards, so that the perspective narrowed its roofs, its peering upper windows. The bones of a dead clematis clutched the flaking paint and cowering within this fibrous frame was a pair of wooden doors that were also reddish in colour. As I approached, the doors swooned inwards and there was only blackness beyond. I felt wary yet not afraid. Perceiving a light within the darkness, I stepped onto the threshold, and realised that ahead of me was an open door, through which poured molten daylight. Only a vast unseen chamber lay between me and the light. I could feel the space even if I could not see it. I extended one foot into the house and the darkness hugged my bare lower leg. I felt somehow... *chewed.*

That was all, at first.

Vezi is one of my oldest friends. He annoys me greatly – always has – because of the puppylike wincing he's given to and the mournful expressions. I told him he should be a poet, behaving like that, but he's not creative at all. Anyway, despite his flaws, I suppose I love him as one loves a sibling – there's always an element of despising in such relationships, I think.

A young man with the unlikely name of Nimrod Queneau had invited Vezi to spend some summer weeks at *Le Nid des Rêves*, his parents' country house in Southwestern France. A nest of dreams: intriguing. Vezi asked me to go with him as he knows my tastes and felt I'd find artistic inspiration in the old place – perhaps commissions too. He insisted he'd pay for the trip. I thanked him for his thoughtfulness, aware there was no doubt an ulterior motive – as in he was scared of going alone. I'm frequently called upon as 'muscle' for Vezi, a backup staring meaningfully over his shoulder at would-be trouble-makers, even if that's only his mulish cat-sitter. But... free holiday. I'd be delighted to go. Of course.

We were both living in London at the time, in our late twenties and each – in our own particular way – eager for adventure. For Vezi, I was quite sure this would involve the finding of 'true love'. (He'd never accept my advice that this scabrous emotion was not real and all to do with chemicals, part of DNA's survival mechanism, with no morals or sense.) You see, poor pup, he had a poet's heart in an engineer's body. Cruel. As for me, all I wanted was to stumble upon things strange and unexpected. This only required being open to the possibility. If it frightened Vezi, all to the good, as this might enhance the experience.

Travelling on a train through rural France and the bleaching light of what I call 'the child's summer', (i.e. endless perfect sunlight in memory that rarely actually happened), I asked Vezi about the quirkily-named Nimrod.

"We were at university together," he said. "Everyone loved him."

*But particularly you*, I thought.

"He was... beautiful," Vezi continued, looking poetically pained.

Ah, the thorns of unrequited love, desiccated into obscurity, but now already reviving with the faintest drop of water; they scraped once more at his heart.

"Don't worry, Vez," I said cheerily. "It was years ago. He's probably started to get fat and lose his hair."

"You're not always right," Vezi snapped. "He might be the same – or better."

I sincerely hoped not. Another of Vezi's annoyances was that he aimed to find romance with people who would instinctively despise him – people like me, I suppose, although not as tolerant and without the shared history. Inevitably, I was the sin-eater of his tragic romances, and by now had automatic responses, which I knew would soothe him but meant I could be thinking about something else while he poured out his woes.

The house stood on a hill at the apex of a long driveway lined by poplars. I was not surprised to find it painted yellow, but that was where similarities with my dream ended. Many houses in the area were that colour. Also, there was no dead clematis clinging to the walls, and the doors were painted a glossy black. There were turrets too, one to east and west, and the house in my dream had been square. This was not an immense chateau, long abandoned by aristocrats who were now headless ghosts – it was rather more a glorified farmhouse, the abode of a successful land-owner.

Vezi and I were disgorged by our taxi – ancient, creaking, in keeping with the theme of our story – in the sweep of driveway before the house. But where I'd hoped for further eeriness in the edifice before me, I found instead evidence of cosy domesticity. Windows were flung open on all of its stories, and I saw vases of fresh flowers on the sills of several of them. The drive was well kept, and stunted bay trees in pots were arranged with apparently obsessive precision along the house's frontage. The place was neither creepy nor run-down. I found this rather disappointing, but the adventure was new, so I wasn't ready to give up hope.

We approached the doors, at the head of three wide, worn steps and Vezi used the door-knocker. This furniture was of iron, in the shape of a gargoyle, and I approved of it. We could hear the knock echo within the house, quite ponderously.

"*That* will wake the dead," I whispered, grinning at Vezi.

He grinned back.

We heard no footsteps approach, but presently one of the doors was opened by a beautifully peculiar creature. She stood well over six foot in height and wore a tailored, black trouser suit with a startlingly white shirt. Her hair hung to her shoulders, thick, and cut severely straight, like an Ancient Egyptian wig. Her milk-pale face was sculptured and bony – handsome, you'd call it – and marred only by one thing: her nostrils. The nose was long, perhaps slightly too much, but well-shaped. The flared nostrils, however, were inordinately large, so much so the appendage didn't really look like a nose but more like some alien organ that served functions in addition to smelling. Such a deformity might make a person shy or awkward around others, or even hostile and defensive, but this individual appeared unaware of her difference. She smiled at us and said in English, "You must be Vezi Torres and er Ms…?"

"Just Alex," I said and stepped past Vezi into the house.

The hall was panelled in wood the colour of dark honey, and sunlight fell in through a round, stained-glass window high up over the door. The hall itself was the height of two stories. A graceful oak stair swept seductively up to the second floor, like a beautiful woman in a ball gown with a train. The warmth in the chamber seemed to hum; this felt very welcoming. "What a lovely house," I said.

"Yes," said the woman. "I'm Posy Sala, the housekeeper for the family."

*Posy*? I had to stifle amusement. I had never met anyone less suited to such a name. I couldn't place her accent. Eastern European perhaps? But then… maybe not. Certainly not French, anyway.

"M. Queneau sends his apologies he was unable to be here to greet you. So please spend some time settling in. I'll show you your rooms, then perhaps you'd like refreshment." Posy indicated the stairs. We followed her up them.

Our rooms were situated next to one another on the first floor, at the back of the house. Vezi bustled into his and shut the door on me, no doubt to undergo rituals of preparation before meeting again with Nimrod. I went into my room but left the door ajar. Through the open window, which reached down to the wainscot, I could see neat gardens that descended in terraces to woodland, and beyond that – it seemed – into primal landscape, untouched by humanity. If only. My room was comfortable but disappointingly like one you'd find in a decent hotel – no brooding heavy furniture, no canopied bed, nor even a creepy ancestral portrait on the wall that would monitor my movements across the thickly-carpeted floor.

I flopped onto the bed and lay on my back with arms outflung, staring at the cream-painted ceiling. Sounds from outside were few: birdsong, and a kind of subliminal roar in the landscape itself.

After some minutes of daydreaming, followed by a visit to the bathroom to throw water on my face, I went back downstairs. The front door had been left open and summer light pooled on the warm wooden floor. I could hear someone singing in a far corner of the house, not a tune I knew – wistful yet repetitive, like a charm. It could have been the voice of a woman or a child. Now the ticking of a grandfather clock intruded; it stood beside the stairs. I went to stare up into its face, which was decorated with the sun, the moon, the stars. I heard the sound of soft shoes on tiles and then Posy Sala emerged from a corridor – this sumptuous gargoyle of a woman.

"Would you like tea?" she asked me. "Or something cold?"

"Tea, please," I said.

"Outside or in… to sit, I mean."

"I'd like to see the house."

"I'll show you to the sitting room."

This was a feminine chamber, which I decided was – or had been – the province of Nimrod's mother. It was a museum of a room, all chintz and florid flower patterns, but was not uncomfortable. "Who lives in the house?" I asked Posy Sala.

"The Queneau family," she replied rather acidly, then softened. "Nimrod, his sister, their aunt and their parents. He's alone while the rest of them are summer travelling."

I assumed the younger Queneaus did not work. What *did* they do, out here in the middle of nowhere? Perhaps they only came home at certain times of year. I wondered then exactly why Nimrod wasn't here to greet us, seeing as we'd come so far to stay with him, and thought I might as well ask where he was.

"He'll be back for dinner," Posy Sala said. "He had an unavoidable commitment today."

And then Vezi came into the room. When our gazes collided, I saw a message in his eyes, and interpreted it as: *What's going on?* He was mildly perturbed, but that might not mean anything. Vezi is easily perturbed.

Posy went away to prepare our refreshment and we explored the room. There were several large paintings on the walls – intriguingly unusual. While the style was similar to that found in typical 19th century family portraits, the pictures were far from conventional. One resembled a photographic close-up of a woman's hands resting on a prayer book – her fingers curled loosely over the body of a dead dove. Another was of horses, but not typical of its period. The picture depicted merely galloping hooves, the grey legs of the horses muddied and bloodied, as if fleeing a massacre.

While Vezi examined ancient woodcuts around the fireplace, I sauntered to a huge mahogany sideboard on the darkest side of the room, where framed photographs were packed like tombstones in an over-crowded graveyard. I hoped to find historic photos of family corpses among the faces, as was the custom in centuries past, but no such luck. The people I assumed to be Nimrod and his sister – recent, high-definition pictures near the front of the throng – were attenuated and elegant: thoroughbreds. They had a faint resemblance to Posy Sala, I thought, but for the nose. They were very tanned, in all the seasons of their recorded life so far, smiling ravenously at the camera, through fringes of thick, dark blonde hair, with brown eyes glinting and sardonic eyebrows cocked. I could see at once that Vezi would have no chance with Nimrod, or with the sister either, for that matter. Vezi came to join me, stared at the photograph in my hand, sighed deeply. I replaced it in the crowd.

After consuming cups of excellent Assam tea, and the divinely sticky cakes that accompanied it, we went out to walk around the gardens, arm in arm, until it was time for dinner. There were elaborate follies in the Classical style, and an ornamental lake with a fabricated island in its centre, where fake ruined arches crumbled into the moss. At the lake's edge, within a den of shifting willow withes, there was a boathouse, peeling and old, oozing memories of childhood I could almost see. We found a dilapidated rowing-boat named *Pygmy* moored inside.

"What do you think, Alex?" Vezi asked me.

"About what?"

He extended his arms to indicate the house and its grounds. "This place."

"I take it you don't want weird..."

"It's *not*, though, is it? But there's something... something..." He shook his head.

I suspected he was looking for ghosts, the tragic spirit of love, a mirror in time for his heart.

"It's a very nice house," I said, aware this was a remark below my usual standard.

"I don't think he's away," Vezi said. "I think he's *in there*." He glanced up at the house on its hill above us.

"Nimrod? Really?"

"Yes. I don't know why I feel it, but I do. Can't *you* have a... feel about?"

I snorted. "I've never met Nimrod Queneau, so despite my unparalleled occult talents it's unlikely I'd *feel* him. Perhaps he *is* here, but simply wants time to finish up with something before he meets us." I grinned. "Perhaps he has to steel himself to see you again."

Vezi did not share my amusement. He frowned. "I know you'll laugh, because what I'm about to say isn't typical of me, but I had a dream about this place before we came here..." He looked at me with the expression of a man about to be whipped.

"So did I," I said, clearly surprising him. "How empathic of us. Mine was quite dull, but what was yours?"

"I dreamed we never met him, but he was all around us all the time. I can't explain."

"That's only your fears," I said, taking his arm and shaking him mildly. "Really, Vezi, you must stop investing so much energy into someone you've hardly seen for years. It's good to retain a youthful spirit, and I applaud that in you, but it's also essential to grow up. From his photos, I imagine Nimrod Queneau has a glut of casual lovers. Please be realistic for once."

He nodded, his expression glum. "I know you're right. It's just…" He shivered in the warmth of the day. "So, what was your dream?"

"Oh, just that the only thing inside the house was a way out, but it was through darkness."

That made him laugh. "I don't know why I asked."

We went back to the house.

Posy Sala hit a gong in the hallway to call us to dinner from the sitting room. This was at 7 pm, quite early by French standards. We wandered into the hall like tourists and saw Ms Sala standing by the entrance to another room, holding a small mallet with a felt-covered head. The gong on the table beside her still hummed softly as its bloom died away. The housekeeper gestured with the mallet for us to cross the hall and enter the dining room.

I expected to see Nimrod already seated, even though it was still odd he hadn't come down and introduced himself before the meal. But the dining room was empty. Two places had been set at a large glossy table, opposite each other at one end. No place was laid at the head.

"Is Nimrod not back?" Vezi asked.

Posy Sala inclined her head. "No, he sends his apologies and hopes you enjoy your meal."

"When *will* he be back?" Vezi insisted.

"Perhaps later, but you might not see him until tomorrow."

Vezi sat down with his back to the door, looking sullen. I sat opposite him and gave him a stern glance. He shrugged.

I had imagined the house empty but for Ms Sala, but now a brace of servants arrived, carrying trays of covered dishes. They both wore black uniforms and white aprons. These individuals were young, in their teens, a boy and a girl, both ink-haired and beautiful. They were silent but had mysterious smiles. Natural tricksters. How delightful.

Posy Sala introduced them: "This is Ailie and Troyes, who run the house with me. If you should need anything, and I'm not here, you may ask them."

"Thank you," Vezi said coldly.

I smiled at Posy's familiars. They grinned back slyly.

The meal they brought was delicious; chicken cradled in an exquisite sauce, perfectly-cooked vegetables. There was a cool, greenish-white wine, so pure as to be almost without taste, but for its fire. The dessert, when it came, was pears clad in spiced syrup and chocolate shavings.

I was wondering by now whether Vezi had been somewhat selective with the truth when inviting me on this trip. It seemed likely he'd bumped into Nimrod somewhere and, with the cunning of the truly besotted, had engineered an invitation to *Le Nid des Rêves*, perhaps a little against Nimrod's wishes. This to me seemed the explanation for our host's non-appearance. He must be making it clear to Vezi there was nothing to hope for in respect of dalliances. I felt some sympathy for Nimrod. Vezi can be truly terrifying in the grip of feverish desire.

Behind the dining room, there was a chamber dedicated to the viewing of television and here a TV set only slightly smaller than a cinema screen stood waiting to open the doors of the world to us. Vezi and I spent the evening watching films we'd seen before and went to bed fairly early. I drifted to sleep quickly, tired by the earlier journey, and then began to dream.

It began as my first dream of the house had – me walking up the driveway – only now the building resembled reality more than the dilapidated edifice I had imagined. I was aware I was dreaming and was intrigued as to what I might discover. As before, the doors of the house opened to me. I expected to find Nimrod inside, so he could speak to me, tell me the truth, offer an excuse. But there was only darkness beyond the threshold, and that distant light of another open door. I ran across the hallway, down a corridor. Shadows clutched at my ankles, but they were weak and insubstantial, couldn't stop me. I fell into the daylight and found myself on the drive to another house – the place of my previous dream. Was this collapse into ruin what lay behind the façade of domesticity and contentment?

Bells woke me: hundreds of bells. Surfacing from sleep, I realised this was the ringing of telephones – all of them the old-fashioned kind rather than those equipped with modern bleeps and tunes. It seemed every phone in the house clamoured for attention, and there must be a lot of them. "Answer it!" I snapped at the air. If there'd been a handset in my room, I would've done so myself.

Then, silence. Someone had got to a phone, or whoever had called had given up.

The hush was too deep, as if the house held its breath, afraid to utter a sound in case it was *noticed*. I turned on the bedside lamp and peered at the compact alarm clock that stood beside it. The time was 3 a.m. Somewhat discomforted, I got out of bed. The distance between me and the windows seemed vast. The curtains shivered, but I knew this was only because one of the panes was open. I padded across the carpet and looked out.

My walk with Vezi hadn't taken me to this part of the garden. The trees looked unreal, like bizarre formations of coral or lichen. I knew I wasn't dreaming; my perception was skewed. I saw a large white object, which I realised was a bulky statue, situated within a circular wall upon the lawn. This was around 100 yards away from the house, but I could perceive it clearly in the light of a half moon. What I couldn't make out was what the statue represented; it seemed ungainly, awkward, as if frozen in embarrassment. Was it a beast, an ancient god, or simply a rough-hewn block of stone?

Then I heard laughter and across the lawn ran two slender figures, hand in hand. Even from a distance I recognised them as Ailie and Troyes. She was dressed in a simple shift that fell to mid-calf; its fabric appeared to glimmer, starlight blue. He was wearing only dark, loose trousers. Both had bare feet, which flickered pale against the shorn grass. I was sure these eldritch creatures would dance around the statue and they did so – pagan creatures from an earlier time. I wondered then if what I observed existed in real time and space. I was prone to glimpses into otherwheres.

I opened the window wider and yelled, "Hello!".

The couple became still, turned to me as one, then grinned and waved heartily. I waved back. Ailie blew me a kiss before the pair of them scampered off, away from the lawn and into the grasping shadows of shrubs and trees.

The next morning, there was still no Nimrod. Posy Sala served us breakfast, and Vezi snapped, "M Queneau's business must be serious. Did he get home very late last night?"

Posy smiled patiently. "He didn't come home last night. His

*serious* business detained him. Perhaps he will be here today."

"This is all very... odd," Vezi grumbled. "He knew we were coming. Is it all too inconvenient for him? Should we perhaps leave?"

Posy Sala raised her brows, but her voice remained level. "M. Queneau deeply regrets the inconvenience. He has stressed you should regard the house as your own. He asks that you enjoy your stay, despite this setback. The countryside is beautiful. There is much to see."

"Did he call you last night?" I asked.

Posy flicked me a speculating glance. "Excuse me?"

"The phone rang in the middle of the night – many phones. The noise woke me."

"Yes," the housekeeper said, then added briskly. "I'll bring you more coffee." She glided out.

Vezi was staring at me.

"What?" I asked.

"I didn't hear any phones," he said.

I shrugged. "Well, it's hardly surprising. You sleep like a drunk."

"This is all so peculiar."

I sighed. "We have a simple choice, my dear. We take advantage of the facilities and have a holiday – Nimrod or no Nimrod – or we waste your money and go home, you in a grump, me bitterly resigned to your stupidity."

I could see Vezi's lower lip was on the brink of trembling. "He'll have to show up eventually – won't he?"

I wasn't sure about that.

The day passed uneventfully. Vezi and I took bicycles from the stable yard and cycled into a nearby village where we ate lunch at the bar. The locals nodded and smiled at us but were not moved to make conversation. After lunch, we strolled along lanes, gazing out over the vineyards and the swatches of sunflower fields placed between them. We drifted through clots of shadowy woodland, which appeared supernaturally dumped between the viniculture and flowers. I hoped grotesque fairy-tale creatures might lurk among the trees. If they did, they hid from me. I was aware of the antiquity of the countryside, the weight of its fecundity, the intoxicating witchery of its perfumes. As we walked, Vezi and I discussed the house and its mysteries. I told Vezi about the statue in the garden and how I saw the servants gambolling round it.

"We might be seeing mystery because we want it to be there," Vezi said, trying hard to be sensible, but sounding only prim.

"Perhaps," I said, "but if we plaster mundane explanations over everything, we shut the mystery out. We should simply remain neutral on the matter, our minds wide open to anything."

When we returned to *Le Nid des Rêves* we went into the garden to look at the statue. By day, it was unremarkable, a roughly-hewn lump of stone, with some strange scorings on it, like engraved claw marks. It didn't resemble a creature of any kind.

Posy Sala later enlightened us after we asked her about it. "It's a very old boulder, believed to be from the Ice Age. It was found somewhere in the grounds, and Nimrod's great grand-father had it moved to the lawn. It's said he had the marks sculpted into it then, to make it look like an ancient sacred object."

I was disappointed by the relatively mundane explanation, but perhaps Posy Sala warped the truth. I could only hope so.

And yet, from that moment, it was as if the mystery of *Le Nid des Rêves* reined itself in – perhaps suspicious of us. Vezi and I passed the evening watching more TV. We went to bed and slept peacefully. In the morning, still no Nimrod. This continued for three days. Despite the lack of bizarre events, however, I did have a faint sense of being observed. It was not unpleasant but kept me alert.

On the fourth morning, I awoke unusually early, full of energy. I was in no mood to try and go back to sleep, so got up and dressed. It wasn't yet time for breakfast. I decided to stroll around the garden for an hour or so, soak up the atmosphere of the morning.

Outside, a frill of mist hugged the lawns and spilled into the valleys beyond the grounds. It seethed and rippled as if alive. The air smelled rich, full of promise. Soon the sun would burn through the mist and retake the land. Summer would reclaim its territory.

I'd wandered over to the lumpen statue, hoping I'd feel something unusual about it. Beneath my hand, the stone thrummed with faint energy but had nothing to say to me. Then I became aware of the sounds of hoofbeats; a horse galloping towards me. The thunder drew nearer and nearer, until I could hear the animal's snorting breath. It loomed out of the clotted air, black and immense, appearing slightly later than it should have done – but sound might warp in the mist. Its rider pulled the beast to a dramatic halt, although I'd been in no danger of being trampled. It would've had to smash through the statue to achieve that.

The horse pranced towards me and its rider took off a wide-brimmed hat, in a strangely formal manner of greeting. This revealed the sculptured face of Nimrod Queneau. I was grudgingly impressed by the flamboyance of his arrival and almost clapped my hands to him but realised this might appear rude.

"Hello," I said, before he tried to speak to me in French. "You must be Nimrod. I'm Alex, Vezi's friend."

"Good morning," he said in a rich, musical voice. "You're an early riser."

"Sometimes." I wanted to appear aloof and mysterious but found myself smiling.

"I'm sorry I haven't been here," Nimrod said. "Business… you know."

"Not really, but I've heard of people doing such things." My smile widened unstoppably into a grin. "There's no need to apologise. Vezi and I have been exploring. This is a beautiful place."

Nimrod dismounted and offered me his arm. "Let's walk to the house. I shall order Posy to conjure us an immense breakfast."

We walked for some seconds in silence, the horse plodding dozily beside us, then I asked, "Have you travelled over night?"

He laughed at the idea. "No. I've ridden from a friend's place, nearby. I stayed the night there."

"How disappointing. I hoped I'd wandered into a pleasing fantasy, where the master of the domain thunders through the dark on horseback."

He patted my hand that was linked through his arm. "Then by all means believe so, if you'd prefer it."

"Thank you."

By the time we reached the house, I knew that I had in my hands a weapon to inflict a mortal wound on Vezi. How annoying that I was too fond of him to use it. Nimrod, I felt, *knew* me, as most people didn't or couldn't. He wanted to know more too; that was clear.

Over breakfast, we had much to say to one another. Nimrod talked about the history of the house, claiming he could tell I'd be interested.

"I have an ancestor who used to speak to heads that hung hidden in the ivy outside her bedroom window," he said. "The legend goes they told her the deepest secrets of everyone in the house."

"Whose heads were they?"

"She didn't know. Eventually, she married and moved away, and no one saw or heard the heads thereafter. Then the ivy was taken down from the house. No heads were found."

"What a shame."

"We have several ghosts, though. My favourite is that of a woman dressed in gauzy black robes and a veil, who rides a grey lion along the edge of the forest, just inside the tree line." He grimaced sweetly. "Well, maybe she's more of a local goddess than a ghost. We call her *La Ténébreuse*."

"Have you ever seen her?"

He grinned. "I'm not sure. I wanted to so badly as a boy, I might've dreamed her up now and again. I once saw a dour female face staring at me from the rhododendrons, but she turned into leaves and flowers."

By this point, I could almost have fallen in love with him, but I was no Vezi. It takes a very strong magic to work on me and I'm always cautious. He fascinated me, though – the way he identified my preferences and wove these into a clever seduction.

We were still sitting at the table talking when Vezi came down to breakfast. He greeted Nimrod in a reserved manner.

Nimrod stood up and embraced him briefly. "You must've thought I was dead!" he exclaimed with glee.

That day, Nimrod took us out to in his car – a black, vintage Mercedes convertible – to visit a local vineyard, which the Queneaus owned. Vezi and I got mildly drunk over lunch in the restaurant there. Then we drove on to a ruined chateau, which clung to a cliffside above a serene lake where Nimrod told us many people had killed themselves by drowning. "This land is drenched in history," he said, "some of it deliciously dark."

I asked about the Ice Age boulder.

"You mean the lion?" he said.

"It doesn't look much like a lion, more like a lump."

He laughed. "Perhaps. But that's the mount of *La Ténébreuse*, the dark lady who rides in the forest."

"I think you made that up!" I said. "The fantasies of a little boy."

Nimrod held my gaze. "They might be. I can't remember."

When we got home, Vezi went to the bathroom and, wasting no time, Nimrod slid close to me in the sitting-room and murmured. "May I come to your room tonight?"

I regarded him steadily. "I was hoping you'd take me outside once everyone's gone to sleep – to see ghosts, to see a boulder turn into a lion."

He returned my gaze unflinchingly. "If those are your conditions."

"They are not conditions, merely requests."

"As your host, I shall fulfil your requests."

At 2 a.m. I got out of bed, where I'd lain sleepless, and went to the window. The bright moon burned the lawns, and the ugly statue glowed white. Nimrod and I had made no specific arrangements, so it must all be part of an adventure. I put on a long, white linen dress and went barefoot down into the garden.

I was drawn to the boulder but, try as I might, perceived no lion in its awkward lines. I reached out to touch it, and then a hand was laid over mine. A chill threshed through me. Turning quickly, I found Nimrod close behind me. "You walk like a ghost," I said.

He said nothing, but jumped up onto the plinth of the boulder, reaching down to pull me up beside him. The boulder seemed larger now, and more potent. Effortlessly, Nimrod put his hands around my waist and somehow threw me onto the boulder so I was astride it, riding it. I felt slightly disorientated; the world shifted.

"Will you lead me to the tree-line of the forest?" I asked, aware of the high tone of my voice. I didn't want to be afraid, fought it.

"If you want to ride that beast, you must become *La Ténébreuse*, and she is without ambivalence. Could you sacrifice that, Alex?"

"Not funny," I said.

"It's not meant to be. Can you feel the power of the land?" He opened his arms wide. "Smell, it, breathe it in."

My head had begun to ache. The air was fractured. I didn't know what I was dealing with, but sensed it was powerful. Shadows clustered and writhed at the edge of the trees. I felt eyes upon me, but realised it was simply one enormous eye. The land watched.

What did Nimrod want from me? It couldn't be the obvious, could it? I wanted to get down from the boulder, because I felt exposed and vulnerable up there, yet when I tried to move, my body froze. "Help me down, Nimrod."

He stared at me, his mouth curved into a lunar smile that had no feeling, his white teeth glowing. His hair was a nimbus of moonlight. He neither moved nor spoke.

The ground seemed so far away. My brain seemed to lurch in my skull. I knew I must take back control, be brave enough to make the jump and trust I'd not be badly hurt. I closed my eyes and half threw myself, half clambered, from the back of the lion. I fell to the lawn and sprawled there.

Nimrod looked down at me, his smile never wavering, but now he spoke. "Oh, how disappointing, as *you* might say. You're not prepared to ride?"

I stood up. My dress was streaked with grass stains, and the scent of turned earth was strong in my nose. "Perhaps not with you," I snapped. I brushed with futility at the marks on my clothes and noticed my hands were covered in soil, as if they'd been plunged in damp earth to the wrists.

"You know," Nimrod said in a casual tone, "I didn't intend to meet with you and Vezi at all while you were staying in the house."

"But…?"

He shrugged. "Vezi seemed desperate to come here. I allowed it. It's a place of dreams, after all, and I'm generous with them. But then… *you*. I like unusual things."

"No," I said, flatly. "Whatever you're thinking, no."

There was a brief moment of staring, like hostile cats sizing each other up.

Then, he said, "I'm sorry, I've been inappropriate." He offered me a hand, which I took; his so clean, mine a golem paw. "Come.

We'll walk."

We went down through the flowing landscape into the patchwork of vines, and then into crowds of giant sunflowers, some of which were already withered, and left to rot in the fields. Alive or dead, these flowers were huge and oppressive; I could sense their awareness, and a kind of lunacy. But of course – they feared the moon.

Tufts of boscage littered the land, within them teeming herds of deer, whose eyes glowed green, even if their motionless bodies could not be seen. Here were trees infested with mistletoe, species I could not identify but which were not oak. The woods seemed tiny somehow, despite their swarming population of deer, mere islands in an endless sea of vines and flowers. Primal landscape – ordered, yet not.

Nimrod and I did not speak, merely walked, or drifted. Eventually, I heard someone singing, as I had on my first day in the house. We came to a field where the flowers lay slaughtered on the ground. These were not spent, rotten blooms, but recently vibrant, at their peak. I smelled their blood, the rich sap; it smelled yellow.

A crowd was gathered there, dressed in dark clothes, yet they were blurry figures. I couldn't see them clearly. The only ones who were distinct were Ailie and Troyes, who stood facing us. And then Posy Sala appeared behind them, as if in a photograph developing. She loomed tall like a guard. Her face wasn't remotely human. Why had I ever thought otherwise?

The strangely-shifting crowd surrounded a small shrine, which was fashioned of slender white columns and had no roof. And in the centre of the shrine, piled upon the floor, *She* reclined. She was comprised of shadow, buzzing lines of darkness, which made my eyes ache. She appeared to be naked, lissom as a panther and three times as big. Her face, what I could see of it, was a gargoyle mask, from which a long tongue lolled. She writhed about like a restless, hungry serpent yet had the tenuous shape of a woman. Her hair was smoke upon the air, tangling around her worshippers.

*La Ténébreuse.*

I knew her kind, fashioned of what lies within the earth; that which hides in the light and shadow of forests, which slumbers beneath the crop fields, and can be conjured forth by need.

"Now you see," Nimrod murmured to me, clearly proud of revealing his great secret. "Isn't this what you wanted, what you've *always* wanted, grubbing through little mysteries, but never finding the source?"

"Oh," I said, "I've seen the source before. This is but one rendition, like the song you sing to her." I looked into his eyes. "You've shaped her well."

He paused for a moment, then said smoothly, "I'm glad you've surprised me. I thought you would be shocked."

"No... Perhaps, in some curious way, by some accident of formation, I was born of the same stuff as entities such as this. I don't fear them. *Your* creature, however, is ravenous. Perhaps this is her special night."

"It is..."

I sighed, resigned. "And now, I suppose, the climax comes. It's the moment when my life could end, or I could be transformed in mind or body, and the land will go on for ever. Which version of the story is it?"

He laughed. "Neither of them. You've already said no, Alex. This... is simply a gift. An invitation to our party as a guest, that's all."

I frowned. "Am I seeing what you're seeing?"

"I have no idea. How can I?"

Ailie came to me with a goblet, which I took but offered to Nimrod first. He drank from it without hesitation, then I did also. The dark wine within this vessel affected me, but did not take away my senses, merely muddled them a little.

I remember a bonfire was lit and there was singing and dancing. Shadows flickered against the flames, sometimes looking like people, but most often not. Dreams of the slumbering earth that had taken on flesh. I felt the attention of *La Ténébreuse* upon me and knew that she could see me, and where I'd been, what I'd done. I had to make her feel we already knew one another, because I was not wholly safe.

After some hours, while I drank and occasionally danced, Nimrod took me into the trees at the edge of the field and there kissed me. It was as if he were a shadow. I felt nothing.

"I know who you are, *La Ténébreuse*," he said. "A walker in shadows."

He wasn't entirely wrong, but it was irrelevant. He was a

phantom, nothing more than the suggestion of a man.

I thought then, *the first image of the house was true.*

I left a memory of myself to make love to him, then walked back to the sunflower shrine. There was no one there, and only a few sullen embers remained of the bonfire. I didn't pause, but ran through the fields of vines and flowers, all the way to the nest of dreams, where the plinth of the boulder lay empty, and the eyes of the house were open in the dark.

I climbed the stair to Vezi's room and crawled into bed beside him. "Tomorrow we leave," I said.

His arm went about me. "Yes."

"We must leave before it all changes, and dreams become true."

"Yes..."

I knew, for now, it was safe to sleep, and did so.

We rose early, just after dawn. Barely speaking, we each packed a few things into a small bag, and left everything else behind. We scurried out through the open door of the house like robbers. I glanced at the door knocker; the sleeping face of Posy Sala. The whole house slept now, didn't even open an eye. I was concerned there would be some impediment to our departure, because now, by daylight, it seemed we'd escaped too easily – and on waking I was sure it *was* an escape, no matter how Nimrod had attempted to reassure me. I'd pacified this landscape once, perhaps, but didn't want to risk it twice.

Vezi and I stole bikes from the stables and pedalled fast into the village and beyond it. We would go to a town. We mustn't think of anything behind us, anything that might pursue. Also, we mustn't yet talk of what had occurred. In silence we were invisible.

By 6.00 am we came to a larger village, not quite a town, and it had a station. All the time we'd been in the house, we'd never been that far from civilisation.

Once we were on a train, heading to an even larger town, from where we could travel further to an airport, Vezi broke the silence with which we'd sealed the topic of Nimrod. "It was never him, Alex. It was... something else."

I reached across to take his hands in mine. "I think it *was* him,

Vezi, just… not how you remembered. *That* perhaps was never him."

Vezi shook his head. "No, you're wrong. We never saw Nimrod in that house."

There are two pictures. In one of them, Nimrod Queneau awakes to a house empty of guests and realises he went too far with his games. Or… we were seduced and glamorised, and if Vezi and I should ever go back to that nest of dreams, all we'd find is the ruin I'd visited in sleep, dead leaves scratching along the driveway. I'd raise my eyes to the windows and feel someone staring back. We wouldn't stay there long.

# THROUGH THE LIGHTED GARDENS

*Story History:*

This piece first appeared online as a potential full-length transmedia project. I was playing Rift, an MMORPG (massive, multiplayer, online role-playing game) at the time, which had a facility in game for players to create their own pieces of landscape, utilising all the wonderful art assets that have been used to create the game. My idea was to create characters and write about them, along with pictures of what I built in the game. All went well to start with, and I was able to put two chapters up, along with screen shots of the landscapes and dwellings I'd created. But then, as can strike so many good games, a greedy corporation took over from the original developers and ruined everything. It was no longer feasible for me to continue – I simply couldn't afford it. I had to leave the game because it was no longer free to play and I would be forced to buy with real money the components I needed to create my story locations. Incredibly sad, as I loved spending time in that quirky, colourful world. Unfortunately, I wasn't the only player to be disheartened and disappointed by what happened, and now the game is but a ghost of its former self – if, in fact, it exists anymore. I haven't checked for a couple of years. But anyway, I hate things to go to waste so decided to include in this collection the two chapters I wrote. As I worked on them, I found myself hoping that one day I'll finish the story, perhaps even find out if Rift still exists and take shots of the other locations I created. I don't want to lose all those locations half-created in a wonderful, weird world. It makes me sad to think about them. I've included a couple of screenshots of the locations in this piece.

## 1. The House on the Red Cliffs

There was once a woman who could fuse the elements and her name was Meretrice Bilander. At the age of 37, leaving her history behind, she came to live in a house upon the red cliffs that reared high behind the town of wind sails, known as Rocfeather Sill. Folk said she was a planarist by profession and this proved to be true.

Meretrice's house was old and tall and its chimneys towered above the cliffs. By night, she put strange glowing instruments on the land outside, and spread her fingers flat against the earth. She grew things not of this world. Some twenty yards from her peculiar garden, where plants that looked like insects squirmed out of the hard, red soil, a torrent of water burst out of the rock and hurled itself down the cliff. Sometimes, strange booming sounds could be heard from deep below the ground that were often like moans and less often like laughter.

Below the planarist's domain, a rickety wooden stair creaked down the cliffside to a flat table of rock and sparse grass that overlooked the town. There was no further way down from this point. The only other way was up, by a perilous crumbling path that led past Meretrice's house, and then like a vein along the cliffs, until eventually it slid down again – but not before your legs ached from clinging to the tilted path. This unfriendly thoroughfare kept enemies away, for you'd hear them coming from miles off if they tried to creep up on you there.

At the bottom of the rickety stair, where the water tumbled in a rush into a deep pool, was another house, this one girdled by a wooden veranda, where its occupant, a man named Jeriko Rayce, would sit in the evenings, occasionally glancing up at the tall house above him, where a flash of unearthly light might sporadically splash and shiver. Rayce owned a plant of particular beauty and rarity, which he kept in a tall turquoise pot upon a chest in his lower room. At night, should you approach his dwelling from the bottom of the stair, you might glimpse through his doorway the plant's achingly lovely glow, violet as a bruise, with motes of carmine lifting from it like fey. If Meretrice went to the first landing of the stair and craned right over the fence, she could glimpse the plant in its pot. The sight of it made her hungry.

There was a third inhabitant of this isolated plateau, living in a copse of trees half petrified. And she… she was a shamaness, they said. No one knew her real name, but she was called Catty by the local people. She owned up to nothing, but made her possets and potions, and sometimes folk would brave the crumbling path, edge past the planarist's dwelling and descend the rickety stair, so they might seek life betterments from the shamaness. Pungent smokes hung like a fog around the entrance to her small realm, which was a weave of ancient bones from creatures large and long extinct. There was a banner at this portal, proclaiming a tariff of charges for customers, and before it a low table. People from the town left offerings there – bread, potatoes, wine and even coins. It is best not to vex a shamaness but rather keep her happy. She brewed and made transformations in old mossy tree stumps beside her mixing tent.

The shamaness liked unusual things, as of course did the planarist. Neither woman was unmoved by the violet glow that pulsed from Rayce's house in the dark hours. This was because it awoke in whoever beheld it sweet, painful longings, as if conjuring half of a memory where the feeling came back but not the event, or the face, associated with it.

The women had nothing to do with one another, each seeing in their neighbour a template they despised. Meretrice was to Catty a thin, ascetic bore of a woman, despite her fine features of quaintly foreign caste. While to Meretrice, Catty was a hulking, feral creature who could do more to keep herself clean. The only thing they had in common was a craving for the violet flower. The planarist would have liked to plant it in her garden, among the other strange foliate breeds she reared, to see what happened. She had no doubt the violet flower would influence the soil and its products. The shamaness wished to bed the flower in the richest of her tree stumps, spongy with fragrant moss and nourishing loam. She felt sure that traces of its leaves and petals would do much to enhance her potions. But Rayce wove his own magicks, not least a privacy it was difficult to invade.

Occasionally, Meretrice went to the nearby town, and here learned the name of Catty, along with recommendations about her abilities. She heard that Catty didn't need to leave her domain at all, since townsfolk brought her everything she needed. Meretrice imagined the woman must bury all the coins she was given, for what other use did she have for them? Of the man, the people claimed to know only his name, but Meretrice sensed a reticence in them and wondered if they knew more. Upon repeated questioning, which was to her like smashing great stones with a very small implement too soft for the job, she discovered he didn't rent the house from anyone in town. Occasionally, he'd come to stock up on supplies, but how he earned his income remained a mystery. Perhaps he was in fact very rich, a hermit type. Meretrice kept an eye on the narrow track to the town but never saw her neighbour upon it. There was an aged air balloon tethered behind Rayce's house, buoyed by a core of ignarine, but Meretrice had never seen it move.

Sometimes, in the evenings, Meretrice would stand against the splintery fence at the edge of her garden and gaze down at the house of Jeriko Rayce. Even from this distance, she could see he was tall and spare, with long dark hair and a short, neat beard. He moved gracefully from his house to his well and around the soft ground surrounding the water, apparently tending his land, which was a small yet lush oasis. When he was done, he'd sit on his veranda and stretch out his long legs, then smoke a pipe and drink steadily, or he'd perhaps visit his shrine, which was on a balcony to the side of the house. Meretrice couldn't see very much of it, only the waver of its devotional candles. But sometimes she smelled the incense associated in those lands with the veneration of ancestors.

Meretrice had not come to this isolated spot to be interested in men, but she was intrigued by why he had the plant and what he might do with it. Surely it was not just for decoration?

One evening, just as the sun melted into the red mountains, Meretrice mustered her resolve and broke down the invisible barrier that had somehow prevented her from descending the rickety stair before. As she reached the bottom, she saw that the shamaness was standing beneath the bones marking the entrance to her domain. Meretrice disliked the way this shabby woman stared at her with eyes like an owl's, round and staring. She turned her face away and looked towards Rayce's house, where soft lights gleamed on the veranda and the purple smoke of the flower's light was mist upon the evening air.

"You won't get close," called the shamaness, "so don't try."

Meretrice did not respond immediately, leaving enough time to convey her displeasure. Then she called back, dryly, "You, then, have tried," privately convinced she'd be able to walk right up to the house, climb the steps to its veranda, speak to the man.

"He owns this land," said the shamaness, in a mulish tone. "It obeys him."

Meretrice had not heard of this before, as she'd leased the house from a woman in the town below, who'd not mentioned this fact. "Then who is he, this landowner?"

"A body who likes his privacy," said the shamaness.

"Well, be that as it may…" the planarist said dismissively. She received the distinct impression that the other woman wouldn't move away until Meretrice returned to her home. There was a proprietary air about her. Meretrice turned her back upon the shamaness and picked her way over the rough scrub towards the house of Rayce. Strange, though, that even after a minute, she'd drawn no closer to the irrigated land. She glanced behind her and found that the shamaness, hands on hips and staring at her belligerently, was no further away either.

"I told you!" cried the shamaness.

Meretrice ignored these words and continued to walk, but even though it *appeared* she was moving forward it was plain she was not. It was as if the land beneath her feet was sliding backwards without her feeling it, keeping her in place. Eventually, not wishing to appear more stupid than the shamaness clearly thought her to be, she stood still and stared at the house. She could see no sign of life within it, but for the tall fragile leaves of the plant and the violet flower within it, emitting its motes of carmine. Its perfume was stronger here, redolent of lost days, of future days, of days that will never be. She realised that the only source of information available to her at that moment was her neighbour, so retraced her steps and walked right up to the bone portal. "Have you spoken to him?" she asked.

The shamaness shook her head and crossed her arms. "No one does or can."

"But you have wanted to."

Close to, Meretrice could see that the other woman was quite lovely, in spite of her wild knotted hair and wild knotted garments. She was tall and powerfully-built with skin the colour of blue slate. It was impossible to guess her age exactly but Meretrice felt there was not much difference between them in that respect.

"The flower draws you," said the shamaness, now in a softer tone. "That is the cost of living in this spot, because you can never touch its colour, never draw close enough to hear clearly the song of its perfume. Local people won't live here, because they know its name is sorrow."

"What else do you know of that flower?" Meretrice asked.

"Nothing."

Meretrice sighed and turned back to gaze at Rayce's house. Behind, looming over it, the faded red sails of a tall windmill turned lazily in the night breeze, creaking in a lamenting voice. The balloon vehicle, beyond it, hung listlessly in the air, derelict. Meretrice didn't like to be defeated. Hadn't she come here anyway to further her art, take whatever gifts and surprises the elemental planes might throw at her? The violet flower was not earthly; she had to discover its secret. But how? She glanced at the shamaness, who was still staring at her fiercely. "Catty, isn't it?" she said, forcing a smile.

The shamaness' expression did not change.

"Perhaps we can work together on this matter. Perhaps there are things *we* have that *he* might want."

"He would have taken them already."

Meretrice's face was beginning to ache with her smile. "Perhaps *I* have things that *you* might want. Would you like to visit my garden?"

Meretrice was sure in her veins that the mulish Catty must

become an ally. And she'd sensed correctly that as far as Catty's work was concerned, she was just as curious and – well – greedy as Meretrice was herself. They shared too a suspicion of everything, so Meretrice was sure Catty would recognise the invitation as the gesture it was. Meretrice only had to wait now for her response. Eventually it came.

"All right."

Grudging, but at least an acceptance.

"Come now," Meretrice said, "and bring a container of some kind, so I can give you some samples."

Catty glanced up at the garden above, where spectral flashes bloomed and faded. "You grow unearthly things," she said, "but very well." Briefly, she returned to her domain to fetch a basket.

Meretrice's garden was somewhat chaotic. She'd had equipment transported from her college in far Zenithix, which she'd installed rather haphazardly around her house: pulse conduits and connections, migration chambers and transelemental pods. She harvested energy from the soil and created planar portals, so as to mix the essence of earth with migrating surges and waves.

Catty eyed the equipment with distaste. "Not natural," she said.

"It is," Meretrice replied, "but perhaps not *here*. And it's all quite safe. These are basic experiments."

Florid growths had burst from the ground; nothing like any plant ever seen in that landscape. Cautiously, Catty walked around them, occasionally extending a hand to touch a leaf or a petal or a trailing root, or what appeared to be such. Some of the efflorescences looked like beetles or flies and might occasionally move as if they were.

"Well I expect he's had a good look round all this," Catty said dryly.

"He's not been here," Meretrice replied. "I'd know."

Catty laughed. "Would you, now?" She hunkered down close to the soil. "Is any of this poisonous?"

"The growths you see there are unrefined, so not fit for consumption. Come with me. I have refining chambers on my balcony."

Meretrice led the way up the ramp to the back of her house. Here she had a comfortable place to sit of an evening, but it was also crowded with more of her arcane equipment. Catty trod gingerly between the conduits on the floor that roped incongruously over silk, patterned rugs. Glass globes, connected with pulsing channels of radiance, throbbed mechanically.

"Here," Meretrice said, gesturing at one of the globes. "I'll turn off the surge. Take some of the contents." She bent down and wrestled awkwardly for some moments with a connection. The light within the globe grew dim and Meretrice removed the glass cover. "These florets, here," she said, "are infused with planar nourishment. In their raw state, they are known for their efficacy against infection. Now their distillation should provide twice the healing effect."

"These are rogueberry?" Catty asked, her fingers hovering over the gently-breathing foliage in the nest of the globe.

"They were," Meretrice said, "please, take them. I only infused them to temper the shift of the globe, as it's new."

"What are they infused with?"

"Aquagris," Meretrice replied. "Evolulite from the planar deeps of Ploom."

"None of what you said means anything to me," Catty snapped.

"Ploom is a realm of water. Evolulite is a substance that promotes… well… evolution. Aquagris is a lesser botanical strain, but effective in the treatment of ailments in our realm."

"How do you isolate the planar influences?"

Meretrice was surprised and somewhat pleased at the question. "Generally, through tonal signatures, or light pulses. The water influence is strong in this spot, despite it being a rather arid area – perhaps even because of it. The water existing here is focused."

"The falls."

"Yes." Meretrice paused. "The falls that nourish our neighbour's garden."

"Perhaps you too are nourishing it now."

"That's possible."

Catty raised the bunch of foliage to her nose, sniffed, pulled a quirky smile. "If there's something he wants from you, mistress, he's had it, I'm sure."

"My *name* is Meretrice." She walked to the sagging fence and looked down upon their neighbour's house. "I have an instinctive compulsion to solve mysteries."

Catty had put the modified rogueberry in her basket and had begun to explore the balcony. She'd come to a halt at what appeared to be a human-sized glass coffin with a rounded lid, standing on four legs and pierced by energy conduits. "What's this?"

Meretrice joined her, fearful Catty might try to touch or open the device. "It's a convergence chamber. As you can see, it's absorbed the planar surges of the garden and thus has a watery focus."

"You mean these ocean plant freaks that are growing on it?"

"Yes..."

"Are they safe?"

"As far as I..."

Catty had already cracked off a couple of anemone pods and put them into her basket.

"Help yourself, please... Would you like some tea?"

"Wine or beer," said Catty.

"Of course. Just look around, I won't be long."

The evening then progressed in a fairly convivial way, focusing mainly on speculation about Jeriko Rayce. Perhaps more enquiries could be made in the town, Meretrice suggested. Catty responded that the few people down there who appeared to *know* Rayce were exceedingly tight-lipped and probably couldn't be bribed. But there had to be a way to smash his defences, get inside Rayce's domain, nurture a friendship of sorts, prise his secrets from him. Were they not women, after all, and therefore potentially Rayce's greatest nemesis?

"You're more his type, I expect," Catty said, gesturing at Meretrice with her wine cup. "You look only half human, like a fey creature. Perhaps you should leave some of your samples lying about on the ground near his domain. Plant some specimens for me. I can make a show of attending to them."

"Very well. Tomorrow, then."

"Tomorrow."

A toast was made.

Once Meretrice had gone to bed, however, the night became less friendly. For a start, she found it very difficult to sleep, writhing in her tangled sheets, either too hot or too cold. When she stuck limbs from beneath the coverings, she couldn't help thinking of something grabbing hold of them, so had to pull them back to safety at once. The house groaned miserably, as if drying out from rain, and the falls thundered so loudly they seemed to become part of the beat of her blood as she pressed her hot face against the pillow. Sighing, she eventually gave up the effort of trying to drop off and lit the lamp by her bed. She lay on her back, so as not to be unnerved by the heart-pound in her ears, and stared at the ceiling, where inexplicable shadows crawled – perhaps cast by tree branches outside. She wanted to believe this and not that the shadows were in fact sticklike creatures clambering about her room. The falls continued to growl and crash, and within this cacophony boomed the haunt of laughter and grief.

Had Jeriko Rayce created the falls? she wondered. They gushed as if from a wound in the earth, down a series of pools and smaller falls, to be absorbed by the pond at the foot of the cliffs, beside Rayce's house. The pond was man-made, of metal. Water from it clearly soaked into the land there, but this irrigation was confined. It had not, for example, flowed over to Catty's domain, which was not far off. Why didn't it cascade over the cliff beyond the rock table? Why stop just by Rayce's house?

Sleep, when it finally came, was plagued by repetitive dreams – not of horrors, but of mundane tasks that on waking Meretrice could not recognise as anything a person of her world would do – tasks beyond describing, involving elements unknown to her, ideas that made no sense. She was trying to achieve something, she felt this strongly, but the mind-numbing tasks came to nothing. When she woke, her brain was aching with the effort, her fingers shaking.

Groggily, she lurched into her kitchen to make strong tea, hopefully to restore herself. The world felt strange about her skin. Something was different.

Tea-crock in hand, Meretrice went outside, still in her dressing-gown. The day was motionless and stifling, the roar of the falls muted. She hadn't drunk that much wine with Catty last night, had she? And yet she felt abysmally hung-over, lethargic, her joints painful.

Instinctively, she was drawn to the garden fence. Gazing down upon Rayce's house, she felt a sense of desolation; the air itself seemed changed.

Alerted, she went back inside and dressed, and then hurried

down the rickety stairs. She ran towards Catty's portal of bones, beneath the gruesome arch and into the domain beyond. At first, she could not see Catty, but her senses were assailed by a multitude of scents – some exquisite, some foul. She saw an array of ragged tents positioned around a central cauldron, beneath which a clot of embers winked. Smokes twisted through the air at the level of her knees. She glanced to her left and saw Catty's famous tree stumps, which steamed and smouldered in the dawn light.

From the tent beside them, Meretrice noticed a pair of bare legs sticking out and hastened towards them. They belonged to a sleeping Catty, who was cocooned in furs, but it was clear her slumber was no more restful than Meretrice's had been. The shamaness whimpered and shivered. She had bitten her lower lip and drawn blood.

Pausing only a moment, Meretrice ducked beneath the pungent skins of the tent and shook the shamaness awake, calling her name sternly.

Catty flailed her arms, catching Meretrice across the chest with a sharp blow, but eventually came to her senses and sat there, blinking, looking rather like a peculiar hairy animal.

"Something's happened," Meretrice said.

Catty eyed her with hostility, said nothing, but threw off the skins that covered her naked body and, clad only in her long, tangled hair, plodded out of the tent, presumably to find some kind of restorative or refreshment. Meretrice made a noise of impatience and distaste and turned away.

Eventually, Catty returned, drinking from a flagon, which Meretrice hoped contained water. She had wrapped her tall, muscular body in a cloak. "He's been here," she said.

"What?"

"Come, see for yourself."

Catty led the way up a steep, dirt incline, which lay below Meretrice's house. Here, they came to a number of megaliths, one of which had been toppled. They were surrounded by a fierce, pulsing ring of scarlet fire. "He did that?" Meretrice asked.

Catty grimaced. "The fire, no? I did that. Last night. A circle of augury. But when I went to my bed, all the stones were standing. He came here and tainted the augury, warned me in plain terms to keep out of his business."

"How can you be sure of that?"

Meretrice could not imagine Jeriko Rayce had the strength to topple a rooted stone, but maybe he had recourse to more powerful energies than that of his own flesh and bone.

"I know the smell, taste and feel of my domain," Catty said. "Someone has been here, and it wasn't you. Nobody from the town would dare. So…"

"Did you learn anything from your scrying?"

Catty wrinkled up her nose, pulled a sour face. "Glimpses, maybe. He's hiding here, licking wounds. That's what I think. Maybe he's running from crimes or someone who wishes him dead. Maybe he's running from grief. But the wards around him are weakening. This is why we can wonder about him now."

"I've always wondered about him."

Catty shrugged. "But now we have spoken to one another and have made plans. Now we turn our eyes more keenly towards him. He heard us, smelled us, doing that." She narrowed her eyes. "Now the mystery of him has become provocation."

"If you are right and the wards are weakening…" Meretrice began.

"We might reach him, yes," Catty finished. "Let me dress. It's not clever to meet an enemy unclothed."

"Enemy?"

Catty was already striding away.

Meretrice turned back to the circle of flame, which was now fading into the earth. She saw that the root of the toppled stone was raw, broken. Its stump remained in the ground to one side. She could not help but think of rage pouring through this spot, pulverising rock into dust.

The first thing to become apparent that whatever unseen obstacle Rayce had placed to deter visitors to his house had vanished. Meretrice and Catty walked without difficulty across the plateau and soon were standing beneath the veranda. Meretrice reached out to touch the wood of the rail around it. She felt slightly light-headed.

"He's not here," Catty said.

Meretrice glanced up, for a moment holding her breath. Had the flower gone too? But no, she saw a faint, pulsing glow through the open doorway above her head.

"Round the side," Catty said, "there's an entrance."

As the ground sloped down to the cliff from this point, the side of Rayce's house was flush with the earth, while its other side was suspended on a deck supported by thick wooden beams. The ground by the side door was moist, almost muddy, strewn with blue-green lichenous growths, which to Meretrice looked planar in origin. What she saw rooted on the deck beside the back door confirmed this.

"Catty!" she cried. "He has a convergence chamber, like mine. How is that possible?"

Catty strode over to examine the coffin-shaped instrument, which like Meretrice's was covered by glass. "Not *quite* like yours," she said dryly. While Meretrice's chamber had attracted, or indeed spawned, water affinity growths, this one harboured efflorescences almost identical to those growing in Meretrice's garden. There was a plane, Meretrice explained, where plant life was primitively sentient; part vegetable, part fungus, part animal – primarily cephalopod. The growths on Rayce's chamber resembled those found in that realm. Meretrice had planted varieties of these germinants as part of her experiment but they'd not become attached to her convergence chamber and had merely mutated into watery strains. Rayce had done something different here, perhaps *expanded* upon Meretrice's work. A couple of tentacles waved sinuously above the chamber as if tasting the air.

"Seems he shares your interests," Catty said.

"This…" Meretrice reached out but did not actually touch the device. "It's identical to mine, as if patterned in Zenithix."

Catty shrugged. "So? He must've bought one somewhere."

Meretrice made an exasperated gesture with both hands. "That's not possible. You can't just *buy* these. My college wouldn't allow it."

"Perhaps he has contacts."

Meretrice narrowed her eyes. "Or reproduced mine in some way."

Catty laughed. "Well, I told you he'd had what he wanted from you. I expect we'll find a catalogue of your work inside." She made to go inside the house, for the side door was open, but Meretrice restrained her.

"Wait… Where *is* he? We should be cautious."

"He's not here."

"You can't be sure of that. He could be in the upper room, sleeping."

Catty waved a hand dismissively. "I'd know, trust me. I feel such things."

"You don't seem concerned about his disappearance."

Catty huffed impatiently. "I didn't say he'd disappeared, just that he wasn't here. There's a difference. His wards are down. Something must've happened. He could be seeking aid elsewhere."

Meretrice wondered how safe this area was. The wards were to keep her and Catty out, but what else? Had they instead kept something within? She and Catty had made the assumption Rayce was hostile to them, but maybe he was simply protective. Something became clear to her – he'd *wanted* her to rent that house above his land. He must've watched her, perhaps stolen from her, and had either duplicated her machine himself, or had it patterned for him. But how had he pierced its mechanisms, seen the workings within? He'd have had to dismantle it. She'd have heard, noticed, surely? The thought of Rayce walking silently, unseen, among her unearthly crops was at once unsettling and bizarrely electrifying.

Catty had gone inside and now called to Meretrice. "He left in a hurry."

Meretrice stepped into the single room that was both living space and kitchen, although without running water. Rayce must use the well and pool outside for all his needs. There was a door that no doubt led to the upper room. A fire had been lit and looked fairly fresh, so he couldn't have been gone long. It appeared Rayce had been preparing his breakfast, for some fruit had been cut up and placed on a plate. This too was fresh. Catty tried the door to the upstairs but found it locked. As she made preparations to shoulder it open, Meretrice said, "No!"

Catty paused. "What if he's up there, ill or dead?"

"Not yet, Catty. If he walks in here to find his door battered down, imagine how we'll look to him."

Catty shrugged. "Well, poke around, then. Let's see what we can find." She went out onto the veranda, and shortly afterwards Meretrice heard her pounding up the ramp to the balcony on the other side of the house.

Until this moment, Meretrice had resisted inspecting the violet flower, all the time acutely aware of its proximity. Now she turned and stared at it; it was larger than she'd thought it would be, towering over her, whereas the house was smaller than she'd imagined it. How lovely the flower was, emitting its fragrance and motes of light. The scent was almost a song, a series of half glimpsed memories, a peal of joyous laughter. She found she had closed her eyes without realising it, and now opened them again. Dare she break a petal free, or a leaf? Dare she rummage in its pot to feel its roots, perhaps steal part of one? She was sure her apparatus could conjure an entire plant from such a scrap. And yet, there it was: inviolate. She could not bring herself to ravish that ineffable state.

The chest on which the flower's vase reposed was flanked by two tall bookcases. She drew closer to them to inspect their spines. All of them seemed ancient, dusty. Many of the titles were in a language she didn't know. She prised a book at random from its fellows and opened it. The text was incomprehensible, and the drawings accompanying it could either have been magical or mathematical. Of course, he shared her interests – that could not be denied. Was he older than her, more knowledgeable? She hadn't been able to tell by spying on him from her garden. He didn't move as an older man would, she thought, but neither was he a boy. Until today he'd been an intriguing mystery, an amusement even, but following the events from the evening before, all the way through to this morning, and now her discoveries, she knew he was more than that. Was this a destiny to happen, or something that had already passed, and she'd missed its significance? She was annoyed she hadn't taken him more seriously, not realised he'd been watching her work, invading her territory.

Catty came back into the room, breaking Meretrice's reverie. "Not much to be seen outside," she said. "But he's left us something. We just have to find it."

"How can you possibly know that, or even think it?" Meretrice snapped, irritated. She slid the book back into its place on the shelf. "He's taken great pains to avoid us, while clearly stealing my work, and interfering in yours. Why would he leave us a message or any other evidence?"

Catty regarded Meretrice scornfully. "Because he leased this land to us, you moonkit. He wanted us here. We are part of... whatever it is." She went to a shelf on the wall, picked up a jar from it. "Mine," she said. "Nepentharine, the juice of forgetfulness. I can't recall selling him this, and he certainly didn't leave a donation."

"Part of the rent, maybe," Meretrice said archly. "How do you pay him, anyway?"

Catty shrugged. "A woman from town comes every few months and takes coins from my coffer at the gate. I never really check." She pushed past Meretrice to stand before the flower. "Truly astounding," she said, then reached out and broke off a petal.

"Catty!" Meretrice cried. "Don't."

"Don't what?"

Catty ate the petal.

"Are you insane?" Meretrice screeched. "Spit that out."

"Too late... Aaah." Catty drew in her breath, closed her eyes.

"What? Have you poisoned yourself, you dumb beast?"

Catty blinked. "No, but that was a strange experience. I tasted my own past, and possibly someone else's future. It burned, but in a good way." She grinned. "Dumb beast? What does that make you?"

"I'm sorry," Meretrice said insincerely. "I was worried you'd hurt yourself. In my opinion, that was a stupid and reckless thing to do. Might still be. The poison could act slowly."

"It's not poisonous," Catty said. "I can tell. I know plants." She pushed past Meretrice again and went back outside through the side door.

Meretrice followed her.

"Look up there," Catty said. She pointed to a gently sloping rock beside the falls. Here an awning of patterned cloth had been erected, and there was a large, scarlet cushion beneath it. Nearby, a device that appeared to be a telescope stood. Being close to the cliff, the rock hadn't been visible from Meretrice's garden above, but it was apparent Rayce must sit there sometimes. Catty climbed the rocks nimbly and went to investigate. "There's a book," she said. "Half drunk wine." She picked up a green bottle and drank from it.

Meretrice didn't bother to warn or complain. "Bring the book down," she said.

"In a minute." Catty went to the telescope, looked through it.

Meretrice was faintly disappointed it didn't appear to be pointing up at her house.

"What do you see?"

"I think it's more of a case of what can see *me*," she said. "It shows nothing of this earth."

Meretrice climbed the rocks less elegantly than Catty had done. She brushed down her skirt and went to look into the telescope, half expecting to see some planar view. But there was only roiling mist. The longer she looked, so it seemed attenuated shadows walked within the mist, with sticks for limbs. She was reminded uncomfortably of what she'd imagined in her bedroom the night before.

"Any ideas?" Catty asked.

"A means to view alternate realities," Meretrice said. "My teachers would know more, but that's no help to us here."

"Maybe that's where he's gone."

Meretrice examined the telescope more carefully. Could it create portals? She couldn't see that it did, but then she'd never come across an instrument like this before.

"Someone from town brought me ham yesterday," Catty said. "How about I bring that to your house and cook us breakfast? You can examine the book while I'm doing that." She thrust the book into Meretrice's hands, where it fell open.

Meretrice saw handwriting within. Was it a journal, a thesis, a workbook? She closed it. "Very well. You collect your ham and I'll light the stove."

"We might as well take his fruit," Catty said. "Go to waste, otherwise."

"You have it," Meretrice said. She didn't want to eat anything from Rayce's house.

As they clambered down from the rock, a flickering light caught Meretrice's attention. When she reached the ground, she could see it clearly: a wide and steady beam of radiance, shooting up into the sky from somewhere below the rock table. Had it only just appeared? She couldn't remember it being there before. It was situated roughly where the telescope was directed. "Do you see that?" she asked Catty, pointing.

The shamaness nodded. "Maybe he's dead at the bottom of

the cliff and has turned to light," she said cheerfully.

Without further words, the women walked across the plateau to its lip. Gazing down, Meretrice could see what appeared to be a key-hole shaped door far below, surrounded by peculiar radiance. There was no way down to it without a rope, other than by falling, but she knew at once that this was a portal and Rayce had passed through it.

"*That's* where he went," Catty said.

Meretrice nodded. "Yes."

Catty cooked ham and scallions and fried thick dark bread in the bacon fat. While the shamaness was busy at the stove, Meretrice examined the book. It appeared to be a journal of Rayce's work but was either written in code or a language Meretrice didn't know. However, she was perplexed to find that more recent entries and drawings clearly explored – or attempted to mimic – her own experiments. She also found drawings of tree stumps with indescribable *things* incubating in steaming loam or some other material, which referenced Catty's pharmaceutical concoctions. But there was nothing she understood plainly; Rayce kept his secrets encoded. If this had been left for them, it was a tantalising glimpse, nothing more.

Catty placed the food on the table, and Meretrice had to concede the meal was delicious. It appeared Catty was adept with herbs in all capacities.

"So what did you find in the book?" Catty asked.

"Only that he was definitely watching our work. He made notes, but it's all in code, or a foreign language. I can't read the text, only draw conclusions from the pictures."

Catty picked up the book, and began to leaf through it with greasy fingers, which made Meretrice wince, but she held her tongue.

"Well, the last page seems readable enough to me," said Catty.

"What? Show me." Meretrice grabbed the book from Catty's hands. And there they were: words in her own tongue. She read them out aloud.

"*So now you find the scent, but yet need eyes to see.*
*The flower you crave is both a reflection and a fountain.*
*I offer you this freedom to make discoveries.*
*What is old is new.*

*What is strange is common.*
*This bird that barks, this cat that flies, these horses of shadow.*
*The reflection of a tree on a ceiling becomes a thing that crawls and bites.*
*Follow if you dare.*
*But only you decide whether you come as fearless saviours, or fools to fall into a trap.*
*At journey's end lies knowledge, perhaps bliss, perhaps horror. Both.*
*The world is a fragile bauble of spun glass and spider webs; so easily shattered and torn.*
*Protect it and we save ourselves.*
*The portals will lead you.*
*Wherever you arrive, find first the way out.*
*Then place the pieces of me into a whole.*
*Learn.*
*A cat may be killed by curiosity, but without this faculty we are blind and vulnerable.*
*Find first the place of my birth. Follow the smoke of the flower."*

"What a tantalising creature he is," Catty declared, once Meretrice had finished reading. "And so arrogant. He presumes we're stupid, I suppose."

"But we are not," Meretrice said dryly. "We will not, of course, be stupid enough to enter that portal."

Catty was silent for a moment. "You have knowledge of such things?"

"To a degree. Translocation is not my speciality."

"Can you make us a safety net, a means to return here, should we be stupid?"

Meretrice did in fact have a dismantled travelling device in her cellar, which was rather old. She'd meant to assemble it in order to return to Zenithix when she needed to but hadn't got round to it because she'd had no desire to go back. "I suppose I could," she said. "I can create the base structure here and then clone it when we arrive in a new area."

"How?"

"It's a planar device, and I have tools that replicate such things. I can make a memory of it, which can be projected and used as if it were the real thing. Rayce has his portals, we can have our own. Supposing mine work, of course."

"Well make sure they do! I'll construct wards to protect my

domain while you're working on that. I suggest you do the same."

Meretrice frowned. "Catty, doing as he wants us to really *would* be stupid. We don't know this Rayce, or his motives."

"And of course you have no desire at all to find out what's going on, or how we're involved."

"I do…" Meretrice sighed heavily. "It's all very well going in search of knowledge, but if we have none to begin with, we're putting ourselves at great risk."

Catty's enthusiasm could not be dimmed. "We lack knowledge, true," she said with eager relish, "but it's my belief this is more than made up for by the sum of our skills and instincts. We can't *not* go. Plus, we'll have our safety net. We just have to ensure we can return at any time."

Meretrice felt somewhat slapped, almost dizzy with it. "There's no guarantee that's possible."

"The *potential* of it is possible."

"Now you sound like the maddest of my teachers," Meretrice said. "But I expect she would tell me to go too." She paused. "The violet flower… that was his trap. He drew us in with it, and now has simply left it behind. We could go and steal it if we wanted to, but now… there is something else to draw us onwards."

"We will find even greater wonders," Catty said softly, as if to herself. She looked into Meretrice's eyes. "To me, this isn't a risk, but a door to marvels."

Meretrice rubbed her eyes for a moment, considered. "Oh, very well, we'll follow him, whether fool's road or sage's path. But we must take great care. Promise me you won't eat anything strange, whatever your instincts tell you."

Catty helped Meretrice haul the components of the travelling device out of the cellar and then clean them of dust and grime. Some parts were rusty but had not rotted through. Once this preparatory task was complete, Catty went back down the rickety stair to secure her domain. She said that once the people of Rocfeather Sill realised she and Meretrice were away, they would come to nose around, so Catty's offering table and coin chest must be hidden away. She would go to the town, while Meretrice was working on the travelling device, and pay several months' rent in advance for them both. Meretrice was somewhat surprised

Catty had had such a sensible thought.

As she assembled their portal, Meretrice wondered how much Catty would grate on her nerves as a travelling companion. They had a reason to be allies, yes, but Catty was wilful and reckless. Meretrice was perhaps as full of curiosity, but this was tempered with caution and prudence. They had no idea where they'd be going – would it be to other planes or simply different areas of their own world?

Rayce had hinted at danger in his ramblings, the world at risk. But maybe his words were merely diamonds on the path, glinting lustrously, which when you picked them up were only glass.

By sundown, they were ready to leave. Catty had been away all day, and it had taken Meretrice just as long to finish her portal generator and test it. She and Catty stood looking at it in the evening light. The device looked ancient and unreliable, occasionally spitting out tongues of lightning and uttering sporadic whines.

"Are you sure this is a portal generator and not simply a killing machine?" Catty said.

"No," Meretrice responded. "But the electrocutions it gave me were tiny."

"Can it protect itself from tampering?"

"Yes. The electrocutions for intruders are rather more than tickles. If greatly threatened, it can fold up and burrow."

"Well, then we can go."

Catty took a deep breath, shouldered her backpack and began her descent of the stair.

Meretrice hesitated before following, glancing round her garden and up at her balcony, now empty of apparatus, which she'd stored in the cellar. What if she never came back?

"Are you coming?" Catty called.

At the edge of the plateau, Catty had already hammered a sturdy stake into the ground, from which a rope depended. The portal below still shone steadily, and could no doubt be seen from the town. Slowly – Meretrice uncomfortably – the women descended.

The glowing doorway was in fact a circle above a rectangular shape, apparently constructed of wood and metal, both carved with intricate curling designs. In the centre of the circle was a round window of coloured glass, the central gem of which pulsed slowly. Spectral light swam around the portal, and within it more solid skeins could be seen, like primeval fish or featherless birds. Meretrice stepped up to the portal and put her fingers against the central gem, felt it give beneath her touch, become alive. The whole door began to glow more radiantly, until it became simply a portal of light. "I'll go first," Meretrice said.

"One thing before we leave," Catty said. "I want to tell you."

Meretrice turned, her eyebrows raised.

"Today, I went back to his house, took some of the violet petals and leaves."

Meretrice sighed. "Well, perhaps for the best. They might be of use to us, although it seems wrong to violate the plant."

"Not just that."

Meretrice stared into Catty's face, saw some trouble there. "What else?"

"I broke into the top floor, just to see."

"And?"

"Not *much* of interest, but there was something in the bed."

"Something...?"

Catty breathed in through her nose, exhaled, blowing out her cheeks. "It was a child," she said, "a mummified child."

## 2. Deepmoss Pile

A human body isn't made to squeeze like paste through a gap too small for it. Meretrice tried to calm her mind, tell herself this was simply a part of etheric travel, even though in her experience, such journeys were usually less painful – more like a dream from which you wake up, rather than a torture you're trying to escape.

She found herself expelled abruptly into a new world, where light and colour were too harsh, her body aching and shivering as if from a mortal fever. The sky appeared full of immense yet ghostly flying reptiles, the ground seething like muscles beneath her feet. But after a few moments, her senses righted themselves somewhat, and she saw around her a reassuringly recognisable landscape, if somehow wistful and fading. Buildings, trees, firm ground, a clear sky. A gagging sound alerted her to the fact that Catty was on hands and knees beside her, retching into the grass.

"That was *unnatural*," Catty said, wiping her mouth, a phrase Meretrice had already come to realise was used often by Catty who had rather a narrow view of what was actually natural.

"It was... *bumpy*," Meretrice said. "Perhaps Rayce's device is crude." She was thinking that her aged metallic traveller, despite its electronic eccentricities and antique design, was a lot more comfortable to use than Rayce's portal, with its light effects and jewelled window.

"I need some widowsalve," Catty said, "to calm my nerves *and* my stomach."

"I doubt you'll find it here."

"Just as well I brought powdered with me, then, isn't it? But – still need water." Catty stood up and together the women regarded their place of arrival.

Late afternoon sunlight sloped in mellow rays across the roofs of a small settlement surrounded by high trees. The houses themselves were blanketed in thick emerald moss, so they appeared like burial mounds rising from the earth: if burial mounds could be furnished with small, peering windows and squat chimneys. The place felt deserted. Meretrice concentrated upon her senses, picked up first a strong scent of honey, which she presently linked with the soft humming of bees.

The grassy ground was covered in tall blue wild-flowers that emitted a stringent scent. Feathery, hooked seeds of no plant she knew wafted drunkenly on a faint breeze that wound through the verdant spaces between the dwellings. The breeze, pausing in its journey, caressed the clapper of a bell on a pole nearby, so that it rang in a low tone, as if to itself, for there seemed no one near to summon. Meretrice heard, indistinctly, a rhythmic thump that could have been the beating of a drum or a heart. And quieter still, the whisper of splashing water.

Rough planks had been set into the grass to form a walkway, perhaps essential in wet weather, as there was no proper paving. This led between the buildings to a well, which was housed within an ornate marble gazebo.

Catty began to walk towards the well.

A few steps behind, Meretrice thought the structure had something of a religious feel to it. Perhaps it would be sacrilege to drink from it, but who was here to notice, anyway? She glanced through the open doorways of houses they passed – this must be a community where there was great trust among the inhabitants. No doors were locked, no windows barred. She glimpsed food set out upon tables, displays of fresh flowers and foliage, a lack of dust or stillness, as if whoever lived there had only just departed. Meretrice knew enough to be aware that such a situation could presage danger. People didn't generally disappear or rush off quickly, unless there was something to run from or they were taken unawares.

"Catty, be cautious," she said in the loudest hiss she could manage, knowing these three simple words were probably the most ineffective in her lexicon.

"There's no one here," Catty called back.

"That's odd, don't you think? What you'd call *unnatural*. We should take care."

Catty shrugged as Meretrice caught up with her. "I don't smell fear or distress," she said. "The people just aren't here at the moment." She ducked beneath the arch of the gazebo and lowered a nearby bucket into the well.

Meretrice continued to scan their surroundings for signs of life. "We don't know why they're not here… doesn't feel right to me at all." She was aware also that watchers could be hidden.

Catty had hauled the bucket from the well and was now extracting materials from her backpack – a small wooden bowl and a sachet of powdered herbs. She sniffed the water, shrugged in apparent satisfaction. Then she mixed the herbs with a splash of water and ate the paste with her fingers. "So, this is where Rayce was born," she said, "but perhaps only a picture of it."

"A picture?" Meretrice grimaced. "What do you mean?"

Catty flicked her a glance of mild contempt. "Well, haven't you considered that? You assume the portal led to an actual place, in ordinary time. I'm not so sure."

Meretrice had to concede, grudgingly, that Catty had a point and wished she'd thought of that first. "It's… very beautiful," she said. "So still, so peaceful, and the light… there's a strange but wondrous quality to it." She gestured at the western horizon; the hue of a ripe apricot dribbled with honey. "That is the most perfect of sinking suns."

"A memory of childhood," Catty said. "Wasn't everything golden then? For the lucky ones at least."

"Well, as we're here, let's explore. Rayce said we must first find the way out, so I suppose that's what we should do – seek his portal."

"After you've set yours," Catty reminded her.

Meretrice chose a spot a short distance away from where they'd arrived, in a copse of tall trees. The device looked awkward and out of place in that setting and expelled a few unhappy forks of electricity. Still, it seemed unlikely it would be disturbed – unless everyone who lived here suddenly returned.

Once their escape route had been placed, Meretrice and Catty began to explore the buildings. Most seemed to consist only of single rooms, of various sizes, and while all of them were roughly the same in shape and design, only some bore evidence of being lived in. The rest were workshops, or storage areas, including a hut where honey was bottled; there were hives of bees outside it. One house was larger than the rest, with two rooms, the second of which appeared to be a dormitory, as it contained rows of beds, neatly made. There were no beds in the other buildings, except for one, which consisted of a single large room somewhat grander than the other dwellings. Here, upon a lavish couch, they found a grey cat asleep, which Meretrice at first thought was dead, but it awoke at their approach and stared at them.

"Some life at least," Catty said, bending to stroke the cat's sleek flank.

Beyond the well, to the right, they came across a much larger building of two storeys which, while having white plaster walls, was also roofed with thick, bright moss that hung over its sulking eaves. This place, like the dormitory, appeared to be a communal building. There was a huge central chimney, and on the ground floor a fireplace set into it, where logs were alight.

Catty drew in a deep breath. "Do you catch that scent?" she asked.

Meretrice inhaled. "Yes."

Intoxicating, beguiling, filled with sorrow and sighs, it was the aroma of the violet flower. Catty ran up one of the two flights of stairs that led to the upper storey, Meretrice following.

They came to a landing where there was a stone table, much like an altar, and here stood a purple-glazed pot containing a plant identical to the one that Rayce kept in his house.

187

"So here's a start," Catty said. She rubbed a leaf between her fingers, licked them. "Mmm, this seems... *stronger*. I feel I could fly away quite easily."

Meretrice said nothing, walked past Catty up another few stairs to an open room beyond that was furnished with seating and tables, warmed by the chimney. "It has a good feel," she said. "I have a strong desire to sit here for a while."

A heavy flood of nostalgia poured through Meretrice's veins. She remembered a time that had never happened, yearned for an evening she had never lived. No details: simply the feeling.

"I feel the night coming down. I'm sitting here, drinking a green liquid, soaking the last of the sunlight."

She shook her head. Must be the scent of the flower affecting her. Opposite the flower's altar was a balcony where there were further seats, and a view of the countryside beyond. Meretrice walked out to the balcony rail, leaned on it, took in a deep breath. "Beauty and grief all in one feeling. It must have a name. Can you *feel* beauty, Catty? Can you gaze upon grief?"

Catty had come to stand beside her. "Don't linger here. His memories are strong."

She took Meretrice's arm and half dragged her back down the stairs.

The feelings lingered in Meretrice even when they returned to the open air. If this *was* one of Rayce's memories rather than a real place, it had a strong grip.

Opposite the well, and to the right of the communal building as they came outside, was a much larger tree, with a thick trunk; it would take five people to hold hands around it. The bark was wrapped with fat fraying ropes from which talismans of beaten iron disks hung, and on the far side of the tree, some kind of monument had been erected; a carved monolith of grey stone, dappled with moss and green lichen. Here, the sound of falling water became louder, for opposite the monument was what appeared to be a shrine set into a fabricated grotto. Huge standing stones were arranged in a rough circle, protecting a small cave where water sprang up from the ground, issuing from the stomach of a moss-streaked statue of a woman – an elemental creature with reeds for hair. The water fell into a clear pool, skirted by ferns.

Meretrice was making connections: the falls at the Scarlet Cliffs, and Catty's augury spot.

"Catty," she said, "the stones in your domain – you know, where one was toppled? – I take it they were already there when you moved in?"

Catty rolled her eyes. "Of course. You think I lugged them there?"

"Well, the carvings on them, what I saw... aren't they the same as the marks on these stones here by the grotto?"

Catty went to investigate. "If I didn't know otherwise, I'd say they were the same stones."

"We can't rule anything out," Meretrice said dryly. "And if this is a shrine, as it appears to be, it venerates a water goddess, or at least a water sprite. These features tie in with aspects of the Red Cliffs."

"Doesn't tell us much, though, does it?" Catty wrinkled her nose in annoyance. "What *is* that thumping?"

The dull beat, which had not relented since the women had entered the village, was louder now. Catty set off to discover its nature, and Meretrice followed.

They took a wooden path to the right of the shrine, between more trees, and came to the edge of the settlement. Here, they found two people – a man and a woman – who were dancing around a cauldron. They seemed hypnotised by the pounding rhythm – and where was that coming from? There was no one playing drums that Meretrice could see. The dancers were both wearing tribal costumes of fur and feathers, their skins were laced with blue tattoos of curving sickles, and the woman wore a mask that looked like a skull. The pair didn't pause as Meretrice and Catty approached and seemed oblivious of their presence.

"Hello," Catty said loudly, and for some tense seconds her voice had no consequence.

Then the woman seemed to shake herself from her trance and wobbled to a standstill. She stared at Catty with round, feral eyes through her mask. Meretrice noticed that she and Catty were, in fact, alike, both having slate blue skin and a powerful build.

"I don't know you," said the woman.

"We're looking for Jeriko Rayce," Catty said. "He sent us here."

The woman frowned, "Don't know anyone of that name." She

called to the man who was still dancing. "Blaize, listen. You know a person called Jeriko Rayce?"

The man continued to gyrate, though less energetically. "No. No one of that name."

"Well, he definitely sent us here," Meretrice said. "Are you absolutely sure?"

"A man can use many names," said Catty.

The woman pushed up her mask to reveal her face, which was wide and sculpted like Catty's, and once she did so her eyes didn't appear so large and staring. Her expression, in fact, was cordial. The mask now gaped at the sky atop her head. "Well, what does he look like, then?"

"Tall, spare, dark hair and eyes, unshaven but not exactly bearded... handsome, I suppose," said Catty.

The woman laughed. "Well, that certainly narrows it down!"

"He directed us to a travelling portal," Meretrice said, "which was how we got here. He implied there would be one like it here."

"Oh." The woman's face became oddly expressionless. "He sent you here, you said?"

"We did say that, yes," Meretrice replied, aware of a slow tide of impatience building within her.

"Follow me."

The woman led them to a patch of land that served as a graveyard, yet the graves and monuments were haphazardly placed and most appeared to be ancient and untended, obscured by tall grass and weeds. The path led round the back of the grotto, and Meretrice realised then that the cave wasn't entirely made of rocks, but the trunk of a black-barked tree, immense and aged. Its base was surrounded by shrubs and ferns, some of which had climbed the trunk and now grew from crevices there. Shifting light wavered from the thick leaves, which the woman pulled aside. "A portal such as this?" she asked.

It was, in fact, identical: a key-shaped door with a jewelled window. Shuddering beams of light played around it.

"Yes," Meretrice and Catty said together.

The woman sucked in her lips and nodded thoughtfully. "Then you're saying Azuris Squall sent you here."

"We don't know about that," Meretrice said. "We know him as Jeriko Rayce."

"Azuris is tall and dark," the woman said. "Had no beard

when last we saw him, but he is sometimes younger."

"What *is* this place?" Catty demanded. "Where is everyone? And what do you mean 'sometimes younger'?"

"This is Deepmoss Pile," the woman said, "and I am Glo Lavis. My man over there is Blaize Lavis." She paused. "We have few visitors here. I'll offer you hospitality, for I suppose that is what's expected. Are you hungry? Thirsty? Do your feet hurt?"

"A drink would be welcome," Catty said, "wouldn't it, Meri?"

*Meri?* No one had called her that for years, since she'd left home to go to the college. "Yes, welcome," she replied.

"Come."

Glo Lavis led them back to the communal building, while her partner resumed his dance to the mysterious rhythm.

"Find a seat upstairs," Glo said. "I'll fetch you something."

Meretrice and Catty settled on one of the sofas in the upper room, just above the landing where the violet flower stood. Meretrice was overwhelmed immediately with a desire to sleep. The room's wooden walls seemed to breathe gently around her; this was an enfolding, safe space.

Catty yawned, stretched. "This place is tiring."

Glo returned with a tray, on which stood three tankards, each filled with a green liquid that glowed faintly.

"What's that?" Meretrice asked sharply, pointing at the drink.

"Mossdew," Glo replied. "It'll restore you in every measure." She sat down. "Try it."

Catty and Meretrice did so, exchanged a glance. From the swell of well-being that surged through her, Meretrice guessed this was the fluid she'd imagined drinking before, when they'd first visited the building. Its flavour was somewhat earthy but also reminiscent of fresh hay. It also had a perfumed aftertaste to it, reminiscent of the violet flower. "It's... I like it," she said.

"Is it made from moss here?" Catty asked, and Meretrice deduced Catty was wondering if she could get her hands on some of it before they moved on.

Glo smiled. "Yes. As you probably noticed, we have a lot of the stuff here and it's quite a rare kind. We augment it with the nectar of the umbradisa bloom." She gestured vaguely down towards where the violet flower stood in its pot.

"Did Jeriko Rayce give you the... umbradisa?" Catty asked.

"It belonged to his mother," Glo replied. "He brought it here to serve the community after she left the mortal realms."

"What does...?" Catty began.

Glo closed her eyes briefly and raised a hand to stem Catty's words. "With regard to your questions. I'm not averse to assisting you if I can, but first, I must ask a question of you. Are you agreeable to that?"

Meretrice and Catty indicated that they were.

"When I said we have few visitors, this was true. But those we do have nearly always ask for Azuris, and sometimes we have to lie. My feelings for you are optimistic, not least because you..." She jerked her head towards Catty, "... are clearly a sister of skin and our breed are rarely liars or ne'er do wells. But still I must ask. What business have you with him?"

"He's our landlord," Meretrice said quickly. "Catty and I met because we both lease properties from him in a place known as the Red Cliffs. Last night, he disappeared unexpectedly, but left a message for us, and a portal..."

"We don't know *why* we want him," Catty interrupted, "but are keen to find out."

Glo laughed. "Well, all right. You are in the dark about everything, it seems. This place...? It's what you'd called a halfway province. It is Deepmoss Pile, but also somewhere else entirely. You can't see anyone who lives here, because this is simply a layer of the village, and you're not in the layer where the people live."

There was a silence, then Meretrice said, "I see..."

"Blaize and I see people on every layer. This one is caught in the moment before Manticore Moole took Azuris away. We don't like to change it because it's of course precious to our community."

"So, it's not exactly a *living* layer of Deepmoss Pile," Catty said, "if it's stuck in one moment."

Glo made a gesture with one hand. "The explanation is not quite so simple, but you can look on it that way. The Squalls were the leaders of our people. They were teachers. This place, if you like, is a school, although it is down to Blaize and I to continue its traditions now. Flurris Squall, Azuris' mother, is dead, her brothers and sisters scattered or lost, her husband consumed by... well, let's just say they are all gone. Flurris fought long to keep Azuris by her, but in the end Moole defeated her. She lies in the graveyard all alone."

"Who or what is Manticore Moole?" Meretrice asked.

"A great magus," Glo replied, "with ambitions. Flurris asked him to teach Azuris, because she could tell the boy was a special one, but Moole wanted more than that. He can smell power like we can smell flowers, and it is as sweet to him."

"So Azuris was abducted as a child?" Meretrice asked.

"Not so much that, just taken away, to another school, where he would reveal to Moole the secrets of the umbradisa, the amethyst flame, the bloom known also as the heart of sorrow."

"Now we have three names for the violet flower!" Meretrice exclaimed. "It's clearly part of our... mission."

Glo raised her eyebrows. "Azuris told you about the plant... its properties?"

"No," Meretrice replied. "He has an umbradisa plant in his house. We saw it, *tasted* it in the air."

"Then..." Glo shook her head. "Moole must have discovered how to propagate it – with Azuris' help. There are only certain provinces, in all the realms of existence, where it may thrive, or perhaps simply be permitted to grow. I can't give you a certain answer about that, because no one has yet discovered the extent of the umbradisa's powers and properties. Therefore, it has to be regarded as both a boon and a bane. Moole wanted to break the natural law. It seems likely to me now that he succeeded, although of course that is simply my personal speculation."

"What *is* the umbradisa?" Catty asked. She screwed up her eyes, shook her head, clearly frustrated she lacked the words to form her questions precisely. "What...?"

Meretrice was moved to touch Catty's arm briefly. She smiled and took over the questioning. "Glo, you must know far more about this amazing plant than we do. Please tell us. Perhaps lives depend on it. We're not here by accident. Why is the flower so valuable? It has properties, clearly, but so do many of the other plants that Catty and I grow in our gardens. Is this one really so much more potent than the strongest of our restoratives? Why *can't* it be grown in certain realms?"

Glo paused a moment before answering. "It's very difficult to explain, perhaps easier to experience, but I'll try to tell you. The flower in one way is only an *idea*. It soaks. It collects. It dreams. Within it are all the aspirations and knowledge of everyone who ever lived. It's an endless book, a limitless horizon."

"Then why is it called sorrow?" Meretrice asked.

"Grief and sadness are its defences. In order to access the wonders within, a person must first fight through the very horror of existence."

"Existence is not necessarily horror," Catty said, having restored her composure.

Glo shrugged. "That is your experience of petty indulgences speaking. What greater horror can there be than the fragility of a human life? We can be squashed like insects. We are trapped within inefficient vehicles of flesh and bone that wear out far too soon or become impaired. Our senses are limited, unless we train very hard to extend them, and even then the improvement is relatively small. We think our earthly pleasures are bliss, but they are hardly more than sorrow, for we can't live beyond our senses. These lives we have are necessary, but they are not the pinnacle of existence, far from it. Some of us are custodians of the umbradisa, and it's our function to nurture its growths. Where it grows, so knowledge comes, but at a price. Some, who are not guardians of the flower, cannot wait to see what lies beyond this life. Some, such as Manticore Moole want that knowledge now."

"And should such individuals gain that knowledge, is it a threat to our world?" Meretrice asked.

"Depends on what plans the individual has!" Glo said. "To seek power over others, and dominion over realms of existence, causes imbalance, which can lead to material decay. Manticore knows this, of course, but he doesn't care. The realms themselves are limitless. Should one not survive his experiments, he could always move on to another. But the moment one realm and its inhabitants perish, he would set himself upon a grim path. Perhaps he has already done so and has begun to make of himself a monster."

Meretrice shivered. She didn't disbelieve Glo's words, for in many ways they mirrored those of her teachers, who spoke of different realms of existence, some higher, some lower. She herself had experiences of elemental planes. But in those places, she was aware of the insignificance of human beings; the idea of them controlling a realm or destroying it was unthinkable to her, because she couldn't visualise these small things of flesh being capable of it. But now, undeniably, she *could* believe it. She realised she had already sensed it in the scent of the umbradisa.

"There must always have been people like Moole," she said, thinking aloud. "Who or what deals with them? I assume something does, otherwise there would be no universe at all."

Glo pulled a face. "Well, that's not quite true – creation continually invents, reshapes and extends itself. A million Mooles couldn't end it, but yes, there are powers that are enemies to his type. Part of his dance is to evade them. It hampers his destructive capabilities somewhat."

"Did he kill Flurris Squall?" Catty demanded bluntly, giving Meretrice a brief glance. If they were in some way to follow this man, it was better to know as much about him as possible.

"I'm not sure he did," Glo answered evasively. "I think she threw too much into fighting him and it withered her, but not that Moole sought to do that deliberately. Her death was a consequence of fighting, but she did not die by combat in a literal sense."

"And what of Azuris Squall?" Meretrice asked. "What's his position in all this?"

Glo shrugged. "Azuris walks his own path. I believe he stayed with Moole for many years and learned as much from him as a mentor as no doubt Moole learned in return about the umbradisa. I can't speak for Azuris, for I do not know his mind, but I would not say he is an evil man."

"You said you've seen him since he was taken," Catty said.

"Sometimes," Glo replied. "He comes and goes. He was never a prisoner of Moole's, you understand. He comes to visit his mother's grave, light a candle there."

"Have you any idea why he would want us to follow him, if he's not here?"

Glo shrugged. "How can I say? The plan he has might be long discarded, or yet to be. The halfway provinces are the Nighted Gardens, where time flows and roils like an ocean, and nothing is hard and certain."

"There must be *something* here for us," Meretrice said. "Why would he send us here otherwise?"

"Look for it," Glo said. "You may stay in the Squall house if you wish. It's where he sleeps when he is here. Perhaps you might hear his dreams there."

There were in fact two beds in the Squall house; one was clearly a child's, being small. The larger of the two looked spacious enough for Meretrice and Catty to share without annoying each other. Meretrice suspected Catty was the sort who slept restlessly, flinging limbs about in bed.

Once they'd pulled a curtain over the door opening, Meretrice was doused once again with exhaustion, as if the effects of the mossdew had drained out of her. The grey cat rose from her sleeping spot and sauntered outside, presumably to explore the night.

"It's a strange way to live," Meretrice said. "Only one room."

Catty laughed. "I don't have any rooms at all, and don't consider my living arrangements strange."

"What I meant is that people would usually erect a screen or something to conceal the sleeping place."

"Not everyone is as prudish as you," Catty declared. She sat down on the bed. "This is a watchful place, waiting for our dreams to be loosened by sleep."

Meretrice felt unnerved climbing into that bed. She was aware of who had slept in it before, because Azuris Squall would no longer fit into the child's bed; the feeling this inspired was in some ways thrilling, in other ways disturbing.

Meretrice woke up to utter darkness and stillness, for a moment believing herself to be alone. She reached out tentatively and touched the warm, sleeping bulk of Catty, who did not stir. Meretrice's eyes could not become accustomed to the dark. She didn't feel threatened exactly, simply alert and wary. Presently, small motes of carmine light began to float through the door curtain, bringing with them the scent of the umbradisa. The motes swam towards her, playfully darting this way and that. They brushed against her skin, stinging her face until it tingled all over. This experience, while not entirely pleasant, was not uncomfortable. She held up her hand and the motes formed a sizzling filigree glove upon her. This was beautiful; the tingling felt like her flesh was being renewed, her blood purified. Then, as if having lulled Meretrice sufficiently, the motes began to sink into her skin. She could see them moving beneath the surface, travelling deeper.

At first, her body shivered in delight, but then a feeling of terror formed gradually within her. She could feel it rising like a bubble in her soul, lightless and hopeless. *Work through the sorrow to the light*, she thought, aware the thought was not wholly her own. But how could she, when her only desire was to scream and run, and to keep on doing so until her lungs and feet were worn away?

"Catty," she rasped, barely able to make the word, then louder, raggedly, "Catty!"

Her companion did not wake.

Meretrice got out of bed; the coloured motes had vanished.

She felt her way cautiously around the edges of the room, afraid of the space in the middle of it. Something lurked there unseen; motionless. She had to keep moving, for this dulled the fear a little.

She went to the doorway, seeking the tranquillity of the village outside, but when she lifted the curtain, she beheld only a lightless abyss, seething with winds. The darkness was so complete she knew that if she stepped over the threshold of the Squall house she would be blown away into eternal shadow, twisting like a leaf on the winds of autumn.

She dropped the curtain back in place, resumed her pacing.

*This can't be real*, she told herself, but hadn't she already accepted the unthinkable could be real? Had Rayce, Squall, or whatever he was called, brought her here simply to destroy her? Why? Or was this the manifestation of an enemy of his – Manticore Moole? Seeking explanations in her mind kept the fear under control as much as moving, but she could feel it growing in power. Soon, these simple human actions would not be enough to prevent it engulfing her.

She made her way back to the bed and climbed beneath the blankets. If she could just shut her eyes and will herself to sleep, maybe she would wake up in the morning and find this was nothing more than a vivid dream. But her eyes were unwilling to close, peering always into the darkness seeking shapes. And eventually she saw one.

To the left of the bed, some feet away from her, a blurred grey shape was moving rhythmically. As Meretrice focused on this, it resolved into the image of a woman sitting in a rocking chair, which was moving too fast to be restful. The woman was staring at Meretrice, devoid of expression. Gradually, she became more distinct, glowing blue-white. Meretrice saw she had no lower body but appeared to be growing from the seat of the chair itself.

"Are you a ghost?" Meretrice asked. "Will you speak to me?"

The woman continued to stare, now with a faint air of disapproval. Her face was thin, its expression sour. As she rocked violently in the chair, she left flickering after-images of herself in the darkness.

Meretrice felt something hit her, an object small and sharp. She winced, and then another few missiles landed on her shoulders and face. She could hear now a sound like rain all around her, or more like hail stones. Was that what was hitting her? But the projectiles were neither cold nor wet. She pulled the blanket over her head to protect herself.

Presently, the sound died down and Meretrice dared to look beyond her sanctuary. She yelped in shock, for the woman's ghostly face was waiting there, inches from her own. "If I am dreaming, let me wake," Meretrice said, "and if I do not dream, I ask you to tell me what you want."

"What are you doing in his bed?" the woman demanded, and it was as if several voices spoke at once.

"I'm a guest," Meretrice replied. "I was given leave to sleep here."

The woman narrowed her eyes. "Yes... I see. Don't go without taking the waters."

Abruptly, she was gone.

Meretrice exhaled, realising she'd been holding her breath, and sat up in bed. She could see vague light beyond the door curtain.

Whatever episode she'd experienced had passed. A dream? She got out of bed, winced. It felt like the floor was covered in glass. She put on her shoes and coat and crunched her way to the door. Flinging back the curtain, she allowed moonlight to enter, which was bright and revealed that the floor of the house was covered in white particles. When she bent to inspect them, she saw that they weren't shards of glass at all, but tiny, pointed shells.

Outside, the night was serene. Meretrice heard the ululation of wolves in the distance, which was more like a song than a predatory call. She was impelled to leave the shelter of the house and walk in the moonlight. The buildings seemed to breathe gently around her, as if in sleep; their mossy mounds prickled and steamed.

Meretrice was led by her instincts to the water between the looming stones, sure that the ghostly woman had been referring to this spot when she'd spoken of 'taking the waters'.

The statue at the grotto was faintly illuminated by floating green motes that were perhaps tiny luminescent insects. Water poured from the statue's belly into the pool, which beyond the ripples was as smooth as a perfect crystal mirror, reflecting the tall stones and the foliage between them with astonishingly clear detail. Meretrice knelt at the pool's edge and scooped up the water in her hands, gulped what she could before it trickled away. The water was icy and tasted green but had no noticeable effect on her.

She remained where she was, her hands plunged between her knees, staring at the statue. The woman's face was beautiful, if a little sly.

"Are you the ghost?" she murmured.

"No," a voice replied. "She's a goddess."

Meretrice turned at once and saw to her right a young boy huddled up to one of the stones, regarding her with a grave expression. He was dressed in dark shirt and trousers, with thick black hair, unbrushed.

"Oh, hello," she said. "Is this *your* goddess?"

The boy nodded.

"What's her name?"

The boy came towards Meretrice a few steps. "She's Aahn-Kesh, Lady of the Living Waters."

"Do you live here in Deepmoss Pile?"

199

Again, the boy nodded. "For now."

"What's your name?"

The boy pulled a sour face and shook his head. "Mustn't say that. You're a stranger."

Meretrice wondered whether he'd wandered through from another layer of the village. "Shouldn't you be in bed? Won't your parents worry if they find you're not there?"

"No..." The boy waded into the water and went to put his hands upon the belly of the statue. "Mamma lies in honey, fast asleep."

"How unusual to sleep in honey!" Meretrice exclaimed.

"Not here," the boy replied. "It's always like that." He strode back through the water to stand before Meretrice.

She felt uncomfortable in the beam of his direct stare.

The boy looked as if he was about to speak, but then suddenly stiffened and glanced over his shoulder. "Oh no, he's here!"

Meretrice stood up. "Who? What's the matter?" A protective urge swept through her.

"He takes me. There's nothing you can do." The boy began to run away, towards the rough graveyard.

"Wait!" Meretrice called.

Then she saw a man step from the shadows of the great tree that formed the grotto. He was dressed in strange robes, with a stiff high collar and flared skirt. His hair was red, and he looked hungry. Had he come from Squall's portal? The man did not walk but flickered towards the boy, a series of images one after the other. Meretrice could do nothing but observe as he caught hold of the boy's arm, dangled him in mid-air. There was no sound to this scene, no cries from the boy, no words from the man, although she could see the boy's mouth wide in a scream, and the man's lips moving as if he were speaking.

Then the man grew still, for a moment frozen, before he slowly turned his head towards Meretrice. She wished desperately she had run away the minute he'd manifested. He smiled at her, inclined his head, *bowed*, and then was gone, taking the boy with him.

Meretrice was panting, as if she'd been running. Her chest ached. The red-haired man, she had no doubt, was Manticore Moole. She had witnessed the abduction of Azuris Squall.

Catty was still sleeping soundly when Meretrice returned to the

Squall house. Meretrice noticed that the tiny shells had vanished, and there was no rocking chair beside the bed. Wearily, she climbed back beneath the blankets, her mind strangely blank.

When next she opened her eyes, it was morning, and Glo Lavis was standing at the threshold, bringing them breakfast.

"Good morning," Glo said, sauntering across the room. She placed a laden tray on the wide bed and then sat down beside it. "How were your dreams?"

"A woman came to me," Meretrice said, "and then I think I saw the moment when Moole carried out his abduction."

"Hmm, Azuris does trust you, then, to allow that." She glanced at Catty. "And you?"

Catty pushed tangled hair back from her face. "I was underwater," she said, "walking on shells…"

"There were shells here, in this room, on the floor!" Meretrice cried, then sobered a little. "In my dream, I mean."

"I can't remember much of mine," Catty continued, "only endless walking, but there was a female presence, perhaps the water itself."

"Who is Aahn-Kesh?" Meretrice demanded.

Glo Lavis raised her brows in surprise. "You know of her?"

"A boy told me, a boy I think was Azuris. He said the statue in the grotto is of her."

"I feel I know that name," Catty said, "yet I've never heard it."

"She *is* a goddess," Glo said, "yet a secret one. She is both mother and destroyer. Here in Deepmoss Pile, we work in her name. She is the principle of life."

"What has Moole to do with her?" Meretrice asked.

"She is intricately linked with the umbradisa, its avatar, I suppose. He will be interested in her because of that. They say…" Glo frowned, "…he took Azuris to several places of learning. One of them is in an endless red desert where, in the only known oasis, there is a shrine to Aahn-Kesh. Moole built a dwelling for himself there, or so it's said. But I can't see how. It's isolated, and in a realm that's dead, but for that one spot. To build there would take much effort and manipulation of materials." She shrugged. "Still, stories will shape themselves from facts. The only people who can confirm them as real are Moole himself – and Azuris, of course."

"One of them must've told someone else about it," Catty said, "or else it's entirely made up. How else do stories start?"

Glo put her head to one side. "Through dreams and ghosts perhaps?"

"The woman I saw last night," Meretrice said. "She sat in a rocking chair beside my bed. Dark and thin. Was she Flurris Squall, do you think?"

"Most likely," Glo replied. "This is her house, after all."

"Azuris said his mother lies sleeping in honey. What does that mean?"

"Quite simply, she was embalmed in honey and her casket was filled with it, along with the flowers from whose nectar it came." Glo indicated the tray. "Please, eat, drink, then be on your way. I've no objection to you walking round Deepmoss Pile again before you leave, but you can't stay much longer."

"Why?" Meretrice asked.

"This layer is not fashioned for long-term visitors. Your presence disturbs it. I'll leave you to your meal."

As Catty and Meretrice consumed the breakfast, they compared more details of their dreams. "He's leading us to this goddess," Catty said. "But why?"

"It's a game," Meretrice decided. "I feel strongly he hopes to lead us all over the place."

"It's intriguing," Catty said. "I want to see the next Nighted Garden, and all the others after it." She got out of bed. "First, I'm going out with my satchel and my cutting knife. I'm not leaving here without samples."

Meretrice smiled. "Go ahead. I want to look around a little more. Let's meet at the portal in an hour or so."

When Meretrice went outside, she saw that the light was that of late afternoon, exactly how it had appeared yesterday. Time must move here in some way, though, for she had experienced night and darkness.

An almost inaudible humming led her into a building that appeared to be a dining area. The food looked fresh and tempting – whole roasted animals and steaming vegetables – and yet these must be the same meals that had lain here the day before. Not really fresh at all. In the far corner of this building, Meretrice notice a convergence chamber like the one she used at home and that Jeriko Rayce had had by his house. This one appeared inactive, rather dusty, but still, it showed this community was familiar with planar activity.

She wandered on towards the dormitory building, but there wasn't much to see, no further clues. In the second room, she stood at the threshold, thinking there was no point in exploring here, but then felt compelled to look behind the green wooden screen that concealed the first bed to her right.

Someone – or something – was lying on it. Meretrice approached slowly, her flesh contracting against her bones as she grew nearer. Was that a body on the bed? There was a figure lying down, small as a child, and it appeared to be cocooned, as if in thick spider webs. But there was no sign of webs elsewhere in the room. Perhaps they were simply wrappings, but why had this child been left here? Was it real?

Meretrice stood close to the bed, looking down. The cocoon appeared desiccated, ancient, dead insects caught within its fibres. There was a gruesome suggestion of human bones within it, a small skull, a tiny skeletal hand pushing against the webs. Then there was a jerk of movement within the dusty sheath and Meretrice heard a hideous mewling sound that would never be emitted by a human child. She was filled with revulsion. She fled.

Meretrice ran around the village, searching for Catty, but couldn't find her, even though she called her name. She called for Glo too, but the grassy lawn around the cauldron was devoid of life. Neither Glo nor Blaize were there. Deepmoss Pile felt utterly empty of life; it was as if she had walked into a picture and was now trapped there. Nothing looked real.

*Calm*, Meretrice told herself. *Panic won't help.* She took deep breaths to slow her frantic heart. As she did so, the trees, the light, the buildings took on a more natural appearance. "Glo!" she called again. "Are you here?"

This time, Glo Lavis appeared from one of the smaller mossy buildings nearby, wiping her hands on a rag. She raised her eyebrows in surprise when she saw Meretrice. "I thought you'd be gone," she said.

"There's a child… or *something!*" Meretrice cried, pointing back towards the dormitory. "Wrapped up… I thought it was dead, but then it made a sound… moved…"

Glo blinked slowly. "What?"

"Come, see," Meretrice said, and took hold of Glo's arm,

began to drag her along the path.

Glo pulled her arm free; she was stronger than Meretrice. "There won't be anything there!" she said sternly.

"There will!" Meretrice insisted. "Catty saw something similar in Rayce's house. A mummified child. This one seemed cocooned, but it's not dead. It moved and…"

"No!" Glo yelled.

At that moment, the strange drum-beat rhythm began again, coming from nowhere, but everywhere.

"You must go, now!" Glo said, a note of hysteria in her voice.

"What is that child?" Meretrice insisted. "I know you know. I'm not leaving till you tell me."

"It doesn't belong here," Glo said. "Nothing like that. You brought it here, and now we must dance, and you must go!"

"Dance?" Meretrice grimaced. "Where are the drums?"

Blaize Lavis appeared from between the buildings. "We dance to contain it," he said. "Now go, or I'll push you through the portal myself."

"Contain what?"

Blaize began to walk towards here in a menacing manner.

"I'm not leaving without Catty!"

"Meri!"

Meretrice turned and saw Catty's tall shape silhouetted against the setting sun, some distance off among the graves.

"Come here, let's go! I've got our bags. Just come!"

Glancing back once at Glo and Blaize, Meretrice ran to where Catty was waiting. "What did you find?" she asked.

Catty shook her head. "Never mind! The portal! Now!"

Together they ran to the back of the great tree and while Catty pulled the foliage apart that concealed the portal, Meretrice threw herself against it, pressed the jewelled window.

A gush of dazzling light rays spiralled out, and an etheric wind took them in its clutches, but before Deepmoss Pile disappeared, Meretrice heard the village scream, the air pulsing with pain and terror.

Then it was far, far behind and all that existed was the mad swirl of etheric travel and another portal drawing her to it.

*I welcome you,* she thought, *show me everything. Experience my worthiness.*

A hand closed over her heart.

# PRIESTESS OF PORSENNA

*Story History:*

This story is one of the earliest I ever finished and was written during my English O Level exam in 1972. I'd finished the requirements of the exam itself, so sat writing this, waiting to be able to leave the hall where everyone was still working away. This piece shows the beginning of my interest in Wraeththu, in the androgynous captive/warrior of Strymonis. At the age of 14-16, I had begun to write fragments of fiction and poems about the Wraeththu, who didn't yet have a racial name. I wasn't really sure what they were in terms of their gender – that took a while to develop. Strymonis was based largely upon the illustrations I'd found in an early edition of *The Jungle Book* by Rudyard Kipling. Mowgli, the wolf boy, naked in the jungle with hair to his feet. Yes, it's clear how things were developing!

I've had to polish this piece quite a bit in making it ready for this collection but strove to keep the original feeling and some of "clumsiness" of a writer new to her trade. Back then, I'd been content to write fragments, draw pictures to go with them, or write poems. Now, I was starting to move on – actually crafting a complete story with a beginning, middle and end.

I was only sixteen when first I left the dusty town of my birth and the white, speckled pillars of the temples of Porsenna and Claros. For three years I had been bound to the half-life of a temple priestess and already I was middle-aged, lacking the vivacity and sparkle of my common town contemporaries. How much gold my father had received for selling me to this life I neither knew nor cared. My family had long since rejected me, and I know only the indifferent adoration of the gods.

It was a hungry, hot afternoon when the high priestess, Porsenna Incarnate, berobed in purple, wafted into the cool, scented interior of the temple to find me. The outside world screamed and writhed in the heat, yet the lofty pillars of the temple only regarded it stonily in their coolness. I was seated in the centre of the stone floored Limmerat; the room set aside as the residence of the gods in their inanimate earthly forms of stone. I was in prayer to the white marble figure of Porsenna, who towered over all the others who shared her dwelling: Abdito, with his hounds and spear; Esquilina, with her face of wisdom, and beautiful Chloelia, her eyes of ruby fire shining dully, and many more standing so still, yet somehow living, in the semi-darkness.

"My child," said the priestess in her slow, ringing tone. "Callia…" She sounded so like the Esquilian Bell that rang with the voice of the goddess in the wind.

"I hear, Porsenna Incarnate," I answered.

"You are to go away," she said and at once turned to leave.

"What? Why?" I cried, too loudly, shattering the strong holy silence. My body filled up with the dark wine of fear.

The priestess spun back to me and, with the rage of the gods, dragged me from the desecrated room.

"How dare you pollute the aura of the Blessed Ones with your harsh cries!" she snapped, sounding even more like the baleful tolling of the Bell. "I pray that Claros doesn't take his revenge, you witless child!"

I cringed. "Forgive me, oh Revered One, but I was afraid… Please, why do you send me away?"

The priestess ignored my audacity and turned, once more, to leave. If she had been anything but a body supposedly possessed by the goddess, I would have shouted after her, but this could not be so. I looked once more into the Limmerat and saw the red jewelled eyes of Chloelia regarding me with a dangerous glitter.

"We have our duties, Callia," the priestess said. "Yours are to serve Mimallonides in Velia. That is all."

So, I was to be sent east, across the mountains to the town of Velia, near the sea. I would take up residence in the temple of Mimallonides, with its domes and porticos of azure, like the ocean. Below it spread the town with its white roofed villas and splendid palaces, and the gigantic obsidian statue of Mimallonides himself, standing regal in the centre of the town. I'd heard he was so beautiful, his smile serene, yet he was surrounded by the remains of the young men they sacrificed in his honour. Blood had poured over the statue's feet, through the long, elegant toes and into the drains. At specific religious festivals, this blood supplied the nearby fountain, which for a while spouted a torrent of blood.

A wagon had been supplied for my party, which at first I thought was wholly mine. But it wasn't. The wagon was quite luxurious, with seats and beds and places to store supplies. It was drawn by four beautiful black horses with long manes, crinkly from plaiting. They were friendly, gentle beasts, which often horses are not. Some are bred to kill along with the soldiers who ride them.

Three others came with me to Velia: Traxit, a decrepit old priest who was no doubt being farmed out to retire, Naevia, my handmaiden and a youth named Strymonis, who was a gift from Porsenna Incarnate to the High Priest of Mimallonides. Strymonis was a captive of war, who had been taken from the side of King Obruncalat by my people during battle. I abhorred death and killing, but there was something in this wild, dark-eyed creature that drained me of pity. Never had I seen such calm, calculated bitterness in a human being. I knew he would kill all of us if he had a chance, but he was bound, disempowered. His hair hung wild to his hips in hanks like unravelled ropes, which was unusual and heathen. Perhaps he knew magic. At night I lay awake, thinking about that. Maybe he could blow us all to bits with a glance from those hate-filled eyes. He would soon be dead, of course. That was his function. A pretty gift to be dismantled. Apart from his overall strangeness, he was weirdly effeminate. Sometimes, he seemed female entirely, and not a female I would want to know. He smiled viciously at Naevia and me, perhaps sure he'd put an end to us before journey's end. He wouldn't, though. We had guards. There was nothing to fear.

The journey, at first, was a convivial affair. We were driven out of town in our wagon, whose wood was gilded. The horses tossed their heads proudly, as if aware of their beauty. People of the town came to the gate to see us off. A few gave us offerings to lay at the feet of Mimallonides, whispering for boons. He was supposed to be a generous god.

As we approached the town gates, our driver whipped the horses into a faster gait, and we thundered beneath the arch, throwing up an aura of dust. I gazed for the last time upon the sparkling, stone pillars of the temples, forever vigilant over the town from their hills. For the first time since I'd been deprived of my proper childhood, I felt exuberant. In some strange way, I was free. And yet I was not.

The awning of the wagon was rolled up far enough that people could see my companions and I standing at the rear, looking back at the town. Naevia waved at them, smiling, shouting goodbyes, catching the flowers they threw, burying her face in the already wilting petals. I didn't do any of those things. I clutched the gilded rim of the wagon's frame and stood proudly, with my head high, my long black hair escaping from my veil. I realised that here began my womanhood, a haughty, pious priestess ploughing through the land in a glittering vehicle of gold.

After two days, we reached a small temple of Chloelia in the foothills of the mountains. It was late afternoon; the sun was beginning to seek the western horizon for his rest. Beneath the trees of the sacred grove, the air was cooler and tasted blue. There was a natural spring with sparkling, shivering water that splashed up and moistened the leaves that hung over it. Through the damp, viridian foliage I could see the white walls of the temple; shafts of sunlight like golden bars poking through the branches. Only when I parted the branches did I see that the building wasn't much more than a ruin. There were no priests or priestesses in attendance, not even a caretaker to keep the shrine swept and maintain the flames of the holy lamps.

Behind the temple, surrounded by a wall, was a pool, which Traxit told me must be used for ritual bathing. I wanted to immerse myself in water more than anything. Naevia and I were dusty and our clothes filthy; we'd not realised the powder of the beaten road, kicked up by the horses so we travelled in a constant cloud, would besmirch us like this. We persuaded Traxit that our bathing was in fact essential and a ritual; a young priestess and her attendant should be purified constantly for the gods we served.

Traxit reluctantly agreed and set the guards to protect us from anyone who might try to spy – although the mountain road seemed deserted. We'd not passed any other travellers for days. After our bath, Naevia and I brushed and plaited each other's hair, as normal girls do. It was the best time of my life so far. I felt happy, free. My skin tingled from the scrubbing Naevia had given me, and my hair smelled of fresh grass, as she'd rubbed it clean with the handfuls of the rough lawn around us. We dressed in cleaner, less dusty robes, warm from being packed in the stuffy chests we had brought with us, and very creased. Our other robes we washed in the hallowed pool – taking care to ask forgiveness from Chloelia for tainting her water in this way. The place was neglected, though, and the water itself, on close inspection, wasn't that clean either. No one tended to this pool, other than the wild creatures who came to drink from it. I felt no sense of Chloelia in the air – and her presence is generally very strong in her sacred places. And yet, that little shrine and its meagre garden was perhaps the most blessed place I'd ever visited, or ever will. It was a holy place.

Our toilet finished, we walked back to the road. Traxit had built a fire and was preparing a dinner for us. The guards had killed rabbits earlier in the day and had gathered some wild vegetables from an abandoned farm.

Strymonis had been tethered to the wagon. He sat with his knees up, staring at the dirt of the road. The bindings that confined him didn't look very strong to me, which made me nervous. I wanted to hurry past him as quickly as possible but Naevia slowed down, touched the long, wet plait hanging over her shoulder, in a distinctly provocative way. I don't know what possessed her at that moment – perhaps simply a sort of intoxication from the pleasure of a good bath and the prospect of fresh meat for dinner – but she blew a kiss to Strymonis and said, "Don't look so glum. The evening is beautiful. Take the blessings of our goddess."

"Sssh!" I hissed at her. I wanted to slap her.

Strymonis raised his head, regarding us with utter distaste. My stomach clenched in fear. He might break free. Naevia was a fool to provoke him. He put back his head and smiled down his nose at Naevia. Then he laughed; the most humourless sound I'd ever heard.

"Naevia!" I hissed. "Come along!"

I dragged her away towards the cooking fire.

While Strymonis" reaction had been unexpectedly mild, (in

truth, I don't know what I'd expected), I didn't think he'd forget Naevia's behaviour. It was insulting. He was on his way to die – he must know that. But then, he did not act like a person facing their own extinction. What other fate could there be for him?

For three more days, we travelled without incident. The air smelled different as we descended from the mountains. You could tell that a town was near. There were no more abandoned farms, but thriving sheep smallholdings, whose hardy livestock wandered about freely in the landscape. In a day's time, we'd be in Velia, and the discomfort of travelling would be over. I'd miss some aspects of it, though. As we began the long gentle descent to the valley below, I thought wistfully of the freedom I'd experienced. I wondered what it would be like to be the daughter of sheep farmers, whose only duty was to keep an eye on the hardy animals, lying most day on the grass, staring at the sky, daydreaming.

On the last night, we camped near a roadside spring, placed for the convenience of travellers. The horses cropped gladly at the lush grass which grew around it. The night came down cool and gently. Everyone seemed at ease, cheerful because journey's end was close, but I felt tense and uneasy.

I was apprehensive of our escort's lax invigilation of Strymonis. Over the journey, they'd almost befriended him, sharing their liquor. Sometimes he'd laughed at their jokes. What was he thinking... planning? Like Traxit, our guards were older men, and I feared they might not cope, should Strymonis decide to take matters into his own hands. We should have had some younger, stronger soldiers to guide us and control the youth, I thought. This was folly. Our objective no longer seemed real or feasible. Velia would have captives enough to sacrifice. Strymonis wasn't special. His king had been conquered swiftly because he had been an inept ruler with feckless generals. Now, his people were my people too. I drew in my breath. Since when had I justified war and murder?

I got up from where we sat around the fire and walked to the perimeter of its comforting light. One of the soldiers called to me, in the informal way we'd adopted between us during the journey (unthinkable normally). "Don't go too far, lass. Velia is near but wolves and panthers will hunt here, seeking easy prey."

"I won't go far, Garos," I said.

He smiled at me like a kindly uncle. I would miss him once I was installed in Velia. Priestesses did not have personal bodyguards within the temple complexes.

As I walked past Strymonis, I caught his eye. He smiled at me too, but mordantly. This was not a person fearing death. Perhaps he wanted to die. How would *I* know? He was a bitter, cold creature who hated my people, and I was certain that such a person wouldn't be so calm if he intended to complete the journey to Velia.

The night would be over soon. I wouldn't sleep. I'd keep watch. He mustn't know that, though.

Naevia came to join me among a copse of willows. This annoyed me. I'd wanted to stand among the trees, breathe their scent, *sense* them – then sit down among them to dream a little. Our last night…

"What's wrong, Callia?" Naevia asked. "We're nearly there now. Do you fear your new colleagues might not like you, or something? What is it?"

That was the extent of Naevia's concerns – being liked by others. I shook my head. "I don't know. I feel a strange breath upon me."

Naevia sighed. "It's nearly over. Stop worrying. All the predators and bandits are past. We made the journey. We're safe."

But what if the predator and bandit hid among us? What, then?

"You should come back to the fire," Naevia said. "Have my blanket. I'll sing you to sleep."

"In a while," I said. "You go back."

"Don't stay here alone too long."

I smiled at her weakly. I dreaded going back to the fire. I couldn't explain exactly why.

Eventually I sat down upon the short spiky grass that had been nibbled away by the sheep. Maybe I could stay here forever or walk back into the mountains. Would they come after me? I expected Naevia at least would do so. Sometimes, I thought she was only kind to me because it was her job, but other times I sensed she really did care. I was fond of her too, even if her incautious ways were irritating sometimes. I would go back. I would sleep with my head in her lap while she stroked my hair and sang to me, and tomorrow we would be in Velia at the beginning of a new life. I must believe it would be better than the one we had left behind.

I stood up and brushed down my robes. A shape was coming towards me, outlined against the dim light of the fire, which was now burning low. "Naevia," I said.

"No."

It was Strymonis who stood before me, hardly more than a dark shadow against the night.

I took a step back, could manage nothing more. "Get away from me!" I cried.

He smiled. "Hush. You have nothing to fear from me. I rarely have time for pathetic creatures, but in your case, I feel a shred of pity. I will take you to the town. What you do beyond is your concern."

Suddenly, a strange cold spear of horror ripped through me. I ran past him towards the fire.

I knew what I'd find, what I'd always known lay waiting at journey's end.

Dark forms upon the ground, limbs splayed in awkward postures of death. I didn't want to look too closely. I was afraid. I was aware of making noises that were a combination of grief and hoarse animal cries.

"Stop it!" Strymonis said coldly, who had followed me back. "I don't want to listen to that. Grow up, girl. What did you think lay in store for you?"

"I'm a priestess, I said. "They will look for us. They will kill you!"

"Not if I finish the job and kill you first." He hunkered down beside me.

I uttered a moan, sank to my knees, my hands flexing against the dusty grass. I could see Traxit lying nearby on his back, his eyes open, his head at an odd angle. The guards were pinned to the wagon by their own spears. Naevia lay at their feet, on her belly, arms flung out. I don't know how he'd killed her.

"Why wait this long?" I managed to say. "Why not kill us in the mountains?"

"Why not indeed?" Strymonis said. "It makes little difference. I wanted to watch you all, I suppose. *You* were ignorant, unaware of your fate in every way."

"Oh no," I said bitterly. "I *knew*. I always did."

"No," Strymonis said. "You believe I was being sent as a sacrifice to one of your gods, but that wasn't the story. They had a fate for me in the temple of Mimallonides, but it didn't involve death. That was your privilege, Priestess Callia. Didn't you know?"

"What do you mean?"

He shrugged. "You were marked for the sacrificial altar, not me. They thought I was weak, a simpering creature of my Lord. They were wrong. I watched you and felt pity."

"It's not pity to kill my people and leave me alive," I said. "I shall carry the burden of their deaths with me forever. I should have spoken to them of my fears. You murderer! You beast!" I struggled up as if to strike him, but he pushed me back roughly.

"Pointless. They wouldn't have believed you. And I'm no more a murderer than the soldier who killed my Lord." He stood up. "We'll move from this place. Get in the wagon. I'll harness the horses."

Somehow, I struggled into the wagon, crawling like a feeble baby.

He watched me, didn't help.

As I scrabbled for my sleeping blanket and my travelling cloak, he said, "We are both free now, Priestess. No one governs us. It's up to you to do with that gift what you will. But it *is* a gift. One day you'll see that."

"No!" I said. "I don't believe you. I don't care what you say. You're a murderer, and one day you'll see that too – and pay."

He laughed. "You'll kill me, will you? Grow up, Priestess. Take this night to think carefully about your future – and your past."

"Go away."

He did so.

In the darkness, I drew my heavy cloak about me. Everything was wrong. Everything.

I prayed to Ablitis to come with his hounds and rip Strymonis to pieces. I begged for Claros" steely thunderbolts to strike him down. But the night remained calm and my weeping was like a shudder of the earth, almost too faint to be heard.

# THE TESTAMENT OF THE

# KeLLCOMM

*Story History:*

This story was written back in the late 70s, when I was working for a construction company. Things were changing dramatically in all industries at that time. Jobs could be found easily, but everyone knew this would change, and so it did. My employers ran into difficulty and were set upon by a band of creditors and threatened with liquidation. It all came to a head one afternoon, when we were literally holed up in the office premises, while creditors looted the yard of machinery, tools and supplies. My employers sought aid from another company, in the hope it could save them, but treachery was afoot all round – it was astounding – and eventually the company lost everything and was dismantled, amidst quite an emotional departure. It was all rather dramatic at the time, and I was young and naïve and undoubtedly never got to know the full story behind the scenes. However, this tale records my feelings on the matter, and stands as a memorial to the company and my friends and colleagues there. I'm not sure how much reading this helped with the shock of losing their jobs, but it was a mark of solidarity between us all. The story did not end unrecorded – and it did make them laugh... some of them.

One of the older women was certainly not a friend and throughout my couple of years working there sought every opportunity she could to present me in a bad light to my employers – for the most trivial of reasons. I'm actually grateful to this person as she gave me the template for many a nasty piece of work in my writing! She sought to make my working life a misery, but to no avail. I think I was just too weird for her and didn't fit into the mould of 'young office woman'. The pettiness of that individual was overwhelming, but I left her out of the story itself. Names in this piece were based on real people, with their permission back then, as were the actions, but obviously everything is heavily fictionalised.

The picture accompanying this story was drawn by me at the time, inspired by how excavators can look uncannily like dinosaurs – or monsters.

*(Taken from the few recovered fragments of the "Book of the Terrors of the Liquaceous Marauders", that was found among the ruins of a mighty city, and recounts the tale of the struggle of a courageous band of Kings against the aforementioned terrors, many millennia ago.)*

...so the time came when the Kings of Kehllcomm did come together in the great chambers of the mighty redoubt of Stahl-Banz-Rowed, that which lies upon the territory of the impenetrable Ford of the Staff that is formed of the rushing river of Sour, and did they sit themselves around a rune-carven table to discuss their Troubles.

Dire was their predicament, as the huge and sable wings of the Powers of Darkness did beat most dolefully over their Kingdoms. Even though they had thrown the entire might of the armies of Kehllcomm against the marauding hordes, little effect had it taken upon their dour attackers. Even now, the black and milling vanguards of the Krey-Di-Torrs did darken the fair green flanks of Stahl-Banz-Rowed's surrounding hills, and their filth and corruption did ooze down like crawling fingers into the outlying villages and, wherever that awful shadow fell, death and terror lurked. People fled in fear towards the last hope that was the enclosing walls of Stahl-Banz-Rowed.

Therefore, in the camerated vaults of the redoubt did the valiant Kings and their stalwart Knights shake their heads most dismally, for they had tried every counterattack to no avail. At the head of this venerable gathering was seated the High King, Kriss T'Opherr, and at his right hand his squire Kaay-Di-Piy whose unerring sword arm was ever defending his Lord's person and whose sharp and vital-piercing tongue had many times hopelessly pulverised insistent members of the Krey-di-Torrs until they crawled away, gibbering and completely crushed.

At the High King's left was seated the mysterious high priest Pieter Dog-Throat of whom it was said that he could be in all places at all times, and his wizardry and steely orbs were feared above all things in the Halls of the Kehllcomm. His name was spoken only in whispers, lest his vengeful, omnipotent wrath fall upon an unfortunate head that desecrated his sacred name.

From farther down the table King Ayshess Caide did speak: "Tell us, then, Oh Dog-Throat, what is the nature of this terrible threat that bays at the flesh of Kehllcomm?"

The High Priest then got to his feet and from beneath his cowl his petrifying eyes glimmered with untapped power. His voice was as chilling as the howl of the wolf and for this he was named. Out it boomed over the heads of the gathered Kings. "The Krey-Di-Torrs!" he bellowed and paused dramatically, lowering his voice to a mere whisper, so that all ears were forced to strain to catch his words. "They spawned from the crawling Chaos of Beyond. They thirst and crave for the wealth and splendour of the Kehllcomm empire. Though long eons it may have taken to build the mighty cities, temple warrens and palaces of our realm, this filthy power, riddled as it is with primal evil, will waste no time in razing our grand edifices to the ground.

"Aye!" interrupted King Peetakell of the Western Isles. He thumped the table with his powerful fist even as he spoke. "So fell the fair ivory towers of the Summerwain, lofty dwelling of King Dai-Sii. Even now he is in hiding, mulling over the ruins of lost Summerwain."

Pieter Dog-Throat glowered, as he waited to continue, for another had spoken up.

"Where will it all end?" demanded Squire Kaay-Di-Piy. "I would like to know that most deeply. As the foulness of the Krey-Di-Torrs howl at our throats, almost ready to cross the torrents of the Ford, do we still futilely sacrifice our people to the graven shrine of Reedun-Daansi, that voracious Goddess!"

Dog-Throat scowled even deeper so that his face fulminated with anger. Blasphemy of the potent deity's name could cause terrible consequences. Hungry She was, and many souls had been consumed to sate Her divine appetite.

Thereafter, petty arguments broke out and Dog Throat darkly

trembled with annoyance until the High King was forced to bang the table with his oaken staff for silence.

"Let Dog-Throat continue!" he roared, and the gathering fell to uneasy quiet.

"As I was saying," the lean priest continued smoothly, controlling his voice, "the hideous foe has great and supernal powers, and so far our massed forces have done little to deflect its surging onslaught. Only the sorcerous fires fed by the Goddess Reedun-Daansi, (and he fixed his opposers with a keen eye), have kept the unpleasant battalions from our hearths in Stahl-Banz-Rowed, and even here the power wavers. But after much consultation with our Adviser to the Wise, Prince Kaer-Sohnn, we have decided there is only one course of action left open to us. The Krey-Di-Torrs are at our very doorsteps and positive action is imperative. Therefore, let Prince Kaer-Sohnn give you a brief outline of our plans." He sat down triumphantly in his great maple-wood chair, amid a stifled murmuring.

Prince Kaer-Sohnn rose and strode restlessly about the Hall, pondering upon the information he had to tell.

The Kings followed him with their eyes.

Eventually, he sighed and said, "As you know, our terrible mechanimals, the Xcavatons have had little or no effect upon these unmentionable foes. Where they would indeed strike terror into the heart of ordinary mortals, the dread creatures of the Krey-Di-Torrs smash them as if they were of matchwood. These mechanimals have always been our prime defence, as I am sure I have no need to remind you, but due to the bad year of last, when many of them fell sick, and now the preposterous toll the Krey-Di-Torrs have taken of them we are, I am afraid, utterly defenceless!" He waited for the impact of his words to sink in. "Therefore, we have had to make a terrible decision, and but for your word, oh Kings, the plans are ready. We have no choice now but to seek the aid of the Nameless Night Creatures, those terrifying denizens of the Clawed Cork Canyon, far South, that uncharted and unholy abyss, they that are feared even by the crawling Chaos of Beyond..."

All at once a terrified gasp gusted round the chamber and silvern-haired High King Kriss T'Opherr was moved to speak. "Really, Prince Kaer-sohn, is this the only channel left open to us, the Kings of the glorious empire of Kehllcomm? Are you not aware of the dreadful danger that can be incurred whilst dealing with these sorcerous beasts? They are as unstable as the air. Might they not become a worse threat to us than the Krey-di-Torrs themselves?"

Prince Kaer-sohn stroked his chin thoughtfully. "Not, my Lord, if the payment is right."

"And what might that payment be?" thundered Squire Kaay-di-Piy in astonishment.

"That," murmured the Prince, "is for the spawn of Clawed Cork Canyon to decide."

"And who will brave the terrible night of the Abyss to procure us this doubtful aid?" enquired King Ayshess Kaide maliciously, knowing full well that his colleagues and relatives would be embarrassingly afraid of braving that cavernous blackness.

"Ah," said King Peetakell with a smirking smile, "Do we not have many fine Knights ready for excursions just as dangerous as this one shall be? Let me see... Shall we elect to send Beam Loather, that intrepid little warrior of the north or shock the Creatures of the Abyss into co-operation by inflicting that fearless Knight, Clawl of Coundon, upon them?"

"Don't be absurd," snapped Dog Throat. "I myself have decided to undertake this perilous mission. With the aid of one of the High King's magical steeds, bred on the viridian fields of Puul Cottaj, and my own true sword, Calculator, it will prove a straightforward mission." And he bowed to King Kriss T'Opherr. "If you see fit to furnish me with a mount, sire."

The High King caught a glimpse of the splendid rune-sword against which no man may stand, glinting among Dog Throat's black, rune-embroidered robes. He nodded slowly and then, with a great heaviness upon their shoulders, the Kings dispersed.

And so it came to pass that the camps of the Krey-di-Torrs were blackened by a gigantic shadow that spread across the land. The Night Creatures had responded to Kehllcomm's pleas for aid. The stunted, misshapen warriors of the Krey-di-Torrs scuttled into their ragged, ill-cured leather tents, squeaking and howling in terror. Only their fearless and foul-featured generals, more stalwart than the rest, were courageous enough to stand upon the highest hill and declare that they witnessed the coming of the Creatures of the Canyon. "The Kehllcomm will not be able to control the power of these beings," they whispered amongst themselves to kindle hope in their ghastly breasts, but the wisest of them scowled apprehensively at the sky.

With enormous velutinous wings did the dire Night Creatures flap northwards to alight eventually upon the spires of Stahl-Banz-Rowed, furling their tremendous pinions and lashing their serpentine tails. Their hides were dark and appeared polished, inlaid with jewels of obsidian and jet. Their clothes were minimal, mere sashes of the blackest, most supple silk. It was difficult to distinguish their features, but for the glorious flash of a dark eye, or a glimpse of the ruby maw of their mouths. Their strange harsh but melodious cries rang over the land as they awaited council with the Kings of Kehllcomm.

And so the Kings wound their way up many twisting staircases onto the lofty roof of Stahl-Banz-Rowed. Controlling an urge to flee quickly in the opposite direction, they focused upon their need to speak most seriously with the grim denizens of the South.

And the ranks of those fell creatures were swelled most ponderously by a variety of Strange Acolytes and sub-species that had attached themselves to their aerial formation on the flight northwards. This was a common feature of the Night Creatures' excursions. They were popular and revered among certain kinds of entity.

And lo, did the Kings of the Kehllcomm look upon these massing bands of unearthly creatures and their hearts beat most fearfully in their breasts.

With great night-black wings furled upon their backs, the tall Lords of the Canyon were seated amongst the grinning gargoyles that were carved into the spires. To their left sprawled the ambassadors from the Elsee-Haahn, a race that was older than the Earth and allied to the Night Creatures genetically at some distant part of their evolution. At their splayed, claw-bearing toes were coiled two terrifying creatures of the Comun-Fischh community, beings who were scavengers, and could live upon land and within water.

The Kings of Kehllcomm gazed upon these unspeakable characters in utter silence, until the revered Captain of the Night Creatures twitched his rustling pinions, causing them to crackle like dead leaves in the wind. He spake thus, "We are here, oh

Kings, in response to your summons." And his voice was of the great clouds, and his breath fire-tainted, and this was why he was named Hallburn by humankind, for as all fire-breathing creatures he had a penchant for razing combustible buildings.

Kay-di-Piy, as spokesman for the Kings, replied, "Know you of our troubles?"

And the beasts nodded amongst themselves, rolling their enormous eyes that were as big as Lady Jiin's china saucers.

"High Priest Pïeter Dog-Throat, your emissary, did enlighten us most eloquently as to your misfortunes," murmured Hallburn dolorously, his quiet voice carrying far.

And one of the pale lizard-people of Elsee-Haahn roared, "Aye. And cut off the tail of one of our councillors to prove the Kehllcomm did need us most urgently!" He spoke with the nearest a lizard-man could get to sarcasm, which to the undiscerning, is hardly very much, since most of their dialogue is conducted in a sibilant monotone.

The High King smiled at that and offered the Creatures hospitality of the Hall, if they would deign to descend from the roof of the castle. But, as is well known, the evolutionarily more superior races of the south are most distrustful of the barbarians of the north. They shuffled from foot to foot on their cyclopean perches and grumbled amongst themselves, so that the Kehllcomm had to send forth two ladies of the court to tempt the beasts to enter the precincts of the castle.

Therein, did the beasts deliver the plans they had thought up during their boreal-bound travels. "There is but one choice left open to you!" said Hallburn, untangling his enormous plumes which had somehow come to snag themselves on the splendid candelabra lighting the chamber. Oily, gleaming feathers and small cast-iron roses fell with spots of melted wax onto the table in a gentle miasma of ancient dust. Amongst this, the Creatures strove to look impressive, while younger members of the Kehllcomm crept forth from beneath the table to steal the strange yet wonderful feathers.

"We must go to war with the Krey-di-Torrs, and smash their questionable might with our superior force..."

He sounded almost convincing and the Kings of the Kehllcomm were both distraught and pleased at this suggestion. It was inbred into their mighty hearts of generations to crave war and victory, but such awesome yet questionable allies as these – Ah, it would be no great pleasure to wield a sword beside them. Mistrust could not be dispelled completely. And the languorous graceful snake-people of Elsee-Haahn – over what unearthly powers did they hold sway? But as had been so clearly portrayed, there was hardly any other choice.

On the morn, the Kings of Kehllcomm and their Knights did rise from their beds with heavy hearts. In sombre company did the defenders of Stahl-Banz-Rowed gather to break their fast. And in that chamber of consumption were brought together all the noble heads of the Kehllcomm, in their finest raiment and dressed for war.

Down the table were they lined. Beam Loather of the town Conceal, Clawl of Coundon, Fgreen Luter his fearless compatriot, and beside them, with drawn blade laid upon the table, the intrepid Arlan Hawkilogram. Opposite him, cracking pewter mugs with his bare fists, sat Beam Loather's famed archer, Leri Lurch, and Rich the Pessimist scowled innocuously about the room, grunting in reply to conversational comments offered by the court jester, Aygee Atlas. The Kings gazed upon these somewhat down-hearted Knights from their High Table and sighed.

Eventually they trooped down to their waiting battalions, with their horses skittishly avoiding the Night Creatures that slithered around to examine exactly what they had been given to play with. Ladies of the Court did bring to them steaming bowls of bubbling broth, while trusty prancing steeds were brought to them too – not that many of the Night Creatures made use of this gift, since they could fly. The Elsee-Haahn, however appeared to appreciate the foaming, rolling eyed steeds.

Thus did the cavalcade of that massy army set forth from the creaking oak gates of Stahl-Banz-Rowed and ride out to the plain beyond. Upon far hills opposite did scouts of the Krey-di-Torrs scurry back most hurriedly to their Lords and speak hastily of the great force that rode out from the great white walls of the Kehll-comm, shadowed by the momentous fuse of the Creatures of the Canyon, their wings beating mightily and coldly in the chill, bright air.

Clawl of Coundon reined in his magnificent blue stallion, Cortina, beside the mount of Kaay-di-Piy. "Where then is his mightiness, Dog-Throat?" he enquired "I saw the fearless horse, Granada, being led, bare-backed by another. Is the High Priest not to seal our ranks?" he sneered.

Kaay-di-Piy shot him a look of chastisement. "Look aloft, Oh Clawl," he said in a low voice. "He rides even upon the mighty back of Hallburn himself."

He of Coundon gasped and indeed, gripping the flowing locks of black fur, Dog-Throat sat upon the back of that fearful Lord.

From his lofty vantage point Dog-Throat indeed had a clear view of the land. He could see the repulsive hordes of Krey-di-Torrs rushing madly to secure their arms, mounting their misshapen, hoglike steeds to counterattack the forces of Kehllcomm.

He sighed miserably for their appalling, slithering ranks seemed endless, blighting the green of the land for many miles ahead.

Suddenly, with a reptant surge, that disgusting pool of darkness advanced onto the fair plain. Hideous noises that were their war cries fell from the distorted lips, beaks and sphincters of the Krey-di-Torrs. They rode, ran, scuttled, hopped and crawled forward in a revolting wave, waving their warped limbs that were armed with unmentionable weapons. Their foul chittering was enough to turn the minds of the sanest of men, and the stout-hearted steeds of the Kehllcomm snorted and plunged fearfully, their glossy hides all marked with the dew of terror.

But King Peetakell did draw his mighty long-sword and bellow out the chant of his ancestors, thus impelling the forces of the Kehllcomm into battle.

Swift and terrible was that mighty fray and the green plain did run red with the courageous blood of the Kehllcomm. Many brave warriors gave up their lives that day and the wondrous powers of the Creatures of the Abyss were only strong enough to hold back the unspeakable hordes from the actual walls of Stahl-Banz-Rowed. Victory, it seemed, was beyond them.

Bolts of sorcerous green fire flew from the eyes of the Night Creatures, but where they struck the wriggling mass of the Krey-di-Torrs, more stomach-turning abominations sprang up to fill the gap.

At length, the Kehllcomm were pressed back to the very walls of their redoubt, leaving behind them a litter of crushed warriors and dismembered Krey-di-Torrs

"Get back, foul monsters!" yelled King Peetakell, waving his sword, his black brows bristling.

But the foul attackers ignored his commands. A sleek and firm-limbed Night Creature swooped to his side and addressed the Krey-di-Torrs. They fell to silence for they were still in awe, slightly, of the Creatures.

"Grant the Kehllcomm time to muster their ranks!" he roared and they were almost ready to comply, but for a frightful brute who muscled to the front line and had the nerve to actually shake his warty fist in the face of the Night Creatures.

"We'll give 'em no more bloody time, Bat-boy. We've waited long enough, we 'ave, for our share of the Kehllcomm's goodies," it leered unpleasantly.

The Night Creature, name of Puuri, flicked his wings impatiently. "Enough scum," he said acidly and uttering a Word of Power he froze the front ranks of the Krey-di-Torrs to immobility, thus granting the Kehllcomm warriors time to clamour back inside the protective walls of Stahl-Banz-Rowed.

"What a waste of time and energy that was!" spat Dog-Throat to the Council that evening.

Hallburn (who had sore shoulders where the High Priest had furiously pulled out his fur), stared gloomily at the gathered Kings. "Their might is strong, yes, but we could have beaten them if it wasn't for those few who have more courage than the rest. If we could squash those leaders, maybe..."

"Maybe? Maybe! Is that all we're to hear?" interrupted King Ayshess Kaide. "You're supposed to be here to help us, aren't you? I think this has all gone too far for 'maybes'."

His compatriots muttered their agreement.

"Wait," called a soft hiss. "I have a suggestion." One of the pale denizens of Elsee-Haahn rose ophidiously from his chair. Stooping, he furtively regarded the depressed Kings. "If you were to sell off your lands and possessions to other Kingdoms, they would possibly come to your aid and..."

"*What?!*" Roared Dog-Throat, leaping up and looming over the obsequious serpent. "We are fighting for just those aforementioned articles, are we not? Whose side are you on, you… you creeping *worms*!"

The creature shrank and cringed right under the table and remained there for the rest of the meeting, shaking in terror.

"All *right*, Dog-Throat," muttered Prince Kaer-Sohn placatingly, half fearing that violence would ensue. He noticed the High Priest occasionally kicking the cringing creature under the table whenever the action would not be noticed by anyone else.

"Now then, my Lords," sighed Puuri, getting to his feet. "It is plain we have failed by employing force. Subtler methods are now called for. If you will permit, honoured sirs," he said silkily, "we will send out to the Krey-di-Torrs our emissary, E'mmjai Cappitall. He will set the attackers a riddle that will fox their minds. For he is a veritable sphinx among our kind. His strange space-bending ideas will totally confuse the Krey-di-Torrs. They will struggle to find the meaning of his words, eventually falling into a dazed stupor. Then we can dispose of them."

"Aha, sense at last," said Dog-Throat, brightly, but there was a touch of cynicism in his voice.

And so, in the fusc of evening, did the wide wings of E'mmjai Cappittall flap down from the spires of Stahl-Banz-Rowed, dipped ruddy in the glare of the campfires dotted about the plain.

The Krey-di-Torrs looked up and dropped their half-chewed hams, the light reflecting from their beady eyes as they watched him.

And the words he spake were thus:

"What is this thing:
That dwells in the bosom of avarice,
That is as the black widow,
That is taken upon the crowned heads of the realm,
Thrice-barbed with the tongue of the serpent,
Black and yet transparent to the light?
What is this thing, I ask you?"

The Krey-di-Torrs muttered among themselves puzzling over the riddle. And one of them said, "If we answer this question – what of it? Why do you ask?"

The Night Creature's eyes sparked evilly. "If you guess the meaning of my words, then the wealth of the Kehllcomm shall be yours. To you shall we hand this booty."

Even some of the Krey-di-Torrs have souls and were stunned at this treachery. But the cleverest and sneakiest of them spoke up. "Then do you reveal the answer yourself, spawn of evil. The answer is none other than the greed and avarice of the Night Creatures themselves. Revelling in destruction."

The Night Creature's manic laugh echoed round the sleeping hills.

Then did it happen that Puuri went to the Kings of Kehllcomm in the middle of the night, woke them and warned them of his peer's treachery and sickening behaviour. "I will lead you to safety," he said, fluttering his wings to release a confetti of his smaller, gleaming feathers. "Follow me. Gather your possessions and follow me."

So quickly the people of Stahl-Banz-Rowed hurried to leave their beloved precincts, perhaps forever. Packing their belongings into horse-carts and loading down donkeys with blankets and food, they sought to creep away from their apparently invincible enemies.

Puuri led the people of Kehllcomm into the deep dark hills, where not many ever went, for strange things did lurk abroad there. All of them bore heavy hearts but with hope inside them still, trusting the wisdom of the renegade Night Creature.

Camping in a green valley, they relaxed and looked to their futures. But the Kings and their remaining Knights went to a high rock, whereupon sat the Night Creature, Puuri. "How can we thank you?" they enquired gratefully in unison. "You have saved our lives."

With a faint and lazy rustling of his vast wings, Puuri gave an imperceptible twitch of his wide dark nostrils, turned around and without further ado, proceeded to eat them.

# METAMORPHOSIS:
## OR the LARVAL STAGE OF VULGARITY

*Story History:*

Again, this is a piece inspired by one of the offices I worked at during the late 70s/early 80s. I had my share of horrible bosses, and this construction company harboured one of them. Among his many 'crimes', he started a 'relationship' with one of my best friends, which the pair claimed was an innocent friendship, yet for some reason had to be kept a secret from me – unsuccessfully. What my friend saw in this boorish, narcissistic man I couldn't fathom. Also, I didn't understand why it had to be secret, as I knew about another of his 'close' female friends, who sometimes sought information about her rival. Such lovely cups of tea during lazy afternoons in the office, while all the men were out on their jobs. I felt sorry for the woman – who was attractive and vivacious. How did he manage to enchant his conquests? The secret 'friendships' was conducted clumsily right beneath everyone's noses – and because lies and deception never bring good things, it ruined my relationship with my friend.

Mr Ecks treated all his staff with a kind of cheerful contempt. He maltreated and humiliated the male workers – both white collar and blue. He would verbally abuse them, put them down constantly, apparently truly believing he was somehow above them upon the evolutionary scale.

I was the only woman employed by the company, and you can imagine what that was like back in the day. I did nearly everything connected with admin, and it stung like mad when I was working on the wages, seeing all the pay rises for everyone else, while I never got one, all the time I was working there. When I asked the other two partners in the company about this, they mumbled feeble excuses, and that my turn would come 'one day'. It never did. Were they afraid of Mr Ecks? All the other men were great colleagues, incidentally, and I made friends with them easily. They treated me with respect, in their own somewhat sweetly awkward way. I had to put up with pictures of busty women pinned to the walls – such as the old-fashioned page 3 from The Sun – but was cheerfully allowed my own naked man picture as a laugh – Jean-Jacques Burnel from The Stranglers, posing nude for a centre spread in the NME. If you can't beat 'em... This was not typical for the 1970s, yet the guys thought it was funny. But Mr Ecks, though... if you didn't succumb to *his* "charms", he got nasty. So, I got my own back in fiction a little bit.

Luckily, another friend eventually managed to help me get a job working for the local college, so I could wave this vile beast goodbye. It was a pity though – apart from the boss I loved the job. I had the place to myself but for first thing in the morning when all the workers gathered to get their orders for the day, and late in the afternoon, when everyone came back to the office for a final cup of tea and a chat. Every day, I could finish up my work in the morning, then have the rest of the day to write. Luxury, really. In many ways I was sorry to leave. I'd made good friends there. And to be fair to the odious Mr Ecks, his good side could be very good. He could be kind, fun and extremely generous. And he dealt efficiently with idiots bigger than himself. But I shudder to think what might have happened to him over the years... Maybe there are, or have been, a few "metoos" running around after him. Or maybe a passing demon?

Again, names have been changed for this fiction piece.

Mr. Ecks was very, very nasty. He stared at the world from a pair of twinkling, lecherous blue eyes, below a premature tendency to baldness, and grew fat in his vileness. Having constructed for himself a towering ordure heap of corruption, swindlings, general deceits and unpleasantnesses of all kinds, (even genocide was not beyond him), he had now climbed to The Top. So basic as to be verging on the primordial, so accomplished a scoundrel he even believed his own outrageous lies and deceptions, this faintly typical man had hauled himself from the pauperous depths of primitive obscurity to the portals of the glittering Fane of Success. He was complete – almost.

Behind him a crooked trail led back to a childhood of base backstreets, of dirty necks and hardly any pocket money, merciless, Victorian-style parents of zealous sadistic caste, unexciting large helpings of potatoes and listening to the wireless on Sundays. Before him a glorious vista stretched invitingly out towards the very horizon of his life, sparkling with the colours of comfort and affluence. He should have been content, but, unhappily for him, this was not so. There was yet one thing he scrabbled and yearned to attain, yet one evasive, unutterable thing.

More than anything in the world, more than wealth, success or fame, Mr. Ecks craved to be A Gentleman.

Oh true, when he answered the phone, for at least five minutes, his voice could retain a semblance of culture, but gradually his origins rumbled to the surface in a veritable froth of dropped aitches and shiftless vowels. Expletives laced his speech like cherries in a Martini. In short, to anyone unfortunate enough to be within earshot, he became embarrassing.

Some years ago, once he had asserted himself in the world of business, Mr. Ecks had set about accumulating all the accoutrements of good breeding. A gentle wife was duly sorted out and installed in a semi-detached modern residence of estimable charm. Through gradual succession Mr Ecks' cars had reached enviable speed and price. Sensitive to the symbols of success, he purchased several horses and earnestly ingratiated himself upon the equine fraternity, finding, with a rare burst of humour, that money could buy nearly everything. Everything, that is, but for a pleasant mode of address and the interior grace that denotes true breeding.

However, oblivious to the dreadful reality of his failings, he cultivated an image that he thought represented a boisterous, good-time, sporting, philanthropic camaraderie, unaware that to those even with the faintest shred of common sense he appeared merely coarse, brutish, foul-mouthed and rather offensive.

In rare moods of benevolence, he could be remarkably generous, yet sink to alarming depths of petty ruthlessness when seeking to humiliate those, though usually his superiors in all respects, he chose to dislike.

This, then, is a scant *résumé* of Mr. Ecks life and character. It does not do him justice, I fear, for the complexities of his being would fill too many pages and doubtless bore the reader with their absolute unlikeliness. But that is not the story. What follows, is.

Mr. Ecks sat alone in his office, half visible in a cloud of reeking cigarette smoke, which swirled rather picturesquely in the morning sunlight that was fighting for admission through the fly-blown windows. He pondered deeply, squatting comfortably in the grand vacancy of his mind, thinking about how wonderful it would be if tonight he was to hob-nob with the elite of the town. (Next to philandering, his prime channel of thought). To drink with solicitors; charm building society managers with his ineffable wit, nibble *pâté* on toast with eminent architects and entrance councillors' wives at starchy functions, dressed to kill with a big bowtie...

Mr. Ecks sighed. Occasionally, a spark of true intelligence would remind him that he lacked that certain something he needed to be accepted. His reverie evaporated in a flatulent puff of despair.

The telephone rang, as if in agreement. Mr. Ecks rarely conceded to actually work for his salary nowadays. He left all the chores to his two partners, who he secretly disliked, as they excelled him in all things, including – most galling of all – appearance. They appeared unaffected by his constant allusions to the contrary. The telephone continued to ring patiently. Mr Ecks glared at the offending instrument with resentment. Usually, when answering the phone, he pretended to be somebody else. This prevented any irksome, time-consuming conversations, and avoided circumstances of embarrassment. He could lie with dexterity that was appalling, if not rather awe-inspiring in its daring.

With a brisk, irritated movement, he lifted the receiver and before he could utter a word, false or otherwise, a supernally hoarse voice lisped into his ear,

"Today, Mr. Ecks, today arrive your just desserts; and you shall have your heart's desire... You are to be... a Gentleman."

There was a brisk click and then the jarring purr of a dead line.

Mr. Ecks was momentarily stunned. He held the telephone at arm's length and stared at it. Although he liked to believe he was a popular sort of fellow, when he really thought about it, he honestly could not think of anyone who would wish him luck, never mind his heart's desire. Could it be one of his rugby-playing mates playing some kind of trick? No – unlikely. That voice. He could not tell, or even remember, if it was male or female.

In a mental whirl, Mr. Ecks stood up, carelessly pushing the chair back, and walked out of his office somewhat dizzily. In the hallway, all was quiet. He stood motionless for a moment and took several deep breaths in order to calm down. A joke. A trick… *Her*, maybe.

From habit, although still in a daze, he tiptoed up to his secretary's room and quickly, with a silent blast of triumph, threw open the door, hoping to catch her talking on the phone about him.

He knew, without doubt, that she did this, and to the people he'd rather she didn't, but had so far failed to catch her. The young lady looked up sweetly from the ledger she was writing in, wearing a tired smile composed mainly of suppressed contempt and loathing. "Yes, Mr. Ecks?" she enquired in a strained voice.

"You've got the phones on night service again," he replied smugly. "A call just came straight through to me."

The girl put her pen down precisely on the table, shuddering at the visage in front of her. A young man, old for his years, hideously pocked by dissipation: a Dorian Gray in reverse. "I think you are wrong," she said politely. "Please take the liberty of examining the switchboard."

Grumpily, Mr. Ecks did so.

"Hrrrmmph!" he gargled; his face twisted with annoyance at having been proved wrong. "You've obviously just switched it back to normal."

The girl shrugged. "Oh, obviously," she said, being in no mood for bickering. She was aware, through bitter experience, that Mr. Ecks just could not bear to lose an argument, and to try and best him betokened only long, circling wranglings of cataclysmic proportions, when her employer mutated simple facts with mind-blowing monosyllabic English. He could swear, indeed present scientific proof, that black was white, until in a fit of frustrated pique his opponent was forced to leave the room and busy herself in the kitchen, shuddering to the clarion reverberations of, "when you bloody know enough, then you bloody argue with me!" He would nod and grin as he announced this, which made it all the more infuriating.

No, it was just not worth it. Picking up her pen, Mr Eck's secretary resumed her work and Mr. Ecks walked jubilantly out.

"I'll be back soon," he said, jangling his car-keys.

"Right," she affirmed, knowing full well that he wouldn't.

Mr. Ecks owned a beautiful, sleek, silver-grey, expensive car. It instilled within him a sense of superiority. He could sneer with convincing aloofness from the tinted windows at scurrying pedestrians. He could play contemporary, 'trendy' music on the discrete stereo, whilst admiring himself in the rear-view mirror. He could parp his well-spoken horn at passing girls, who always looked up smiling when they saw the car but looked the other way when they caught sight of the oafish idiot grinning stupidly at them through the glass. It was a lovely machine.

Disconsolately, Mr. Ecks climbed behind the wheel. He felt uneasy, as if the Earth had just moved beneath his feet. It was that bloody girl! Because it was so obvious, he could not help but be aware of her concentrated loathing of him. He had power over her, because he kept her on a wage so low she was too ashamed to quote it on application forms when trying to find alternative employment. And anyway, jobs were harder to come by nowadays. Yes, he had power over her, but he could not gain her respect. This annoyed him. He seriously thought he deserved it. Thus, he sought to torment her constantly, because she needed the job, by waving fat wads of money in her face and giving everybody else pay rises. However, it failed to assuage him because he walked eternally under her curse. Wearily, he turned the ignition and the car purred to life.

From deep-rooted instinct, rather than any particular need, he drove round to the nearest garage where the Company held an account.

"Fill "er up!" he yelled from the window, lighting a cigarette.

"The usual, sir?" an oily, ingratiating voice enquired.

"The usual, mate," Mr. Ecks replied, not looking up at the attendant, which was unfortunate really, because instead of the habitual oil-stained, jovial, middle-aged man who worked the pumps, an eight-foot bipedal reptile was industriously filling Mr. Ecks" tanks with a substance that did not smell at all like petrol.

"Nice day," the creature commented.

"Bloody nice, if you 'aven't any worries," Mr. Ecks replied, sounding as though he had just come from a strenuous session of wrestling with contracts and estimates. The habitual middle-aged man would have believed him and made soothing noises. The eight-foot reptile knew better but said nothing, although his silence felt bemused.

Mr. Ecks veered off the service station forecourt and turned right. A bevy of pubescent schoolgirls, from the rabid jungle of a local comprehensive, was just walking past. They gawped at the beautiful car. The approaching traffic lights were on green. Parping his horn, grinning lecherously through the window, Mr. Ecks revved forward and... shot into another dimension.

The schoolgirls were non-plussed. All they'd seen was the grinning face in the car then an explosion of what appeared to be vivid green slime and radiance. The effects had lasted only a second but afterwards the car was gone.

"Did you see that?" one of the girls ventured breathlessly.

"Yeah! Bloody good job an' all," another chirped in with a voice and a face like cracked granite. She sounded strangely knowledgeable on the subject. "*They* got 'im, that's what. Bloody good job. It's types like 'im that makes yer afraid to go out at night..."

"Who's *they*?" yet another asked.

The hard-faced girl shrugged and her friend, of astounding and beautiful innocence, whispered, "Makes you think there is a god, dunnit?"

Back in the office, Mr. Ecks' secretary tidied the papers on her desk. She was smiling. "Well, that's got rid of him!" she said gleefully.

"Mr. Ecks' adventures have just begun," her companion, unseen to any eyes but hers, murmured mysteriously.

Mr. Ecks was amazed, stunned, appalled. From streaking gloatingly past a green traffic light on a pale autumn afternoon, his beloved car was now shuddering to a halt, to an accompaniment of severe grinding noises, in a vista that even to his unromantic nature could only be called purple midnight. The sky and horizon met in a maelstrom of weird indigo light. He could perceive no details of the landscape, sure that there were some, which he should be able to see, if only his eyes weren't watering so much, nor his stomach roiling with hideous noises.

Of course, most people, when finding themselves mysteriously catapulted into such bizarre circumstances would either lose consciousness, scream themselves to madness or else sit tight nervously and wait for something to happen.

Mr. Ecks did none of these things. He was blessed with a remarkable lack of imagination and believed in nothing remotely strange or supernatural. He blinked firmly for a minute or so until he could see the short velvety blue grass that furred the ground and the tall spindly trees that grew from it. He accepted the situation immediately, convinced there must be some logical explanation for his dilemma, and resolved to find someone to remonstrate with about it. He got out of the car, and after putting on his heavy-duty anorak, carefully locked the door. Dropping the keys into his pocket, he sauntered off along a vaguely defined pathway just discernible in the gloom.

The air was neither warm nor cool, and the landscape stretched dimly away to all horizons, occasionally punctuated by the gnarled, alien trees. The sky now pulsed with an eery luminescence that cast no light on the land. There were no moon nor stars nor sun. In fact, the whole area seemed lifeless, uninhabited.

Mr. Ecks walked for what seemed almost ten miles, blankly wondering how much grazing land there was in this place and how much it might cost to rent, before he came across anything even slightly animated. What he did find, however, was incongruous and probably frightening. A resident of this realm, whose appearance would no doubt send most inhabitants of earth insane. However, Mr. Ecks addressed it sternly.

"My car seems to have sodding well packed up. Would you mind directin' me to the nearest garage?"

The creature regarded him stonily. It closely resembled a giant sea-urchin, although thistle-down light. It swayed and rolled gently on the road in front of him, pulsating a parade of different colours and twirling its eyestalks. Unfortunately, Pudgrins, and the creature was one, communicate solely by subtle variations in their colouring. Its dreamy conversation was, therefore, lost on Mr. Ecks, despite the fact that it emitted several loud bursts of violent purple and red, plus a colour that Mr. Ecks did not recognise but which gave him a headache.

Luckily a Stroop happened to be passing and halted its league-covering strides to watch the ineffectual conversation. It extended a friendly finger and tapped Mr. Ecks on the shoulder.

Ecks turned. "Bloody 'ell!" he exclaimed.

The Stroop, however, all eight feet of him, was not offended. He was used to receiving aggressive reactions from straying humans and merely smiled graciously. "Do not be alarmed," he said. "I only wish to inform you that the Pudgrin you are attempting to question is unreceptive to aural stimulation. Notice the colour change among its fibrils. It has just informed you that it fails to understand your limited conversation and wishes to pass."

So far, Mr. Ecks had only turned red. Obligingly he moved out of the creature's way and it bounded past him, displaying a sickly shade of yellow. He turned back to the tall, black creature standing with its branch-like arms crossed, studying him from red eyes. A fearsome beast to look at, Mr Ecks thought; but quite polite. He liked politeness. He deserved it, even from a thing like that.

"To be honest, I don't recognise this place," said Mr Ecks. "Is it that new development near the bypass?"

The Stroop shrugged. "Might be. I have no idea how our realities cross."

Mr Ecks did not find this answer satisfactory. "Where's Monk's Walk."

"Never been told," said the Stroop. "I'll ask him next time I see him."

Mr Ecks felt his blood pressure rising. "Talk bloody sense, mate," he said. "Monk's Walk is a *place*, where my office… company premises are."

"Keep walking, then," said the Stroop.

"But my car…"

Uttering a sigh of ennui, the Stroop turned round. His long skinny legs sprouted wheels where his feet should be, and away he rolled, very fast.

"Bugger me!" exclaimed Mr Ecks.

All he could do was follow the advice he'd been given and keep walking.

Time seemed to pass in an odd way. In fact Mr Ecks wasn't sure it was passing at all, but rather just hanging around shiftlessly. He could employ time, he thought. It would get on well with his feckless workers.

Nothing changed and the only thing that moved was Mr Ecks walking along the road.

Then everything had changed completely.

It was more or less Monk's Walk, with the converted end terrace house that was his office. Mr Ecks focused on that. He was feeling a bit sick now, his eyes swimming with caustic tears as he struggled across the car park, which – in normal earthly reality – was now nothing more than a dull plate of concrete but had once been a much-loved garden. Here, the carpark was composed of oyster shells, which shattered as Mr Ecks walked over them. Arms flailing to help him keep his balance, he felt his way through the whirling air towards the metal fire escape stairs, even though they looked almost rusted away. Why hadn't he noticed this earlier?

Everything was back to front, although Mr Ecks didn't follow this thought through.

He climbed the stairs with effort, finding two frosted glass paned doors at the top rather than one. They both had bold and elaborate name plaques. One bore the word "Louts", the other "Gentlemen."

This... *this* was what that voice on the phone had meant, thought Mr Ecks. Perhaps some secret businessmen's society had *noticed* him. This was his invitation.

He opened the door of the Gentlemen.

A gout of flame roared out.

Everything was back to front here.

# About the Author

Storm Constantine has written stories ever since she was a child and first went to school. Before that, she made them up in her head. She is the creator of the Wraeththu Mythos, the first trilogy of which was published in the 1980s. However, the influences and inspirations for the Wraeththu world go much further back than that and continue into the future as she plans more stories for it.

Her other full length works cross genres from science fiction, to dark fantasy, to epic fantasy, to slipstream. She has written over thirty books, including full length novels, novellas, short story collections and non-fiction titles. Her short stories, which she continues to write prolifically, appear in diverse magazines and anthologies.

Storm is the founder of Immanion Press, created initially to publish her out-of-print back catalogue, but which evolved into the thriving venture it is today. Her interests include magic and spirituality, movies, music and MMOs. She lives in the Midlands of the UK with her husband and four cats.

# Publishing History of the Stories

The Bone Fire – *The Mammoth Book of Halloween Stories*, edited by Steve Jones, Skyhorse Publishing, 2018.

Haven – *Splinters of Truth*, ed. by Ian Whates, NewCon Press, 2016

Dimmed by a Scattering Cloud – 2018, previously unpublished

Violet's House, or Songs the Martyrs Sang – *Splinters of Truth*, ed. by Ian Whates, NewCon Press, 2016

Down into Silence, *What October Brings: A Lovecraftian Celebration of Halloween*, ed. by Douglas Draa, Caeleno Press, USA, 2018.

In the Speed of Their Wings Keep Pace, 2015, previously unpublished

Spirit of Place, *Splinters of Truth*, ed. by Ian Whates, NewCon Press, 2016

When He Comes Home Through the Snow – *The Darkest Midnight in December*, ed. by Story Constantine, Immanion Press, 2017

Colin's Cough – *Splinters of Truth*, ed. by Ian Whates, NewCon Press, 2016

When the Angels Came: Novacon 22 booklet, 1988; *Splinters of Truth* collection, ed. By Ian Whates, NewCon Press, 2016

La Ténébreuse – *The Alchemy Press Book of Horrors*, ed. by Peter Coleburn and Jan Edwards, Alchemy Press, 2018,

Through the Nighted Gardens – Two joined stories "The House on the Red Cliffs" and "Deepmoss Pile", previously only published online, as the transmedia project *"Through the Night Gardens"*.

Priestess of Porsenna, 1971, previously unpublished

The Testament of the Kehllcomm, mid 1970s, previously unpublished

Metamorphosis, or The Larval Stage of Vulgarity, late 1970s, previously unpublished